Wickedly His

A MARRIAGE OF CONVENIENCE BILLIONAIRE ROMANCE

WICKED & WED

MAUDE WINTERS

Cover By: Gwendolyn Sams

ISBN: 978-1-969247-05-7

For the readers who want the yearning, broody hero who gets greedy. And for all of you who refuse to blanch at 206 "fucks".

Author's Note

This first book in Wicked & Wed can be read as a standalone, but those who have been with me awhile, should be delighted to recognize some familiar faces.

This is Lanie's story. For those of you who read Lakeshore Empire, you'll recognize her as the fast-talking, no-fucks-given second youngest Delphine Daughter. And if you read *Love Match*, then you will relish the conflict that draws Lanie to Baz.

This is also my spiciest book. **Readers, please stop if you want to avoid spoilers. But if you are concerned about triggers, read for content expectations.**

CONTENT EXPECTATIONS

- Explicit language and open-door scenes
- Consensual, ethical non-monogamy
- Kink, voyeurism, cuckolding, and impact play
- Discussion of loss of parents
- Mentions of emotional and physical abuse of the MMC (off the page)
- Pregnancy and birth

LANIE

At the start of a short day that felt impossibly long, my best friend's face popped up on my phone for the third time. Still unsure what to say, but homesick as hell, I answered.

"Oh my god, I thought you were dead! Why are you ignoring me, babes?" Chloe asked.

The sound of her voice brought relief. I took a deep breath and answered, "Sorry. It has been wild here with all the rehearsals and Sam's schedule and everything."

"Plus, the dinner party. How did that go?"

I took a deep breath, "I don't want to talk about it."

"Lanie Delphine, if you don't—"

"We survived it. Okay?"

Chloe paused, concerned but debating if she could push me. She knew my tone. She read my voice better than anyone. We grew up together—our lives always intertwined. We knew everything about one another. Her older brother married my eldest sister about a year ago, making her more sister than friend.

She took the cue and changed the subject cheerfully, "So, spill! how is training going on the dances?"

"I spent two hours at the studio, and I *think* I'm getting the hang of it, you know?"

"You will be amazing. It kills me you must go through all of this for a scene or two."

"The life of a woman in a period piece. The network wanting more ballroom shots is not my decision. But hey, why not?"

We just finished shooting our first season of *Dollar Princesses*, a show based on a book series about American heiresses leaving Gilded Age America to be passed through the marriage mart of London. I played the daughter of a Chicago railroad tycoon sold off by her parents for a title.

"I still don't understand the idea of reshoots," Chloe said. "Why not do it all at once? A shoot costs a mint."

"I know. The network wanted more of me learning to waltz and having a dance card full of hot men my mother turned down. Leah said it was something about giving them more Prestige Porn or whatever. She's the boss and it's their money, so no one says no."

Leah Roughy was an EGOT-chasing legend. She was also the Queen's niece and came armed with a blank cheque with the network no other nepobaby could touch.

"I suppose it doesn't hurt to dance with a bunch of hotties?"

"I could lament my blisters from my shoes or the constant use of a corset, but it's hard to complain. I hope we get renewed. I am hungry to do more."

"Work it. You give a hundred and ten percent on a bad day. I gotta believe that if even the suits don't see it, Leah does."

"She's great to work for and I'm desperate to keep the job. So, I smile and dance even if I'm having flashbacks to Madame Routledge."

Many years before, our mothers enrolled us in dance at the Chicago Ballet School. My mother had been a ballerina in a past life, while Chloe's grew up with nothing and made a beauty empire fit for a queen. By the time Chloe appeared, she was all-in to make her daughter a dancing star. Unfortunately, our teacher was toxic. Chloe never took to it and—to my mother's chagrin—I moved on to acting and musical theater. Neither Chloe nor I enjoyed the rigidity of ballet life. We were both chaos goblins.

"I can still hear her telling me to look less like a hippo on stilts," Chloe said. "I am so glad I didn't listen to her."

"She was the worst. I really hope she's no longer teaching. I'm loving dance, but I am so out of shape. I was honestly worried I was pregnant—"

"Oh, Lanie, are you?"

I murmured, "I thought I was, but no. I took a test before our party and I thought Sam would be excited for us, but he made it clear he was nothing but relieved. I didn't react well."

"Oh, honey, I'm sorry. No wonder the party was hard on you. I cannot imagine that emotional rollercoaster."

"He just shut down. We didn't talk. And this morning when I woke up, he was just gone."

"I am sure you all can talk through it."

"It's for the best."

"Lanie, I—"

"Chloe, don't say you aren't already aware this is like beating a dead horse."

"Can we not mention dead horses?" As our resident competitive equestrian, Chloe was sensitive.

"Sorry. Uh… I just… I am always the last to know. Somehow, this time, I cannot even feel pain. He swore he wanted kids, but I saw the lies there. I could twist myself into something I'm not, but I know in my heart of hearts, he's not in it with me."

"Sometimes it can be a shock. Men may need more time.""

"Nah. He's had time. I think he lied to protect me."

"Explain."

"I was pretty excited after Cordelia was born," I said of our mutual niece. "I found out how badly I wanted a baby, and I sort of went on and on about it. Looking back now… I see he was going through the motions. It came to a head last night when he had no empathy for me and could no longer hide his relief. This won't change. But we've been together for years—"

"And sometimes relationships aren't forever. Lanie, I can see you compromising on many things, but a baby isn't one of them. Watching you with Cordelia made it clear. You want to be a mom someday. You *deserve* motherhood. If Sam doesn't want children, it's not fair to either of you to force the issue."

"Okay, but… it's not like I will be able to avoid him in this industry."

"Yes, that's so unique. Sweetie, it's Hollywood. He's a cinematographer with a following, but you're an actress—"

"One who no one really knows about yet."

"Plenty of people do. And it will change. You're about to blow up."

I doubted her.

"Focus on what is next, okay? Focus on shooting in London and having the network green light everything. I'll come. We will party and live it up. We'll sleep with sexy, rich men who worship us. Maybe it wasn't the plan—"

"But what is a plan if we're miserable?"

"Exactly."

"Chloe, I want to be brave, but I also worry."

"About what?"

"I'm not getting any younger. What if—"

"Come to London and let's just talk about it, okay? We're still babies. We can still freeze our eggs if we want to. We always joked that we'd grow old together. Maybe we can have babies and say fuck those men?"

"I think we both have too high of libidos to make that work," I giggled.

"We can switch off on date nights. You *know* I am not serious."

"Our moms would expire at all of this."

"That makes me want to do it more. Regardless, the fact that you're not crying right now over me mentioning it makes me think that you're ready for the next step. You're brave and strong, Lanie. Go where the road takes you. You're already open to it."

I breathed deeply, knowing what to do. "He deserves to know. We should both get a chance to be happy. I will have a family one way or the other."

PART ONE

All A Game

CHAPTER 1
Eldergrove

LANIE

I NEVER GOT over the excitement of driving up a private lane to a country house. As an American, pastoral British scenes with houses straight out of *Pride and Prejudice* thrilled me. This weekend, I vowed to spend time away on a whim with a cute but sophomoric man I met at a club in Soho. He took me home to his penthouse, and I stayed two nights. The next morning, he decided to go to a friend's shooting weekend and asked me along. Given that I had nothing better to do and didn't think he was a murderer, I texted the family group chat I was going away for a four-day weekend with a potential suitor and packed a bag while Chloe and Dora slept.

We drove to a place called Eldergrove in Somerset. It sounded rather ominous, but I was a sucker for big stone walls and fireplaces big enough to cook an entire sow. The facade of the place didn't disappoint. My escort opened the car door, and I stepped into the cool autumn afternoon air. Staff waited at the door. A man in a suit took our bags from the trunk.

The housekeeper asked, "Mr. Moynahan, welcome. And who is this you have brought with you?"

"This is Miss Lanie Day," he said.

I'd given Caleb my stage name, hoping he would have *no* clue who I was. I hated bringing up my origin story—especially when I planned to get wild. My sister had once been a respectable woman in London circles when she was previously married to a now-disgraced Member of Parliament. Even if people didn't know Daphne from that notoriety and her subsequent legal battle with him, they'd recognize my surname—Delphine—and its connection to one of the finest department stores in London.

"I am Anna and this is Giles," the woman said. "We will take care of you this weekend. Please, come in and settle. Several of our guests are out shooting right now."

"Is Baz about?" Caleb asked.

I died for his posh accent.

"He was tied up with business calls, sir," Giles, the aptly named butler, responded. "And in a meeting with Mr. Callahan."

"Very well," Caleb said.

"Shall we bring you tea while you wait for the others?" Anna asked.

"Not yet. I will check back in if that changes," Caleb said.

Caleb took my hand and walked me through the halls of the massive house.

"What is your connection to this place?" I asked.

"My father's uncle owned it. Growing up, we spent summers here. Some friends of ours bought it out—the friend I was asking for—but he usually invites us up for shooting weekends. The lot of us who grew here are all close."

"That's nice," I said. "We have a family farm. It's nothing like this, but a similar vibe on weekends away."

It was an understatement. While the farm in Western Michigan differed from our gilded-age family home in Chicago, it wasn't a small establishment. My mother renovated the place at least once a decade. We had fruit fields, a vineyard, and a bustling artist market.

"Nice," Caleb said.

We stepped into what I assumed was the library—a cozy, well-appointed room with books and beautiful views of a large pond. I stepped towards the books before Caleb pulled me back towards him with some force. Surprised, I stared at him.

"I am sorry, but I really cannot wait to have you again," he growled.

Caleb took my face and kissed me definitively as if claiming me. I pressed my pelvis against him. He was a good kisser and relatively fun in bed. However, I wasn't sure if that was because he gave me the first orgasm I'd not given myself in months or if it was due to his actual sexual prowess. Even if he wasn't a superb conversationalist, he was well-hung and pushed the right buttons.

Caleb's hand ran to the hem of my dress and dipped up my thighs. He brushed the waistband of my sweater tights. I wanted more. I wanted to get off and moan into his mouth as I came, but we were in someone else's house. I didn't want to be *rude*.

"Caleb, this isn't the place. Can you take me to our room, at least?" I gasped.

"Relax. No one is here. The servants will not bat an eye. No one cares. Besides, it makes it hot, right?"

I wouldn't deny that I had a thing for testing the bounds of propriety. I loved the *idea* of risking getting caught, but did not enjoy having to explain it if I did.

"I want to taste you," Caleb punctuated the statement by biting my earlobe.

I melted.

"Fine. I will let you," I said. "If we get caught, this is on you."

"Yes, ma'am," Caleb said, almost gleefully.

I let him toss my shoes and tights to the side as I sat on the couch. He propped my legs on his shoulders and dug in. I longed for this—to be worshipped. I wanted to be taken over the edge by this mostly stranger who appreciated my curves and knew how to make me cum.

BAZ

I wrapped up my last call and looked at my assistant, Jeremy. I knew not to disrupt his note-taking. He had a *process* and if I bothered him, I'd hear about it. Given that I would probably not survive without Jeremy's organization and planning, I practiced patience. I missed out on the early afternoon shoot to take a call from a developer in Edinburgh. I wasted the day, perhaps, but not the *entire* weekend. I planned to spend that much with my mates.

"Are we good?" Jeremy asked.

"I'm satisfied with their answers for now," I sighed. "But to be this annoying about due diligence frustrates the hell out of me. Either provide it or don't. I don't like them pissing about with it."

"Dodgy. But you know how they are," Jeremy admitted. "If we're done, I will take a walk."

"Sure," I agreed. "I'm going to go walk the house and find the dogs. Rest a bit before supper. Are you coming?"

"We'll see. Are you having lobster?" Jeremy chuckled.

"Yes," I said. "That was Caleb's request."

"Perhaps," Jeremy said. "If my date falls through."

Caleb was a surrogate little brother—the one I wished I had in replacement of my *actual* little brother. I invested in his scheme and sometimes reaped major awards. I suspected his success had more to do with luck, and the ability to fundraise than actual investing talent. This weekend, he asked to drop in. That meant that he needed money for something. I wasn't looking to invest, but I'd give him an audience.

Making my way down the backstairs from my office, I heard people in the library. There was rustling, then the sound of a woman talking. I stopped short and listened. Several of our mates were married and one brought his wife this weekend since she *also* liked to shoot. However, as I listened, I didn't know who the woman was.

I walked towards the door to greet them, catching a glimpse of what I least expected. Caleb and this mystery girl were in the middle of something. He was on his knees eating her out while she lost herself. I ducked back out, heart racing. My curiosity was piqued, but I prayed she didn't think I was up to anything dodgy.

I pressed myself hard into the wall, trying to figure out how I could leave in silence before they knew I was there. As I did so, she got louder. Though unintelligible, Caleb's paramour let out delicious little moans—moans she tried to stifle. Her panting and moaning made me rock hard. I wanted to watch, but knew better.

Then, she gasped, "You were right, Caleb. Of fuck, I'm going to be bad. I don't care who sees us."

Was it an invitation? Had she seen me?

"Oh, don't… god… that's so good," she whimpered.

I walked one more step until I stood in the crack of the library door. I shouldn't have. In view, I could see only the back of Caleb's head while his face was buried in her pussy. She was lost in the pleasure he gave—face flushed and gripping the couch. She was beautiful—alabaster skin, dark ginger hair, and the prettiest nose. I marveled at her full thighs and the way her breasts rose and fell. She was so close. I should have watched myself and stepped away. Instead, I stayed. I wanted so badly to watch her cum for him—to lose it. I wanted to hear her scream his name and fall to pieces.

"That feels amazing!" She panted more as Caleb sucked her clit with clear determination.

Lucky bastard.

"Fuck! Oh, don't… don't stop, Caleb!"

She was so close and I couldn't look away. Keeping her eyes glued to mine in a defiant gaze, she gripped his hair and pressed his face against her. To know I watched her *thrilled* her. Her nostrils flared until her head rolled back and she came with a low growl. I couldn't believe my luck! All I wanted was to watch it again. I wanted to make her scream *my* name.

CHAPTER 2

In the Act

LANIE

I was deep in my head, living for my climax, when I spotted an onlooker. I panicked as I met the eyes of a tall man with broad shoulders momentarily in the doorway. I expected him to apologize or—worse still—yell at us. Instead, he remained calm, just staring. His steely gaze was neither upset nor fussed. Then, he disappeared, looking flustered. I should have ignored him, but I couldn't. If he was game, I wanted to play.

Instead of stopping, I slyly invited him back with a moan. And, return he did. Though timid at first, he came forth, intrigued. I enjoyed the slight smile that crossed his face as I acknowledged his gaze. He had a jaw that could cut glass with an undeniably sexy bit of stubble. His slightly grey hair wasn't fussy and he was dressed down. I had no idea who this stranger was—he wasn't staff. I wondered if he was the owner. As I took him in, I noticed the outline of his substantial erection. The vision of me here aroused him.

When I came, I shuddered—eyes locked on the voyeur until they rolled back with sweet satisfaction. Caleb kissed my thighs, then came to press his body into mine on the couch. I didn't know what to do. His erection suggested he wanted more. In all honesty, I was dying to have him inside me. But, there was the stranger.

"Get in the chair over there," I pointed over his shoulder. "I want to ride you."

The man stepped away just so Caleb didn't see him. Part of me hoped he might remain. The oversized chair faced away from the door. So, if I was on top, all Caleb could see was the books on the opposite wall. Caleb spun fast, pulling a condom out of his wallet and kicking his pants and boxers off. I watched as he rolled the condom slowly over his hard cock and waited patiently for me.

As I climbed astride Caleb, I caught a glance of the mystery man from the corner of my eye. He stood, enraptured. I bit my lip and tried not to stare too obviously. Turning back to my date, I cupped his face in my hands and kissed him slowly as I slid him deep within me.

"Do you like that you can taste yourself?" Caleb asked.

"I don't mind," I said. "I have satisfaction of knowing you wanted nothing more than to have me cum all over your face."

"Oh, fuck," Caleb moaned. "You are amazing."

I smiled, satisfied as I rocked my hips back and forth. The mystery man watched every move I made. Once more there was really nothing more to see beyond my facial expressions. I should have kept it down, but having an audience made me behave even less.

"I wanted to pull over and fuck you on the side of the M5," Caleb kissed my neck. "Who are you? And why are you so fucking good?"

"You spoil me," I said. "I love to be worshipped."

"I'll give you whatever you want," Caleb promised. "If you keep doing what you're doing."

I smiled at him, then looked back at the man in the doorway. Caleb's gaze dropped to my tits bobbing in my dress. I committed to the act. As I found the perfect, glorious spot that sent me over the edge, I stared directly at my audience.

"Oh, God, Caleb! Make me cum!"

I dug my nails into the leather chair back and lost myself, staring into the eyes of this handsome stranger. Thrilled, amused, and a little embarrassed by my high, I came back to Caleb, kissing him. Why did that feel so good?

———

BAZ

Watching this beautiful stranger reach orgasm again—even in the hands of my friend—was enough to send me over the edge. I resisted the urge to touch my cock for fear she'd call it off or I'd get caught. It killed me to refrain. I ached to find release with her screams.

Staring at me, nostrils flaring, she kept going.

In a husky voice, she said, "Cum for me, Caleb."

Her accent alone cut through me. She *tortured* me and *loved* it. Who the hell was this exhibitionist American? And why didn't *I* have her? I pictured her on her knees before me —big eyes looking up. Even worse with her full pink lips wrapped around my cock.

Then, I knew I'd cum. Racing to relieve myself, my palms sweated with an aching need for her. I found the nearest toilet. With a few not-so-generous strokes, I came, thinking about her beautiful face and the way she moaned. I was too old for this shit but couldn't help myself.

Returning to the hall, I struggled to act normal. I heard them now, trying to act like they hadn't just defaced my library. I listened to them laugh down the hall, chatting casually now about something else. She moved on, but I hadn't. Mentally, I found myself unable to separate myself from moment's electricity. This American either didn't recognize the hold she had on me or knew her power and didn't care. If it was the former, I found it cloyingly adorable. If it was the latter, I found it infuriating, yet engrossing.

Hold it together, Baz! It was just a bit of fun!

The desire for answers about this beautiful stranger overwhelmed me as it hadn't in years. Watching her, I *felt* something more than lust. Flustered, I couldn't face her. I fled, unable to string together a sentence. I worried I'd look weak and disappointing. Instead of waiting for them to emerge, I rushed off and focused on dressing for supper.

As I decompressed in my sitting room, a knock sounded. Annoyed, I rose to answer. Caleb stood before me, a shit-eating grin on his face. I wondered why he was here, but didn't want to assume it had to do with the pretty young thing who just eyefucked me while fucking him.

"Hello," I said. "You made it in."

"I did. I hope you don't mind I brought someone."

"I don't. Of course not," I said.

Especially someone young, fit, and downright decadent.

"You're gonna love her."

I cleared my throat. "I am sure I will. Is everything to her liking?"

"She's found the hounds and is in the garden," Caleb answered. "She's American. I think anything remotely old-world tickles her fancy. It's not that. I was coming to ask you about a project."

Predictable.

"I have an opportunity with a building in Islington I have a line from the council that they will approve my request for density."

"But?" I sighed.

"I wanted to see if you might go in with me on it. It has *tons* of potential. There are hip places popping up everywhere. *And* it's close to Exham."

Exham was my family's football club. We'd just built a new stadium because my father was bored of the old one. He had come to approximately two games since then. It was dizzying the things my father would spend money on just because he could.

"I don't know. Numbers would have to make sense, Caleb," I said.

"I think I could change your mind, mate."

"Tell me over dinner," I pinched the bridge of my nose. "It's already been a long day."

"All work and no play will make you a dull boy, Osgoode."

"I am well aware," I said. "Will you come see us play next weekend?"

"We'll see, mate. Depends on if you want to see the build site."

I rolled my eyes. "I will be at club level. Take it or leave it."

Caleb patted my shoulder. "You'll want in on this."

I wanted in on what he had, but it wasn't what he offered that piqued my interest.

CHAPTER 3
The Stranger

LANIE

Dinner required dressing "smart", so I went for a nice cocktail dress. I packed several options—not sure if anyone would dress for dinner. I longed for my American existence where I could get away with jeans no matter what. My aristocrat-born mother only asked for a bare minimum most nights —what Chloe called "hard pants" in the evening. My late father had shaken away her British aristocratic bent by the time I was born, getting her to compromise. The more I hung around wealthy Brits, I understood my mother's neuroses.

Seated by Caleb, I looked at the others at the table. I'd already been introduced to most. Caleb finished that job while we waited for the host who I guessed by now was my mysterious admirer. I was famished and ready to dig into surf and turf. Where was the man of the house?

"It's so like him to be late, you know?" William, a venture capitalized, agonized. "We wait on him."

"Darling, it's his house," Anastasia, his wife, said.

Anastasia was pretty but far older than me. I gathered she was the type who travelled *everywhere* with her husband. While many wives were content to give their spouses space on a boring hunting weekend, she was overbearing. I didn't understand the need to spend every waking moment with your spouse. Then again, I'd never had anyone I longed to travel anywhere with longterm.

"Sorry everyone." A deep voice said.

I looked over my shoulder at the mystery man. I expected him to at least flinch, but he spoke as if directly to me.

"I had a call. It went on too long and I do apologize."

The man sat at the head of the table.

Caleb cleared his throat. "Baz, are you going to be rude to my guest?"

"Oh, no," Baz stood, reaching his hand out. "Basil Osgoode. And you are?"

"This is Lanie Day," Caleb said. "I met her at Koda while she was out partying with her friends. She's a laugh."

"Nice to meet you," I said. "Thank you for hosting."

"And thank you for coming." He put *far* too much emphasis on the last word.

I barely kept a straight face. To distract myself, I patted my skirt until I felt it was sufficiently righted. I wonder if he thought about getting between my thighs. I felt terrible for sitting next to Caleb—a man I genuinely enjoyed—while thinking about his bizarre voyeuristic friend. Unfortunately, Baz ticked all the boxes—he was too old for me, probably a head case, had more money than anyone ought to, his accent melted me, and he was off-limits. I wondered what he'd sound like looming over me in bed. Would he be as rough with me as I hoped?

"What is it that brings you to our little island?" Baz asked.

I shook my stupor and blushed. "My friend, sister, and I are staying on here for a bit at my older sister's place. We've been in and out. I filmed a bit on and off here this year."

"She's an actress," Caleb declared.

"Apologies, I hadn't heard of you."

"Baz, you live under a rock and never watch television," Caleb sighed.

"Oh, television," Baz said with derision.

He tried to take me down a peg. I wasn't having it.

"Actually, while I admit I'm an up-and-comer on the screen, I've done some stage plays and I'm currently in the ensemble cast of Leah Roughy's new project."

"Leah? Really?"

"Do you know her?" I asked.

"Yes. Of course," Basil said.

Of *course* he knew her.

"She's great," I said.

"She's wild," Baz said. "No doubt about it. Are you wild, too, Lanie?"

I sipped my wine, never dropping eye contact. "I don't know. What do you think?"

He chuckled. "I would love to know more. Thankfully, you're stuck with us for the weekend."

CHAPTER 4
The Game

BAZ

THE WAY LANIE sipped excited me. This wasn't a fluke. She knew what she was doing and gave as good as she got. I found opinionated women irresistible. She was too good for Caleb—too clever and too demanding and needed someone more experienced and assertive. In this dress, I'd give anything to run my hand between her thighs and drive her wild.

After dinner, I had to listen to Caleb drone about his opportunity in Islington, but my eyes always fell back to Lanie. And whenever I saw her, she saw me. Whatever we had earlier was electric, but that wasn't all I wanted. I loved to watch, but I wanted to fuck her.

"So, what do you think?" Caleb asked.

That I want to fuck Lanie.

"About what?"

"The deal? The investment I've been going on about! Baz, where are you?"

"Sorry, it's been a long day. Your margins are too small. That's my honest opinion. It's not worth it for me."

"Baz, it could still turn a good profit for you."

"I don't get out of bed for those margins, mate. Sorry."

Caleb shook his head. "It's a premium offer and that area is perfect as a tie-in for the stadium."

"That is *not* how it works and it's not my stadium."

"Not yet," Caleb said. "But it *will* be."

Lanie passed to go grab drinks at the drawing room's corner bar. She stared at me and bit her lip once she made it. I had an idea. My appetite for this woman won out over reason. I changed the subject.

"Let's table this. Let's talk about Lanie," I said. "She's fabulous."

He set his jaw. "That's madness. She came with *me*."

"I know, but *I* fancy her and we both know she's not going to be more than your girl for a week."

He shrugged. Caleb wasn't a fan of commitment as much as he was women who liked him to flash some cash and fawn over them for a bit. Once they got invested, he booked it.

"She's fun for now, though," Caleb said.

"And after?"

Caleb shook his head. "Well, it wouldn't be the first time. If you want my sloppy seconds—"

"There is no way anything about her could ever be sloppy."

"She's completely ridiculous in bed."

That much I'd garnered. I'd try my luck with her once he was out of the picture. I just needed to put her at ease and be a good host. The evening felt easy. Men drank and smoked cigars, but she seemed unbothered. Instead, Lanie seemed at home. She didn't glom onto Anastasia.

"I'm gonna talk to Matt. Maybe *he* will be smarter than you?" Caleb teased.

"Go ahead. It might be big enough for him."

Caleb rolled his eyes and stepped off. Lanie's eyes met mine again and I couldn't help but approach.

"You are an interesting lass," I said.

"Oh, am I?" Lanie raised an eyebrow. "Why?"

"We both know you enjoyed yourself earlier."

"And judging by what I saw, so did you," Lanie said. "I was just playing along."

"Uh-huh."

"I'm with Caleb."

"Really with him or just for the weekend?"

Lanie shrugged. "Only time will tell."

"He's never serious. And we're not particularly territorial."

Lanie's mouth dropped. "I don't like your tone, Baz."

"I should make you call me Lord Osgoode, in all honesty. You're poorly behaved and I would bet you'd get off on it."

She bit her lip. *Damn, what I wouldn't give to see what her lips felt like!*

"You couldn't even respect that I had a profession, what makes you think you've earned an honorarium, Baz? I'm not the one who kept watching me fuck your friend."

"It's my house."

"Oh, so you think you have a claim to any woman who steps into it?"

I knew she was about to walk off.

"I wouldn't dare *claim* you. You're spirited, but I do gather you'd like to play. If I could get him on board, what would you say?"

I expected her to tell me to go fuck myself, the thought of which only excited me more.

Then, to my surprise, Lanie replied. "Get him on board and I'm game."

"I will take your offer and run with it," I tried to hide my glee.

"You should offer to sponsor his project," Lanie said. "If you do, I'll let you watch—nothing more. We'll see about more after."

"Do you even know what you're asking, love?" I asked.

Lanie crossed her arms and shrugged. "You put the idea out there, I made you an offer. Take it or leave it."

———

LANIE

I should have hated his overstep. I should have run. Instead, I longed to be owned. I found his demanding, possessive statement hot. It was misguided and ridiculous, but I wanted him to want me. Torturing him became a treat and I was determined to help Caleb if I could. If his friend was going to be into this, he could put his money where his mouth was. However, I never expected Baz to *go* for it.

"You don't have to. The money is his either way. But I wanted to take the chance. I want you, Lanie."

"How much did you want me?"

"Very much?"

"In money. Real money."

"Twenty-five million."

Twenty-five million. A man gave twenty-five million for the chance to watch me fuck his friend? Who was Baz and how much money did he have to throw around? What should have appalled me was intriguing. I found myself wanting to see just how far he'd go.

"If you're not breaking guy-code and he's not territorial, show me."

"How?"

I didn't buy Caleb was *actually* cool with this, but I simply wanted to fuck with both their heads.

"I won't fuck you," I said. "But if you give him the support he requests, then you can watch him rail me."

Baz's steely gaze never dropped.

He called Caleb over as you might call a naughty dog. "Caleb, come here a moment!"

Baz called the shots, and Caleb fell in line, but then what was this role reversal? How could he stand watching his friend fuck the object of his desire? They were both very fucked up, but I wasn't opposed.

"Yes?" Caleb asked.

"Lanie doesn't believe me," Baz sighed, annoyed. "She

doesn't believe you freely agreed to this, but I will sponsor your project."

"Really?"

"She made a bargain. I think you'd be daft not to take it?"

He raised his brow.

Baz continued, voice low. "I watch you fuck her. I finance your project. Does that suit?"

Caleb laughed nervously and took a long sip from his drink, "Uh… why?"

"Because you want the money and your development and I want something else." Baz spoke to me—not Caleb—in a way that sent a shiver down my spine.

Once more, his desire for even a sliver of my time gave me an unexpected high. I turned my chin up, defiantly waiting for Caleb's response. My desire to watch this play out overran any urge I had to call it off.

"Baz, this is mad, even for you!"

"We have done a lot worse together," Baz reminded him.

I would love to have more details on that bit. What sort of kinky shit are they into?

Caleb looked to me, then Baz. "You'd really front me the money just for that?"

Again, I should have paused and stopped this fucked up game. Instead, this dirty interlude delighted me. I wanted to watch him torture Baz *and* take the money and run. Maybe my moral bankruptcy had finally gotten the better of me, but I wanted to stir the pot and twist the knife.

"Yes," Baz answered without hesitation.

"And you're alright with it, Lanie?" Caleb asked.

He stammered, "Well, we aren't together. I didn't want to… hog you. If I offended you—"

"We're not together. That's correct. And I'm not offended, Caleb. I'm intrigued. I've just never met a man willing to do this."

Caleb thought about it, debating it, and asked Baz, "You don't get involved at all?"

Baz shrugged. "I'll take what I can get. I will sit in the corner like a good boy."

"You don't touch us," Caleb confirmed. "That's really what you want, Lanie?"

"I want to fuck you and punish him for this ridiculous deal he tried to strike. Yes."

"Fine," Caleb agreed. "I suppose it's all he earned."

"Come!" I pulled Caleb by the arm. "I'm bored. I don't want to wait all night."

To my surprise, they both left willingly. I'd never had a threesome, but this was even stranger. I should have been a good girl and stayed far away from such entanglements, but that wasn't my nature.

CHAPTER 5

The Awakening

BAZ

Lanie's complete confidence baffled me. Yes, she was beautiful. Her hair was a slow-burning auburn. She simmered with sexual chemistry, but at only about five feet tall, she was unimposing. It was the way she carried herself—strong, resolute, a little aggressive—that commanded a room. She had a presence few women matched.

I arrived at Caleb's guest room slightly after they'd left to avoid any concerns about why we ran off together. I planned to go back down in a bit after my itch was scratched, but I assumed I'd only want her more after this. Indeed, seeing her in the buff—her whole curvy, lithe body on display—only made me want to take her more. I'd settle for this. Her tits alone were worth it.

I didn't disrobe, choosing to behave myself in a corner chair. It wasn't the first time I'd watched someone else fuck a woman I fancied, but it was the first time I'd let my mate do the honors. Her eyes met mine for a moment before she turned back to Caleb. They kissed, standing completely naked in the quiet of it all. Caleb was nervous. He needed to relax, something Lanie sensed.

"Lie down," She beckoned, laying on the bed.

Caleb followed orders, deliberately ignoring me. This wasn't his bag, but he didn't want me to have her. She played with his half-hard cock, trying to urge him along, He wasn't unimpressive. I now understood more how the man managed to find women like Lanie—if only for a moment.

"Would help it if I blew you?" Lanie asked, slowly pumping his shaft.

"Yes," Caleb said.

She said nothing, straddling his leg and settling in to blow him. From where I sat, all I could see was her ass—slightly in the air—and her mostly-bare pussy. If I didn't respect their boundaries, I would have eaten her out right then and there. I wondered what she tasted like. I bet she was sweet. By the time she began to suck him off in earnest, I was already testing the boundaries of my trousers. I tossed my jacket aside and loosened my tie.

Lanie moaned as I assumed she took him deep in her mouth. I wanted to move forward and rub her clit so badly. The sound of her sucking almost set me off. Caleb let out a low, "Oh, fuck," while they ignored their audience.

Without so much as asking, Lanie climbed astride him, her ass still facing me. "Condom?"

Caleb panicked, finding one he'd stashed in the nightstand, and handed it to Lanie. She slipped it on his cock—out of sight—then slipped him back inside her with a satisfied gasp. I could only slightly see the outline of her right breast as she ground on Caleb's cock. She moaned, then began to pant. She was going to get herself off. I said nothing. I behaved myself, remaining still and silent. She leaned forward, gripping the headboard and growled.

"Oh, fuck."

She was about to cum.

"Yes! Oh, God, Caleb! Your cock… is… so… good," she could barely breathe through her words.

Then, Lanie let out a loud shriek, throwing her head back. She growled as she came back down. Caleb pressed on, pumping her body by her bare hips. I unbuttoned my shirt.

She was so greedy, so free, and so damn confident. It pained me to resist this woman.

————

LANIE

I couldn't focus on Baz from this angle, but felt his eyes bore into my back the whole time I focused on Caleb. I did this to torture him, even if I was having fun on his friend's willing cock. I'd gotten off once, but I wanted more. This time, I longed for the satisfaction of watching Baz's tortured expression. So, I stopped Caleb well before he came.

"Fuck me from behind," I pleaded. "I want your friend to see what he's missing. I want him to feel bad about it."

"Yes, of course," Caleb agreed.

I crawled onto all fours, offering my pussy to Caleb while staring Baz dead in the eyes. I wanted to watch his expression as his friend thrust inside me. I wanted to punish him for using me in a deal. I wasn't going to give him twenty-five-million-pounds of satisfaction. He'd know better than to tangle with me.

"Oh, fuck," I moaned as Caleb settled in, slowly entering me and gripping my hips hard.

"Good?" Caleb asked, as if trying to prove something.

"So good," I looked back at him.

Looking at Baz, I got nary a word. He studied me like a painter might a subject, playing with his stubble only feet from me. I could hear it as his thumbed his chin, trying to distract himself. I bet he was hard as a rock and wishing he were where Caleb was now. In fact, I lived for that thought.

I decided to make it worse. "Oh, Caleb, fuck me. You're so good!"

I said it loud—loud enough for the house to hear, gasping as he picked up speed. Caleb moved one hand down and around to my clit. I parted my legs wider as he slowly ran two fingers over it. The view of Baz enraptured with Caleb inside me was good, but adding this play was better. I longed to cum hard. And when I did, I would scream Caleb's name again to anger Baz more.

"Oh, God, Caleb! Fuck me! Fuck me harder!" I screamed.

He pounded into me with great force, bouncing my tits in every direction with every thrust. I came, eyes rolling back. I barely stayed up on all fours, but I couldn't resist giving over to how good Caleb made me feel. I looked up to see Baz leaning forward—head on his hands which were propped up on his knees. He hung on my every moan.

"Are you enjoying this?" I panted. "Watching him make me lose myself? Watching him give me pleasure?"

"Very, very much," Baz answered with a raspy voice.

"It's what you deserve," I turned back to Caleb. "You're amazing, baby. Pull my hair."

"Oh, she likes it rough," Caleb spanked my ass.

I pushed my legs closer together to give him more room to deepen his thrust. Head pulled slightly back, I never dropped eye contact. Every thrust tickled my G-spot. Every pump brought me closer. And then as I realized Baz was lowly rolling his thumb over his cock through his pants, I crossed over.

Drunk on power, I lost myself in the way Baz watched. I may have had Caleb balls-deep inside me, but I couldn't focus on him. My gaze trained on Baz, I thought about what I did to him. The control overcame me. On paper, the scene was between Caleb and I. Baz was an onlooker. The connection with Baz was the only thing I cared about.

"Oh, fuck," I growled. "Oh God! Yes!"

My eyes rolled back, but before I could realign them with Baz's lurid gaze, he jetted off to the ensuite. As Caleb continued to fuck me—getting closer to his own climax—I heard Baz let out a low, long grunt. In the span of only seconds, I made two men cum. It was a high I'd not expected, but damn it was delicious. Caleb was the loyal surrogate who I'd brought physically to orgasm. Baz came only thinking about what I might be *like*. I'd never done something like this.

Though I expected to feel guilt over this use of Caleb's cock while my mind was elsewhere, I only felt satisfaction. Baz's gaze unlocked something deep inside me I couldn't name yet.

Caleb dropped my hair, gripping my hips and moaning, "Oh, fuck! I'm cumming."

I turned my head. "Good boy."

He pulled out and tapped me a little on one ass cheek as Baz returned, zipping his fly.

I lay on the bed now, looking up at him upside down.

"Are you quite satisfied, Ms. Day?" He asked.

"Yes, quite," I answered. "You were both very good boys."

CHAPTER 6
The Morning After

LANIE

I woke the next morning beside Caleb, worn out from our night of debauchery. We left the party early to again go at it—this time in a room off the main hall. To my grave disappointment, there weren't any onlookers. I couldn't get over the way Baz made me feel when he watched us. Shaking the feeling of pure power, I'd mustered with nothing, but my gaze and a few moans delighted me.

I rolled to find Caleb awake and typing away at what I assumed was an email.

"We should get up and go," I said. "I didn't realize I slept so late."

He looked at me, "Oh, it's no trouble. We have the day to ourselves."

"Really?" I asked, surprised. "Why?"

"Baz is busy—he is *always* busy—and we're free to move about the place. I will not lie. I long to go out for golf with the others."

I pulled a face.

"I figured you weren't interested or—"

"No, it's alright. I'll curl up with a book and enjoy the quiet. Honestly, I'm fine."

He turned back to his phone. The lack of interest in debriefing last night confused me. I didn't understand how he could just move on. I needed more. What had they done together?

I ran my hand across his chest. "So… are we going to talk about last night or…"

Caleb looked back at me, casual as ever.

"Well, what do you want me to say, Lanie?"

"I… I've never done anything like that. Based on what you and Baz spoke about… I figured you had."

"Oh, are you having regrets?" He sweetly stroked my cheek. "I can tell him to fuck off, Lanie."

"No," I said. "I rather like pot-stirring. I'm intrigued that any man would—"

"Baz has a kink," Caleb explained. "I mean, he's never indicated he wanted me to do… that. I've never seen him get off on being cuckolded, but… we've done… some things."

He turned back to his phone nervously.

"Okay, spill. If you are worried about offending me, don't be. I know you and I are both horny people who enjoy getting a little dark."

Caleb turned back and shrugged. "We've had some good times together."

"So, you don't get off on it?"

"Uh… I don't know how to answer that without sounding fucked up."

I curled on his chest, looking up as adorably as I could. "I really don't think you're fucked up. I think all three of us have something in common and I loved the thrill of it—even if I am not sure about doing it again."

His face pulled in a way that suggested this was a one-time thing. "I have little interest in doing this again. I don't know how I feel about him watching."

"Or sharing?" I raised my eyebrow.

"That bit is not as big a bother," Caleb admitted. "Sharing doesn't bother me. It's the way he looked at you that does. I don't mind when we're equals in it, but… something about the way he pursued you is the problem."

"The money or—"

"No. Money is business. And… Lanie, I think we both know what this is, but… it's almost perverse. As I said, I don't mind sharing. We all got what we wanted, but I cannot shake the feeling that—as always—Baz gets everything he desires and it's beyond a little fun. And clearly, it shook you a bit."

It didn't. I'd do it repeatedly.

As redness crept up his cheeks, I backed off. His insecurity or jealousy showed. I didn't poke the bear or push the boundary. Having two men equally invested in my pleasure got me off even if having two men *share* me, didn't. One allowed me control while the other gave it. But if Caleb didn't want it, I'd let it go.

"So, if I can ask, Caleb, what does Baz do that he can just throw the GDP of a small country at anyone for any silly thing?" I asked, running my index finger down Caleb's chest.

"He is a real estate investor. He makes a mint by buying properties at a low price and finding a way to increase their value. He flips them for much more and he charms everyone while he does it."

"How does one luck into that? Or rather, are they born into it?" I figured the answer was the latter.

"Like most of us, he was born into it. His father is a baron."

"Like an actual baron or just… figuratively?"

"His father is literally a Baron from some little place in Scotland. They are English by birth, I suppose, but the family inherited a shit ton of money when his father was named heir to some random aristocrat who was a distant cousin. Baz has more money than god from industry, but will inherit even more. They even own the Exham Dyers."

I was immediately curious—not about the money but about where he was from. The situation described how my mother lost her family estate perfectly—she was one of many daughters and it was willed to a distant, English-raised cousin. Her parents wanted her to marry her father's heir if only to preserve the estate, but she refused. Instead, she chose to marry my father, a plucky American pilot and the heir to a retail and real estate fortune. Could Baz's father be our distant cousin—the one my mother was originally supposed to marry?

"What Barony?" I asked.

"Oh, she knows what a Barony is," Caleb chuckled. "Who are you?"

"I'm an American playing the arranged wife of an Earl. I know *some* things." Of course, that was only half the story.

"Oban, I think."

My jaw dropped.

"What?" Caleb chuckled. "Do you know them?"

I covered up my surprise. "No, I just thought you were… taking the piss."

"No, darling. He's a real-life lord. Our families go *way* back. He's like an uncle to me."

I didn't want to unpack all *those* complicated dynamics, so I moved along, much more curious about the family and estate itself. Not wanting to raise suspicion, I played the silly American.

"Well, it is so interesting to know a real-life lord."

"Don't be too jealous, darling," Caleb chuckled. "He has his own issues and is in a bit of a pickle from the looks of it?"

"Oh?"

"His father is a massive prick. A real wanker! And as such, he makes ridiculous demands of Baz. He always pits him against his boring, daft younger brother. And Baz? Well, he doesn't help himself."

"How so?"

"His father—despite being a notorious womanizer in his day—hates Baz's love of chasing tail. The man may be smart at business, but women will be the end of him."

"Is he the type to fall in love quickly and get burned? That surprises me."

"No. He falls in lust, becomes obsessed with a shiny object, and then gets distracted."

I suddenly understood Caleb's reticence to let this happen again. I suspected *I* was now a bauble to Baz and the reason he did something so stupid as to make a business decision just to watch me cum. While I sensed things between his father and my mother ended *very* badly, I was still stuck here for the weekend with a man who should have been my sworn enemy. I also now knew what Baz's kryptonite was. It didn't just flatter me to be the object of his desire, it gave me another leg up—one Baz didn't even know I had. I sat on that, not wanting to draw attention to my intrigue.

Playing cheerful, I asked, "Do you want to get ready for breakfast? I'd blow you in the shower."

"I'd be delighted," Caleb said. "Why in the hell are you so horny? You're a very cheeky girl."

"I'm insatiable. It's been a complaint before."

"Not from me."

I bit my lip as I left bed. "No, you're very willing to go to hell with me, Caleb. I adore you for it."

As I blew Caleb in the shower, I wasn't thinking about him. I thought about Baz and how hot it might be to be here right now with him in the corner jacking off while I blew Caleb. It was power I held—power to torture a man whose family scorned mine. Suddenly, all I wanted to do was have wild, crazy, slightly vengeful sex. After all, seduction was an art, and I'd already proven myself an excellent painter. I told myself every time I tortured Baz with an orgasm, I avenged my family.

BAZ

I took a call, slipping into the library and pulling the door behind me. My construction manager droned on about job issues and an executive decision he felt I should make with a development in Bath. But as he continued, I felt eyes on me. I turned to see Lanie reading in the nook by the window, staring from her stomach on the couch with her legs kicking behind her. She looked so innocent, yet so seductive all at once. It was that confidence and lack of shame that always stopped my train of thought.

"I don't know what to say," I said once he stopped.

"Well, I'd suggest you come down here tomorrow to at least check it out. We're working around the clock," he explained. "And it would also signal to the crew this isn't all for nothing."

I groaned. "Fine."

Yes, I have nothing better to do on a Saturday morning than to check on a construction site.

"Good. I will be here early—eight, if you can."

"Early is better," I agreed. "I will see you then."

As I hung up, I turned back to Lanie. She pretended to be focused solely on her book, but I knew better.

"Well, Miss Day, apologies for that."

"It's fine. It's your house," Lanie looked at her book.

I wanted to toss the damn thing across the room.

"You're a reader then?"

"I'm not much for golf, Lord Osgoode." She sat her gaze back on me.

"Nor am I. Too slow."

"Oh, you're more for things that go fast?" Lanie raised her eyebrow. "Too fast, perhaps?"

"I'd rather they go fast than drag."

"I couldn't tell. Although, sometimes, it might be wise to take a minute?"

Her advice was sage, but damn if I didn't want to go far too fast with her lips around my cock or to flip her over the arm of a couch and pound into her. Her fearlessness made me nervous, but the way she baited me only made me want to punish her for her bad deeds.

"I don't have much time," I wanted to adjust myself. "That's what my job requires."

"Yes, of course, it's just business. Like last night. Was that really the smartest move?"

"You tell me, love." I prickled at her admonishment.

"Well, was it worth the investment? You're the one who laid it out there. I had no money in the game, just skin, I suppose."

Yes, beautiful, perfect, milky-white skin and nipples I wanted to suck very badly.

"The thing with investments," I said, "is you need to give them time."

"And do you think it will pay off in the end, Lord Osgoode?"

I smiled, confident. "Yes, I think it will. I suspect it will pay dividends. I rarely regret such investments."

"Because you don't like to lose?"

"I never lose, Miss Day." I turned.

I'd have her—all of her—before this was over.

Unfortunately, I worried that without a gesture, she'd assume this was all just a game I ceded to Caleb. I gathered a woman like Lanie became accustomed to a chase. After all, I assumed she could have any younger, rich man she wanted. I wanted to prove it was me she longed to see after this weekend. Yes, we'd shared in some sort of carnal mischief, and I longed to do it again, but it was more than that. Caleb would bore of her, and she deserved better than his usual treatment of discarding a shiny object only days after discovering it. Yes, I'd find a way to impress her. While Lanie tested my resolve and patience with every sideways glance or innuendo, I would get what I wanted sooner or later. I always did.

CHAPTER 7
The Pursuit

LANIE

THINGS WENT quiet after Baz was called to a job site. He declared he needed to leave so he could make a meeting. My heart sank. I wanted to bait him and make Caleb jealous. Still, it didn't take much to play into Caleb's feeling that he ran Baz off after our encounter. Caleb ran the party as if it were his house and he fucked me like I was a glittering trophy later.

I focused on the next day when Baz would return. Satisfied with my reorientation as a sexual vigilante, I attended brunch on day three with a focus on my charm offensive. To my grave disappointment, Baz was nowhere to be found.

"Is Baz just… gone?" I asked. "Has he ditched us?"

Baz's associate, Warner, responded. "He went to check on a job in Bath. He said not to wait for him, and he'd be back to shoot in the afternoon. He wanted to get an early start this morning—hence the evening departure."

"Are you sad to miss him?" Caleb sounded a little threatened.

I squeezed Caleb's knee, "No. I just feel bad since it's his house and we've barely seen him. Doesn't that bother him?"

"No," the others answered.

"He is that way," Caleb explained. "Business before all else. He never stops."

Except for me. He'd do anything to fuck me.

Torture could wait. And either way, we were having fun, weren't we? A leisurely breakfast was served as we waited for our host's return, but I suspected we'd go without Baz.

As I was in the library reading a beautifully gilded copy of *Wuthering Heights*, Caleb appeared.

"Baz is back. If you want to change, now's the time."

"Sure," I said.

I went upstairs to our room and found a neatly wrapped box on the dresser with a note emblazoned "Lanie".

I opened the card.

> *Ms. Day,*
> *You are much agreeable. Please take this as a token of my greatest apology for my bad behavior.*
> *-B*

Baz gave me a *gift? What the hell?*

I undid the ribbon and peeled back the paper to reveal a jewelry box. I opened the clamshell to reveal a necklace. Suspended on a white gold chain was a beautiful emerald. I gasped. This would have been at least five grand in the States. I touched the dazzling teardrop and thought about how I could wear it. He'd done well, but I *hated* him for it. Had he paid for this in blood money? I contemplated sending it back in protest, then stopped. *If it was worn on my skin, wasn't I reclaiming it?*

———

BAZ

"So, do you want to explain why a gift was left for Lanie in my room?" Caleb asked.

I couldn't tell if he was upset with me. Given that they'd been in their room making as much noise as possible this morning, I didn't think he had room to complain. I decided to play another game while I skipped out to Bath with a shaky work excuse.

"Who says it was me?"

"I'm not an idiot, Baz. It was your handwriting."

I sighed, "Look, it's to smooth it over with her. That's all. I feel I offended her."

"I don't. She's quite alright," Caleb said.

"But I've offended you, Caleb?"

"No. I get the feeling this has run its course and that she's interested in neither of us."

I suspected he was hurt but played it off so I'd stop pursuing her. Unfortunately, I was better at strategy than Caleb.

"Is Lanie joining us?" I changed the subject.

"She can shoot, so she says," Caleb said, as if doubting her capabilities.

I turned to see Lanie walking out in a light jacket unfit for the British weather.

"It might rain," I said. "You will want to add something more substantial than that."

"Sorry. I didn't realize it was going to be thick as pea soup. I didn't pack anything more," she replied.

"Come with me," I said.

I led her to the back entry's hall wardrobe that housed extra clothes. I knew we had a coat or two that would probably work. Lanie followed and picked through the options.

"You have very well-heeled leftovers, Baz," she said. "Not that I am surprised."

She held up an older Burberry coat and compared it to her own stature in the mirror behind the door. I gently took it from her and held it so she could slip inside. Lanie quietly obliged, leaving me staring back at her in the mirror. She met my gaze with a hungry expression. I couldn't manage to step away. Nor could I bring myself to do what I wanted. I longed to kiss her neck and breathe in her scent.

Saying nothing, Lanie spun.

"The necklace was nice. You did well, but you shouldn't have gotten it for me. Caleb is jealous."

"I don't care if Caleb is cross. I wanted to spoil you, so I did. Wear it tonight for dinner," I said.

She shook her head. "You don't own me. You realize that, right?"

Her scowl and biting words cut me. Had I overstepped? My intent was genuine. Caleb's discussion of his plans to dissolve everything only supported my desire to make her feel special. Was her act a game or did she hate the gift?

"If it bothers you, I can return it," I assured,

Lanie's face softened and she dropped my gaze momentarily. "I appreciated the gesture. It's beautiful. However, you haven't won me. I'm not yours."

I said softly, "I know. I wish you were."

She met my gaze again, mouth agape, she searched for a snappy comeback. Her resolve weakened.

"I know you're here with Caleb. I'm not about to dream otherwise," I said. "But if you're still in London for a bit, I'd like to take you out properly."

"I should say no," she said. "But do something to wow me. Don't bore me."

I grinned. "I have an idea, yeah."

"Good."

She snapped the jacket and proceeded outside where a staff member herded people into cars. I watched her board a Range Rover with Caleb, but I knew I'd have her, either way. When we finally landed on the shooting grounds, I assessed her behavior with a rifle. Caleb doubted her, but I didn't.

Even with a fine mist and poor visibility, she confidently called, "Pull!"

The pigeon shot into the air and she nailed it. She called a second time, again killing it. Without acknowledging her victory, she adeptly broke the shotgun open to toss the spent shells.

"Your move." She nodded at Caleb.

He'd never best her. Nor would I—more than likely.

"Who taught you to shoot?" I asked as she reloaded.

"My father and grandfather," she answered. "I grew up in Michigan and my grandfather liked to hunt. I know how to shoot. I'd wager I am probably the best of my siblings—minus my older brother who is in the Air Force."

"I am impressed," I said as Caleb missed his second shot.

"She kicked your arse," I razzed.

"Yeah, yeah. She's good," Caleb said. "I'll concede."

Lanie was *very* good. She was never what I expected, but she left me wanting more.

CHAPTER 8

Getting Naked

LANIE

"You just got home and you're leaving again?" Chloe flopped on my bed wearing only a robe. "You are never here."

"Nor are you," I said. "Didn't you go to Ibiza on a lark last week?"

"It was a work trip."

"With a hot guy."

Chloe lived her life always on the move. We made bank as influencers, but it was her main source of income. She specialized in horse content and had a lifestyle brand. People invited her to fly first class to five-star resorts all so she could take a picture in a bikini having a good time. It was nice work if she could get it. She may have been a bombshell, but she was also a shrewd businesswoman and, like me, had quite the appetite for hot men. Her choice in men differed from mine—I preferred them older, while Chloe swore she was open to a sugar daddy but wanted to keep her options open to fit, younger men. Most were fuckboys, but some were fun for a while.

"Where are you going?"

"To shop. Come with."

"I have a headache. I want to rot"

"Uh-huh." I didn't buy the excuse. "You look like you are already made up."

"I'm not feeling social."

"C'mon, I need to buy a dress."

"Fine," she agreed. "Is Dora Elizabeth coming?"

"Dora must work. It's all she does! Apparently, she is exploring some ruins next week."

My baby sister was visiting between volunteer assignments. Lately, she'd been living in a convent in the DRC working with nuns. She was the best person I knew, even if her selflessness would have been annoying with anyone else.

"She wants kids to have clean water. She'll never stop. I guess. C'mon! You'd really leave me to do this alone when you have nothing better to do?"

"Oh, there's the Catholic guilt coming out," Chloe teased.

I giggled. "Light on the Catholic. Heavy on the guilt."

"Fine," Chloe said. "I will come but only if you tell me what you got up to this weekend. You've been so hush-hush."

I rolled my eyes. "I will spill, but you cannot say shit to my sister. She'll freak out."

"Oh, hot. Scandal!" Chloe stood and left while I finished up my lipstick.

I decided to spill on the way in my sister Daphne's "old" Porsche. I drove.

"So, what did the guy do? Are you going out with him again?"

"Probably not," I admitted.

"That bad?"

"No," I answered. "He was good. *Really* good. But it got weird and… I have another interest."

"What?"

"So, Caleb's friend and older brother type is this sexy older guy—they call him Baz. He caught us and just *watched.* And I should have told him to fuck off…"

I stopped as we hit a snag.

"Fucking traffic," Chloe said. "Still somehow better than the Eisenhower in the morning."

I snickered. "I do not miss that."

"Me neither. So, wait… he watched you *fuck* this guy?"

"Yeah. And then he offered his friend 25 million pounds so he could ask me to sleep with him."

"Who the fuck are these guys? This is some *Eyes Wide Shut* bullshit right here."

"I dunno. I thought it was awful—and hot. So, I played along and punished Daddy Vibes a little."

"What? How? Can we *please* call him Daddy Vibes?"

"Yes," I giggled. "Uh, so I told him he couldn't fuck me, but I'd let him watch Caleb plow me. And he did. I blew his friend, got on top, and then let him destroy me from behind looking right at Daddy Vibes in the face. And before Caleb even came, he ran off and got off in the bathroom. No joke. It was strangely so hot and also fucked up."

"So, he's a little kinky. And *this* is the reason you cannot fuck Caleb again?"

"We both agreed there was nothing more there than sex. I suppose I *could* fuck him again, but I think it's pushing the envelope with Daddy Vibes if I do. And damn it! I *want* to fuck Daddy Vibes!"

"So, are we talking like full on silver fox?"

"Mid-forties, maybe. Salt and pepper with impeccable stubble. After that, I just fantasized about him every fucking time I shagged Caleb. God, I cannot help myself."

"He paid twenty-five million to sleep with you?"

"No. Not like that." I shook my head. "It was so he could even have a *shot* with me. Caleb sold his chance off for a condo development in Islington. Except he didn't because we kept fucking like bunnies all weekend. But I'm bored now."

"Lanie, you need help," Chloe said. "I want to meet Daddy Vibes."

"Maybe someday," I said. "He wants to take me on an adventure this week. I said I'm open to it."

"An adventure? Oh, nice. Damn, that was *not* the tea I was expecting this morning."

"Nor was this," I said. "I mean it, do *not* talk to Daphne about this. I don't need the judgement."

"I am certainly not going to talk about this kink of yours with my sister-in-law!"

"It's not my kink!"

"You performed for him and *clearly* enjoyed it. Face it, Delanie, you're *kinky*. It's nothing to be ashamed of. I'm here for it. We're both proud sluts after all."

"God, my mother would be *horrified* by this conversation."

My phone buzzed.

"It's Cassandra," Chloe said.

It was my agent.

"Put it on speaker."

"Hello?" I answered.

"Oh, good! I got you. Well, I have good news."

I felt Chloe vibrate in excitement.

"Is this about *Dollar Princesses*?" I asked.

"It is. Leah and Brian just called. Early ratings are in and they are excited to offer you a main storyline in the next season. The network loved your character. They did want to clarify things with you, though."

I'd done it! I booked a lead role in a season of a prestige drama! I was living my own dream.

"Yes?" I tried to keep my excitement down.

"Well, there's the sex issue," Cassandra said. "This season is planned to be spicier than the last one. I wanted to make sure you were okay with that. There will always be an intimacy coach, but given there was nudity in season one—"

"Sure, that's fine," I said.

"Well, in the past—"

"My Dad is dead," I said. "I promised him as long as he was on this earth, I'd never get naked on camera. I *hated* that rule and I held to my word. No more!"

"Well... okay. I will get the details on the contract ironed out and send it over to your attorney! Congrats!"

"Thanks," I answered.

Chloe hung up. "She's getting naked! Ah!"

CHAPTER 9
The Vesper Room

BAZ

My car approached the address Lanie listed—a very posh Mayfair house. As I took in its scale, I suspected daddy had money and she lived with her family. That was fine. Almost every aristocrat I knew still lived under mummy and daddy's roof—myself excluded. I paid for my current place with my own money. I stepped out, taking in the cool autumn air and walked upstairs to the door. I rang the bell and waited awkwardly.

A young woman answered—but it wasn't Lanie.

"Hello, I'm here for Miss Day," I said.

The pretty blonde looked me over before shouting. "Lanie, Daddy Vibes is here!"

I fought anger and embarrassment as the woman stepped back and crossed her arms. She sized me up. *Daddy vibes*? I wasn't *that* old. Then, again, what was she? Twenty-five. I was almost old enough to be her father. Another girl—a blonde with glasses popped into the picture.

"Who are you?"

"Baz," I said. "I'm taking your sister out."

I assumed and she didn't dispute it.

"At this hour?" The girl asked. "Lanie, he should at least buy you dinner first. Jesus!"

The other blonde snickered as Lanie walked into the picture, looking beautiful in a short dress. Her auburn hair fell around her shoulders in curls I wanted to touch. Before I could even comment on the outfit, she stopped.

"Oh, I forgot my jewelry."

"Can I get it?" The first blonde asked.

"No, I'm good. One sec." Lanie departed, leaving a conversational vacuum where no one knew what to say. The two blondes appraised me suspiciously. They had no inkling of my plans and that was for the best. I was worried even Lanie might blanch when I told her.

Lanie returned with a pair of earrings and held out the necklace I bought her. "I planned my entire outfit around this and just forgot."

The younger girl stepped forward to help, but I spoke up.

"I can do it."

Lanie spun towards me, one eyebrow lifted.

"Well, I bought it for you, so shouldn't I be the one?" I asked.

"Fine," Lanie approached and handed the necklace over.

Lanie spun, holding up her beautiful red hair so I could drape the necklace around her delicate neck—the one I wanted to kiss desperately. I clasped it, satisfied she was now marked. She was mine in a way she hadn't been before. I tried not to gawk, keenly aware of the women watching. The older one seemed entertained, while the younger one's judgmental scowl shook me slightly.

Lanie turned, looking at me, mouth slightly agape. "Well, I guess I'm ready now."

She stepped into her shoes, tossing her hair over her shoulder and pulled on a light coat to shield her from the cool air.

"Don't wait up and fuck off, Dora!"

She pulled the door closed.

"Were those your sisters?" I asked.

"Depends on why you are asking. If you're going to make some sick joke—"

"No. I found them… very American," I noted.

"As American as apple pie," Lanie said in a silly accent. "You could say that. And Dora is right. You should buy me dinner first."

She slid into the open car door and settled. I followed her, the door closing behind me.

"I am taking you somewhere unique and the party starts late," I said. "It's only 10."

"Only? You're taking me on a date. You called it a *proper* date."

"Doesn't mean dinner. Now that I sense your hostility, I will make note I owe you dinner. Do I ever *not* owe you, darling?" I asked.

"No. Because you lust for me, you get a high from being around me, and you'd do anything to impress me. I am very demanding—as you previously stated. I like to be spoiled. So, I will keep asking for things and, I suspect, you will keep giving them."

I missed that wit ever since she left with Caleb. Since then, Caleb left town and was likely hooking up with another woman in Paris. I was glad to have Lanie Day alone. She was still fucking gorgeous. There was something hauntingly familiar about her face—especially those full lips—but I couldn't put my finger on what.

"You always examine me," Lanie said.

"You're beautiful. I enjoy it," I said. "Now, are you ready for something unique? And are you brave?"

"I'm not eating squid. I don't eat things that freak me out. Squid is one of them. I don't care how uncultured that makes me."

"We aren't eating. Are you really that hungry?"

"I will be in approximately 2 hours if I also drink."

"There will be drink," I promised. "And if you're a very

good girl, I will give you your choice of literally all kebab offerings on the way home."

"You think you're taking me home?" She raised her eyebrows.

"I *know* I'm taking you home, Lanie."

"We'll see. Where are you taking me?"

"The Vesper Room," I said.

She did a double take. "I… oh… I don't think I belong at a place like that."

"A place like that? I'm a member, for one."

Her mouth dropped.

"You are a babe in the woods, but I am not, darling. Is it too much for you? If so, that's fine. We can get a drink—"

"No," Lanie said, determined. "I am… open-minded. I just worry that my agent might kill me. Our show got renewed and I'm going to have a big part next year."

"It's very hush-hush. And anyway, if they fire you, it's silly. Your boss has been a member, too. I shouldn't tell you that, of course."

"Leah goes to the Vesper Room?"

"I haven't seen her for a bit. I don't think she'd bat an eye. It's… very interesting."

"Holy shit," Lanie gasped. "Well, good for her, I guess? I suppose if the Queen's niece can make it work, I can."

"Correct. We can leave whenever you want. I'm not bothered. However, I got the feeling you might want to play. And if you do, we have options."

Lanie leaned over, her face close enough to kiss me.

She tilted her head and whispered. "I'm game to play, but I come to win, Baz."

Then, she backed off, not kissing me and not touching me. If she didn't let me have her, I'd be miserable, but on the off chance she let me fuck her, I'd be fine with it.

———

LANIE

The Vesper Room was an exclusive sex club in SoHo with a list of clients that remained secret to only its members. There weren't trial periods and one had to be sponsored by a current member to even be considered for membership. I'd curiously listened to Vesper Room lore, but never thought I'd find myself there. Walking into the concierge area, I wasn't sure what to expect. The lights were low, and the furnishings high-end. The couple ahead of us was dressed to the nines—two women in contrasting Dior. I recognized one as a super-model—Bri Corrigan.

Baz guided me, his hand on the small of my back, and whispered, "There are rules. The first one is they will take your mobile. No phones inside and if you come without one, they don't let you in."

"Makes sense, I guess," I pulled out my phone and handing it to a short, dapper man with a fabulous set of long locks.

He took my coat, locked our belongings up, and handed a keycard to Baz while making small talk, A woman opposite the desk raised an eyebrow.

"Have you brought us fresh meat, Basil?"

"This is Lanie," Baz said. "She may be fresh, but she isn't new to the game."

He expressed such confidence in me. I talked big, but I wasn't sure I'd be able to hang when we passed through the doors. Baz took my hand and pulled me towards the entry. I held on tight. My eyes got wide as dinner plates as the door attendant opened it, but what I saw wasn't what I thought I would. The area inside was a standard bar. People laughed, joked, and a few danced to too-loud, slightly goth techno.

"It's just… a bar," I noted.

"Nah. It's more than that. You can come here just for a drink and privacy, or you can go to the *fun* areas. I will show you around, but you'll want a drink first. I'll discuss Ps and Qs in the interim."

He stepped up to the bar and nodded at me as the bartender approached. "What do you want?"

I quickly ran down the drink menu. "The Gin martini is great."

"I'll have a negroni," Baz said.

The bartender left without a word.

"The staff are so… chill," I noted.

"Their job is to fade into the background to let things happen," Baz said. "It's good we got here a little early—good for you. It's best for people watching."

"How often do you come here?"

Baz shrugged. "Enough. Sometimes I just get bored. Believe it or not, I don't always come here to do something too debaucherous. The bartender is good, people leave you alone, and I enjoy people watching quietly."

"I haven't noticed."

"In all seriousness, Lanie, there are rules here. The first one is a man cannot approach a woman. Women approach men *only*. Consent can obviously be withdrawn at any point during play. You don't have to engage directly. You can always just watch. It legitimately doesn't matter to me *what* we do, Lanie—or don't— but you must leave with me. It becomes a labyrinth back there. You probably want to stick near me at least for now."

"Okay," I said. "Consent is key. For your reference, I like things rough. I don't mind being treated like a bit of a ragdoll, but if I say Kiwi, we're done-zo."

"Kiwi?"

"Do not make fun of my favorite safeword."

"I'm not. It's rather ingenious. So, you're not so precious?"

"I am not precious, Baz. Wise up."

I sipped my drink as people arrived. If you told me that most of hedonist London was already a member of Vesper, I would have laughed. However, on this evening, I recognized several famous faces. Some may have recognized me. Either way, they never said anything, as admitting you knew someone belonged was mutually assured destruction.

We finished our drinks with dedicated, quiet people watching.

"I apologize if I say little," Baz said.

"I generally find it off-putting," I said, "but not here. I am trying to get my bearings."

"You're observant?"

"I must be observant, I guess? You cannot create characters without seeing how other people live."

He nodded. "Well, that makes sense. I am just not much for small talk. If you seek that, you won't get it here."

I considered how that could work, but decided I didn't *need* it to work. This was about torturing *him*, wasn't it?

It was past eleven and people began to file into rooms beyond the bar. As I followed Baz on a more extensive tour, I shook with nerves. Thankfully, it wasn't exactly what I expected. There were a range of activities and no weird initiation ceremony. People flowed through in a relaxed fashion, some hand in hand as if they were just on a date, others clawing at one another. Still, it wasn't all that different than many Soho night spots. While there were dark areas—including a room with what seemed like the world's biggest bed—not all of them were so poorly lit. Some places were more vanilla, while more adventurous folks could access a full-on dungeon.

"I'm good with light bondage but that's a bit much," I whispered to Baz, worried that was what he might be into.

"That's fine. Don't be nervous. Are you alright?" He began to doubt me.

"I… I am. It's honestly not at all what I expected—minus the dungeon. That's not for me."

"This place is nothing," Baz said. "Some people complain about it not being intense enough. I'm not into it, either. I mean, I'd give almost anything to hold you down and fuck you properly, but—"

"But you're willing to let me play?" I arched my eyebrows.

"I wouldn't have brought you if I didn't want to socialize you."

Baz had no idea what he was in for. If he thought I was a build-your-perfect-sub, he was sorely mistaken. I walked away, then turned playfully to look at him. I wanted to get another rise out of him, darting back into a room with another, smaller bar. I ordered another martini and took in the crowd. Baz settled in next to me, but I ignored him. Instead, I focused all my attention on a short but incredibly built man in the corner wearing a nearly painted on button-up shirt. I stirred my drink and met his eye contact. He wanted me and Baz knew it. He said nothing, but I knew I was about to twist the dagger. The mystery man watched like a hawk. I sat my drink down and approached, hoping I was braver than I thought I was.

"Hello," I sipped my drink.

"Hello." A grin spread across his face.

"Are you here alone?"

"My girlfriend is here with *her* girlfriend, but I am free to play as I see fit," he answered. "Where on Earth did you come from?"

I turned and looked back at Baz. "I came with a friend."

The man looked at me like I was a total snack. Which, in this dress, I was.

"Do you want to kiss me?" I asked.

"I'd love to do whatever you'd like, love."

The accent. I was in heaven. I leaned in, kissing him. He responded by pulling me closer. I pressed my hips into him, very aroused by the idea of making out with a stranger and raising the anger of the man who'd brought me here and couldn't leave without me. I ran my hand through his hair as he played with my nipple through my dress.

Moaning, I pulled back and looked over at Baz. Jaw set, he glared.

"Your friend is jealous. Does he want to play, too?"

"He likes to watch," I answered. "I don't think he wants to play with you."

"Well, he can watch. I don't mind."

"I'll ask him," I said.

As much excitement as there was in the thought of shagging a stranger in *front* of Baz, I didn't want to break Baz's heart, either. I stepped back to whisper about what I could and could *not* do.

"Are you going to torture me all night?"

"Didn't you sign up for that? You know I'm a sadist, right?"

Baz smiled slightly. "You kiss a stranger—one who isn't even deserving of you—but ignore me. I've not even gotten to touch you."

"You're greedy. Why bring me here if you don't want to share?" I asked.

"He can go down on you or finger you," Baz said. "But I won't let him fuck you. I plan to—and properly—after I take you home."

I should have told him off for being so possessive, but his cross expression and terse words aroused me. I didn't know what possessed me to agree to it, but I nodded.

"I will let you be a little greedy, but you better fuck me properly, darling."

I walked back to the stranger.

"You can use your hands and mouth, but you cannot fuck me with your cock. And he wants to watch. Is that agreeable?"

The guy chuckled. "Yes, please. I'd like to eat you out."

"Be my guest," I nodded at Baz to follow.

The two accompanied me like lambs to the slaughter into a room with several beds. I collapsed onto one. Mystery Man followed, going in for the kill. It struck me as *so* odd that we were about to publicly engage in the most private act, and I didn't know his name. I didn't *need* to, either. I supposed that was part of the thrill.

Mystery Man parted my legs enough to run his hand up my thigh and reach for my panties. By now, Baz stood at my shoulders. He wanted to observe my gratification and nothing else. *That* was what got him off. I took my panties from where Mystery Man tossed them and handed them to Baz.

"You'll pay for that later," Baz growled. "I'm not here to hold things for you."

His gruff response didn't jive with the erection he was already too pained to hide. For him, this was serious.

I gripped Mystery Man's hair and looked down at him momentarily before turning back to Baz. I again realized I couldn't visualize anyone *but* him. He'd never even had me, but he had all of me. Yes, it was good to have them both and the novelty helped. However, that wasn't all. It was also the gratification on Baz's face. In the end, that was the hottest bit. I locked my eyes on him as each stroke got me closer.

The room was quiet apart from low, ambient music and the sounds of another couple shagging to our right. Normally, I muted porn. Fake screaming didn't do it for me, but I wasn't bothered by listening to a stranger get railed by someone ten feet away while a man went down on me. I looked over, watching her. The man pinned her to the bed hard—wrists above her head tied up by one of his hands as he steadied himself with the other.

Turning back to Baz, I expected he'd be watching the display. Instead, I realized he was watching me watching them. Somehow, I transfixed him. How or why, I didn't know, but it did it for me. I pressed my hips to the man's face. He dug his palms into my hips as I fucked his face with each roll of my hips. I focused my gaze on Baz. My nostrils flared and I moaned louder. I shrieked as I came, surprising myself with the words that rolled out.

"Oh, fuck, Baz!"

It probably surprised both of us—given that he hadn't yet laid a hand on me.

The man backed off, trying to gauge what happened next. He couldn't make the next move, so I was in charge, but all I could think of was Baz and how much I wanted to somehow return the favor. I knew that wasn't the right way to treat someone who just gave you an orgasm. So, I turned back to the man.

"You're lovely," he gave me a quick kiss, before pulling back and standing.

"Thanks. You are, too," I said.

Then, he left, sticking to the boundaries of our agreement. I turned back to Baz, pulling myself to my feet and approaching. Not knowing how to repay him for his patience, I moved toward him, searching for what he was thinking. I took my panties from his hand and pulled them back on. Again clothed, I played with the collar of his shirt and read his expression. The look of wonder in his eyes made me feel all new, even if it wasn't for him. His bewilderment amazed me. Was he just the best actor I'd ever done a love scene with?

Baz gently cupped my face in his hands and kissed me slowly and sweetly, as if this was the first time I'd *ever* been kissed. It was gentle—our lips barely meeting at first. He slowly ran a hand through my hair—careful not to pull it. I realized he was taking me in—properly and slowly. His other hand ran down my neck. I shivered at the sensation, expecting him to cup my breast. Instead, he found the chain to my necklace and pulled.

"This is even more beautiful on you than I anticipated," Baz chuckled slightly.

I nearly shuddered at the mention. The minute he offered to put the necklace on, I knew he thought the war was won. In truth, though, letting him think he won got me off. On the other, I was slightly thrilled by his willingness to spend money to impress me. No man had ever spoiled me like this. I relished the attention I never got from my ex. He never spent much on presents and wouldn't have had a clue what looked nice with my hair or overall aesthetic.

"It's beautiful. You chose well," I admitted. "And, yes, I did buy this dress to go with it."

"Good girl," Baz whispered, kissing me slowly.

The way he sucked on my lower lip made my toes curl. It was a complete experience. He'd never done anything to me.

This was all still very PG on the surface, but deep down, I launched deep into the depths of my own desire. Baz fell before even I had. While I was here to seduce him—to play my game—I lived in this moment where I felt everything was completely new again.

CHAPTER 10

Getting Down To It

BAZ

LANIE'S LIPS were so full and soft, I could have kissed her for hours. At my age, I never thought kissing could feel like such a sensory experience. However, as we stood there, I breathed her in. I tasted the whiskey her conquest drank but also a slight taste of *her*. I wanted more, but I didn't want it here. I didn't want the first time I had all of her to myself to be interrupted by anything—or anyone. She felt precious. It was a rush thinking about how quickly I could get her home and devour all of her. I wanted to worship every inch of this woman. The pull hit me like a brick.

Lanie played with my belt. I grabbed her hand.

"No," I said, voice low. "Not here. I don't want to share you right now. I want to be greedy and have every inch of you to myself."

Lanie looked up at me, her big blue eyes filling my soul with more than lust—I adored her. Stupidly, I'd do almost anything to win her. Like me, Lanie was wicked and depraved, but she was also soft and sweet. I wanted to experience the latter. I'd had enough of the former this evening.

"Okay," Lanie agreed. "You win. We can go to yours. If I bring you back, we'll have no privacy."

At my age, I had no time for a roommate or family situation. I had 5000 square feet of freedom and an untold number of surfaces I could take her on.

"Okay," I took her hand and focusing on getting out.

We had to wait until we reached the lobby for me to ring the driver. I wanted to kiss her again. I wanted to never *stop* kissing Lanie Day, but that wasn't how I managed such things in public. Besides, I didn't think either of us could reliably control ourselves. Thankfully, my driver quickly collected us. After a quick trip through Hyde Park Corner, we were back in Knightsbridge and on my side street off Brompton Road.

He pulled the car into the alley, allowing us an entry through the back door. We arrived in the primary basement in front of the gym.

"Where are we?" Lanie asked.

"Darling, I'd love to show you around at a later date, but I don't have much time on my hands to give you a tour right now." I pressed the button to the lift.

Lanie didn't argue.

We rode to the top floor and right into my primary suite.

"Wow," Lanie said. "This is beautiful. Prime real estate. Did you build this?"

"This was one of my developments, yes."

Normally, I could go on about how I got this place and how it was my baby, but I didn't want to talk real estate. That wasn't the business I wanted right now.

"You don't want to talk, do you?" Lanie read my mind.

"No, Lanie. I want you naked."

She bit her lip. God, I couldn't want anything more than her lips right now. I didn't understand why I was so drawn to that part of her. Keeping eye contact, she ripped off her dress, threw her bra to the side and stood on display.

"Good?" Lanie asked.

"It will more than do," I agreed, following suit.

Lanie settled on the bed, boosted by her elbows. If I said she was anything less than perfect, I'd be lying. She was gorgeous—almost glowing in the low light of the city. I wanted so badly to feel her. If kissing had been unimaginably good, I couldn't imagine how superb things would be with her beneath me.

When I rummaged for a condom in the nightstand, Lanie stopped me.

"I don't think you want that yet."

"What?"

"I want to blow you," Lanie said.

"Lanie—"

"No, I do. I haven't got to play with your cock yet. You'd deny me?" She *pouted*. How could I say no?

"Well, then, get to work," I said, gruffly in a way she'd throw back.

Argument with Lanie was so precious. I loved how good she gave. Younger women were tricky. They rarely felt like my intellectual equal, but Lanie was. She was clever, demanding, and shrewd at negotiation. I could manage a younger woman like that. She was more than a plaything or conquest. She was a constant distraction I couldn't ignore and a pursuit I'd not kick. And after tonight, I worried I'd only be more intoxicated and wrapped up in her. I should have feared that, but I didn't.

Lanie took my cock in her hands, straddling my leg as I'd first imagined her doing to me as she did to Caleb. She slowly rolled her fingers over the head of my cock, grabbing the precum already there. I'd stop her before too long. I was too excited, and I had a feeling she'd be good at this. The feeling of her lubricated hand rolling down my shaft made me shudder.

"Yeah? You like that?" Lanie said, voice husky.

Her accent did it for me every time.

"Yes. Does it please you?" I asked.

"It's very good."

Lanie bent down, licking from my balls up the shaft. Her beautiful lips took me in slowly, making me shiver under her immaculate, delicious torture.

"Fuck," I growled, lacing my right hand through her hair.

Lanie bobbed slowly up and down my cock, moaning as she did. I felt her wetness as she ground against my leg. The woman was so good. As she sped up, I couldn't fight it.

"No," I said, shaking it off. "I don't want to cum in your mouth. Not like this. Later."

Lanie slowly pulled off my cock, but didn't stop. She stared up at me as she licked the head.

"You're playing with fire and being very disobedient, Lanie."

Lanie let go of my cock, grinning cheekily. "You should punish me, then."

"Get on top of me," I growled.

Lanie slowly obliged. I sensed she wanted to be punished, something I'd relish, so I spanked her. That elicited a long moan. Taking her time, she grabbed the condom on the nightstand and slowly rolled it down my shaft. Eventually, her body straddled mine as she slowly enveloped me within her slick, warm center. She shuddered, satisfied with how it felt. I couldn't have complained if I tried.

"Was it all you imagined?" Lanie asked, grinding against me.

"So fucking perfect," I moaned.

"Worth twenty-five million?"

"Worth even more."

"More than this house?"

"Per appraisal value a year ago," I said. "No. Per build cost… yes."

"You would say that to me balls-deep, Baz?"

"I think by the end of this," I admitted. "I will say it's fucking priceless. And for you?"

"I would need more time to know." She played coy.

I spanked her again.

"You'll have to try harder than that."

"Really?"

"I'd say kiwi if you needed to back off, baby."

I spanked her hard enough that I worried it'd bruise her. Lanie responded by bending down to kiss me. She slowly bit my lip, rolling her hips again in the most satisfying way. She knew what she was doing. She knew I needed her to cum—loudly—and that would be the ticket to getting me off.

Lanie pulled back, panting. She was going to cum for me—the first glorious time I'd get to see her *and* feel her simultaneously.

"Fuck me and don't stop," I said. "Get off. Use me, Lanie."

Flushed, she squeaked. "I am… I'm going to cum."

"Good girl. Scream my name."

"Oh, Baz, fuck!"

She did it just as she had at the club. It felt so good to hear it leave her pretty lips. Bobbing her up and down, she reached her climax, digging her nails into my chest. The feeling of her pussy pulsing around my cock was some sort of sweet elixir I'd give anything to have more of.

"Oh my God! Oh fuck!"

Her pleas for some sort of god fell on deaf ears. I didn't want to grant her mercy. Instead, I flipped her on her back, pushing her legs up onto my shoulders with her ankles around my ears. I longed to see her tits in their full glory.

"Fuck me, Baz! Fuck me hard. Just destroy me!" Lanie growled.

"I will. You deserve relentless fucking and a lot of it," I panted.

She bit her lip and grabbed the pillows. I leaned slightly forward, moving my left hand to stroke her pretty little pussy. Lanie arched her back.

"Yeah… more. Please," Lanie whimpered.

"Will you cum for me again, darling?" I asked.

"I… can," Lanie moaned breathlessly.

She was so beautiful. I didn't think anyone could be *angelic* when cumming, but Lanie might have made it possible. I'd never thirsted to make a woman cum more than I did now. Then, Lanie did something even hotter. She gripped one breast with a hungry hand and began sucking her thumb on the other, desperate for something to grab in her release. It was sexy beyond measure. I had to fight my own climax a little longer as her toes curled around my ears.

"Oh, fuck, Baz," she moaned. "Yes!"

Lanie's legs twitched and she was spent. The sound and sight of her orgasm brought me to mine. I held on for a while, just enjoying being inside of her while she recovered. I marveled at how her perfect tits rose and fell and how pink her nipples were even in the low light. She was so beautiful, so delicate, and all mine right now.

I kissed both her ankles and let them fall. Then, unable to resist, I leaned to give her the longest kiss. I basked in how it felt to press my chest against her breasts and all her softness.

"That was worth more than the house, yeah," I confirmed.

CHAPTER 11

The Light of Day

LANIE

I woke in the morning light alone in Baz's palatial bedroom. London awaited me outside—bustling, crowded, alive. I loved this city. I was a stone's throw from my sister's sleepy house in Mayfair, but everything felt new. I peered through the sheers at the road below. The immediate street was quiet, while Brompton Road just up the way bustled. I wasn't in a hurry to return home, so I sent a group text to Chloe and Dora again to let them know I'd survived the evening. Then, I took a photo of the bedroom and sent it off.

God, Baz's place was gorgeous! I wasn't sure how I'd been worth all of this—even in pillow talk—but I was even more flattered in daylight.

Scrolling my messages, I saw one from Leah Roughy.

LEAH

Are you available for a late lunch? I'd like to introduce you to some backstory with your character if you're up for it.

ME

Sure. I could do two maybe? I had a late night.

Same. Long night here. Too much family
drama.

I snickered. I'd have gladly taken my evening over her
woes.

Text me where and when.

2 at Windsor.

I cocked my head, confused.

Where in Windsor?

Windsor Castle. Just bring your ID. I'll put
you on the list.

I stared in disbelief

You're on the cleared list with Scotland Yard
already. Promise.

In one way, that made sense. In another, it did not. I
smiled, then wondered what I could wear. I used the toilet
and perused Baz's massive bathroom, eyeing a tub I bet he
never used, before walking into his extensive closet. There
were suits, ties, and shoes in the most organized fashion. I
wondered if I'd annoy him if I stole a button up shirt. I
figured I didn't care if I annoyed him. He relished torture and
I longed to make him grumpy. The worst he'd do was fuck
me again.

Somewhat clothed, I went downstairs. On next floor
found two guest bedrooms. I heard Baz's voice down the hall
and followed. He sat in his home office talking on the phone

and typing at his computer. I leaned against the doorframe until he saw me. Baz held one finger to tell me he was almost done.

"I know. And I told you I would be there," Baz grumbled. "But I have projects. So it won't be until next week, Alex. Alright?"

He listened to the person drone, then said. "I have a guest and need to go."

More talking.

"Yes, it is. And I'm being dreadfully rude. See you next week."

He hung up and rolled his eyes. "My brother. Apologies."

"You're fine," I said. "It's always a little sexy when you're in a mood."

"I am not in a mood, darling. I just hate my brother. It's different altogether. Now, I can confirm I have nothing for breakfast because I do not cook."

"At all?" I asked.

He furrowed his brow. "And you do?"

"A bit."

"You don't have a staff in that big house?"

"Do you?"

"I have a housekeeper," Baz answered.

"We do, too, but she's only there twice a week. My sister owns the house. She is letting us crash there but she lives abroad with her husband."

"It's your *sister's* house?"

"She inherited it. But we're Americans. We don't really *do* staff. Well, she does, but she's lived here since she was like 17. Our mother is British. I'm not."

"Wild. Odd. Unexpected. Well, that's just like you."

"You could take me to brunch."

"Isn't that all women your age do these days of a Saturday?"

"You sound old when you say that."

"What on Earth would I take you to brunch in, darling?"

I considered that. "Good point."

"We'll order in," Baz said definitively.

I liked a man who made an executive decision without worry. Not choosing everything freed my mind for other tasks. I liked to be taken care of; not because I wanted to be controlled, but because I got so exhausted always having to plan everything. My ex's indecision exhausted me. I didn't miss that. I loved him still even if I hated to admit it, but needed someone willing to plan a date on occasion or make a hard choice. It made sense why he wasn't ready for a baby.

I kissed Baz. "Sure. I can stay a bit. Then, I must go to an appointment."

"I will take any and all time I can get with you today."

"You're still not bored of me?"

He chuckled. "I think it would take some time to bore of you. You're unexpected and quite confounding at times."

"I am the wild card," I admitted.

Baz barely knew me. And he didn't know what I was up to, but he *got* me. He pushed all my buttons. The sex hadn't just been good. It wasn't even just amazing. It was other-worldly. Last night shattered any preconceptions I had about Baz. He outpaced all my expectations.

CHAPTER 12
Stranded at Windsor

.

LANIE

I REMEMBERED Windsor Castle from a childhood trip with my parents. We came on business, twelve-year-old me tagging along. I felt particularly special to be there with them alone. Derrick had school activities while Davey, Dahlia, and Daphne were already grown. Dora was too little to travel. I remembered being amazed at its size and overjoyed to be in an *actual* castle. Mum had laughed about my overwhelm with how pretty it all was. After all, she grew up in the castle Baz's family stole.

As I waited to be received by Leah, I looked around the drawing room where I'd been left by a footman. I wasn't quite *nervous*. I felt whiplash. I had a wild twenty-four hours complete with a sex club, some of the best sex I ever had, a man ordering me breakfast, and now an audience at Windsor Castle with my boss who also happened to be the Queen's niece. I wondered if Leah saw me last night? I wondered if she somehow knew what I'd been up to. I worried about awkwardness.

This was further complicated when a person I least expected ducked in.

"Oh, are you still waiting on Leah?" Queen Natalie

entered in a pair of riding breeches, tall boots, and a Burberry jacket.

I jumped to my feet and did my best curtsy. "Your Majesty, I am *so* sorry. Yes, I was supposed to meet Leah here for something regarding her show."

"Oh, relax, darling. She rang to say she's running late. She said she and Lourdes awaited a reserve force to bail them out. Of course, she got stuck in traffic. I said I'd entertain you on my way out to the stables."

Before I could say more, Leah appeared. "Shit. Oh my god, Lanie, I am so fucking sorry." Leah appeared in her typical fashion—with a big entrance. "Auntie, thanks for entertaining our ingenue."

"Oh, anytime for Danna's daughter," The Queen rose to hug and kiss Leah on the cheek. "How are the babies?"

"They are little devils despite being sick. I am so over it and so behind on production stuff. I called Papa and pleaded with him to help bail us out."

"That would be good for Georgie. Don't feel bad."

The Queen spoke of her twin, Prince George. He *had* been the Prince of Wales until he stepped down to marry Leah's father, Patrick Roughy. Their family was lovely if not colorful. My mother and father knew the Lyons-Roughys for political reasons. They settled in southwest Michigan on the Lake, raising Leah about an hour and a half from where our family farm sat. It was a small world. Leah sounded more like me than her aunt, but she could put on a fabulous English accent. She was a chameleon.

"Well, I will let you get to the barn," Leah said. "Thanks again for letting me abuse the privilege."

"Oh, anytime." The Queen's tone with her niece warmed my heart. She, too, was a proud aunt. "Give your mother my best, darling."

"I will," I agreed. "Thank you, Your Majesty."

The Queen departed and Leah shook her head. "Apologies for looking like a hot mess. I slept with two kids kicking me in the face."

I snickered. "It's totally fine."

She looked perfect as ever. I didn't think Leah ever had a bad day. She was a bombshell.

"Alright, so, come with me. This is related to Annie. I wanted to show you the dress archive we have and show you the tiara we're recreating—much to the chagrin of the network. I will pay for it if I must, but I'm getting fucking tired."

I snickered. "Really? You have clothes here?"

"So, Lady Ruth—Annie—was my great-great-great-somehow great-grandmother. My grandmother was able to get several things back at auction from the estate. It went to her half-brothers and then they auctioned them off when they ran the place into the ground. Her parents bought her the Lady Ruth Tiara back and she chased down several historic dresses she wore to balls at court. Annie—the real Annie—was fabulous."

My character, Lady Ruth Anne, was called Annie. Annie was born the daughter of a wealthy Chicago industrialist, but was sold off to an Earl by her parents only days after her eighteenth birthday. I knew she was related to the monarchy somehow, but I never put two and two together.

"So cool," I said. "Thanks for inviting me."

"The costumers are recreating a few of these dresses, but I find it important to sort of get in the head of these characters, so I thought I'd offer. Really, Delanie, I am *so* excited for you to have the role. You're so great and the studio thought the same. Viewers loved you."

"I am so grateful for the opportunity, Leah. Thanks. I'm honored."

We stepped into a room I remembered from when I last visited. It held a piano usually. Today, it housed an assortment of dresses and two women attended it.

"Delanie Delphine, this is Christine, one of my aunt's dressers. And this is Beatrice, the Palace's clothing historian. She manages the royal collection and all the dresses on display."

"We're going to have these out at St. James's Palace next year," Beatrice said.

"Awesome. Thanks for having me," I said.

The dresses were breathtaking. The trains, decorations, and beautiful fabric were, indeed, fit for a queen.

"What do you think?" Leah asked.

"They're amazing. But they are more vibrant than I expected. Apart from the white one. Is that from her wedding?"

"That is the gown she wore to coronation of my many greats grandmother. So cool, right?"

"Amazing," I murmured. "She was so tiny. My god!"

"She was. It makes sense because my grandmother was a slight woman. She could command a room, but she was short. Grandfather was tall but even my Papa didn't get his full height."

"And this is the most beautiful thing," Leah said. "Lady Ruth's tiara. My grandmother wore it on her wedding day, as did my aunts—when Aunt Natalie wed Uncle Ed and when Aunt Kiersten married Uncle Olav."

Leah's Aunt Kiersten was now Queen of Norway. I felt as though I'd peered through a sheet few got to see. She was an insider, but I wasn't worthy. Though inhabiting the world as a guest in real life, I owned it while playing Annie. To be successful, I needed to get in her head.

I walked the room, thinking about the enormity of these beautiful dresses and the history they held. Did these artifacts exist for our family? Or, had Baz's idiot father destroyed them? Could we get them back? Were there pieces of jewelry he stole from us, too? I know my mother's family tiara had gone to Baz's family. It killed her to part with it. It was her wedding tiara. She looked so beautiful in it.

"It's a substantial piece," I looked the tiara over. "And worn by so many, it's very special."

"I wore this, too," Leah said. "It's heavy—but not as heavy as some of the others my aunt can lend me."

"So, you're going to try to let me wear a recreation?" I asked, a bit gleeful.

"I am. Auntie was going to let me borrow it since it's part of her private collection, but we were told no by the lawyers," Leah laughed.

"Unfortunately, it's a conflict of interest," Beatrice said.

"A shame," Christine added, "because it doesn't get much use and is part of the history."

"But there is *spice*," I giggled. "Scandalous spice."

"Yes. When sex is on the screen, it's too much for the bloody sensors," Leah giggled. "Oh well. I love it. It was so fun to get to wear it once. I felt so special. It was nice to have my fathers give me away and feel somehow connected. I'm in and I'm out, but this made me feel like I was still there with my grandmother somehow. She would have been glad to see me happy and wearing her favorite tiara."

"You should have," I said.

"The provenance of this is interesting," Beatrice said. "It was commissioned by Annie's father upon her engagement to the Earl of Dwyfor. So, it was part of the dowry. She was quite a beauty and the photos you see of her probably reflect it. But there is a lovely portrait of her at the National Gallery. That was from her wedding day."

"Check it out. She was gorgeous—like you—but so young. My God!" Leah shook her head. "Thankfully, we won't have an actual eighteen-year-old going to bed with a man more than a decade her senior. But she was very young."

"It's fine," I joked. "I prefer older men anyhow. But Jesus. Getting engaged at seventeen sounds horrid!"

"It was said her mother was the one who really forced the match," Beatrice said. "Her father was tearful and nervous on the wedding day. Many fathers get that way, of course."

"My fathers both blubbered," Leah said. "And it was our second time doing it—the first time we just went to the courthouse. But they still lost it."

It hit me with a pang of guilt. I'd never get to see my father get choked up on my wedding day. I remembered seeing my own father worried when Daphne married her charlatan of an ex more than a decade before. I struggled more than I ever anticipated on the day she wed Cal. Dad would have died and gone to heaven to know they'd found their way to one another. And he would have been the biggest sap. We lost him too soon. He'd never see any of us get married. I missed him so much in that moment.

I also wanted to know about the history of our family—the stuff Mum refused to discuss. I wondered about the tiara she longed for. I wanted to know more. Unfortunately, since Baz still had no idea who I was, I couldn't exactly ask him. I'd have to do some research on Lady Ruth and Lady Danna Carlisle and her relatives independently. It was all prep for my role, right?

BAZ

"I'm on his shit list again," I sighed. "And he wants me to come home. Alex is guilting me about it. You know how it is with him. Alex swears he's just about to die. I doubt it, though. He pulled this before. Unfortunately, he was still very much alive."

I sat in the club level of my father's football club with Caleb. We spent the afternoon and evening in the owner's box. The Exham Dyers would play tonight against Spurs, their lead rival and trap team. It was high time to drink and take advantage of a pre-game meal served by some celebrity chef we hired for a London Derby for the ages. No doubt we'd lose.

"What is the issue then?" Caleb asked. "What now? Isn't he always on you about your lack of wife and kids?"

"He swears he's about to disinherit me," I said.

My phone buzzed—in Caleb's view. Lanie's name came up on the caller ID. *Shit!*

"You gonna get that?" Caleb asked, eyebrow raised.

"Uh… I'm good." I lied.

Part of me wished she was booty calling me, but I wasn't about to get into that with Caleb.

"She hasn't rung me," Caleb said. "You win?"

"For now. I suspect we will all lose in the end," I said.

"I'm not cross. You can answer it."

A text appeared.

LANIE

Can you please call me? I'm desperate and everyone else is out of town.

Desperate. Well, that was a word I fancied from her pretty lips.

"Ring her or you're going to annoy me," Caleb said. "It will ruin the whole evening. And if you want to invite her around and she's not bothered, that's fine. I spent the last week chatting up that French girl."

"Alright," I groaned, walking to the edge of the box.

Around me, some business associates milled.

Lanie picked up.

"Sorry to bother you, but I'm stranded," she said.

"Where? And how can I help you? Lanie, I'm busy this afternoon and evening."

"Oh, sorry, do you have a date?" She asked flatly.

"Would that bother you?" I asked.

"You'd love me to say yes, but no. Can you send me a car?"

"What?"

"Everyone is elsewhere and I can't get ahold of my brother or sister in-law."

"You've got no backup plan?"

"Don't get angry with me when it's my sister's fault this happened to begin with. I'm stuck. If you're busy, just send the car. I will make it up to you. Everyone at my house decided to go to Paris for the weekend. Bitches! And I am stranded."

"Where? Here in London? There aren't taxis?"

"The bloody M4. I'm near Brentford."

"Why are you on the M4?"

"Well, my sister lost her *good* cars in the divorce. Her husband is a dick. Anyhow, I have this old Porsche. It's been making this noise, but I think it just died for good. I can turn it on, but like I've lost the ability to shift. I am afraid to take a dodgy minicab out here."

"Don't do that," I said. "I can send my driver."

"Thank you!" Lanie sighed in relief.

"Oh, I will make you pay for that favor, love. I assure you."

"I will let you fuck me. Promise. But it's dark and I need to get away from here. I am not hitchhiking."

"No, no. I will send my driver. Are you at least safe to stay there?"

"Yes," she said. "I owe you, Baz. Thank you."

"I will ring you later. Text me when you get home."

"I will. I'll drop you a pin with my location."

"Great."

She hung up and pinged me her current location, which I relayed to my driver before I returned to my seat.

"Everything alright or are you leaving your own match to see her?" Caleb teased.

"No," I said. "I'm staying. She got stranded. Something about her sister's Porsche dying on the M4. She sounded genuinely upset. I get the feeling she doesn't drive a lot."

"Why was she on the bloody M4?"

"I haven't a clue."

"And you're just swooping in to save her?"

I shrugged.

"You're fucking obsessed with her, Baz," Caleb said. "What is wrong with you?"

"And you weren't?"

"Nah. I liked her. A lot. She was *fun*. But to you, this is something else."

"I like the chase," I shrugged.

"It's more than that. You should take her home to your

father and say you're going to marry her. You don't have to mean it, but if he sees her, he'll believe she'd fit right in."

I laughed. "You give her more credit than she deserves. She absolutely would *not*. She's painfully American."

"She's beautiful. He'd buy that you were smitten with some hot young thing with a cute accent."

I shrugged. "Maybe, but it seems too incredible."

"You wanting her is about as credible as anything."

"I'm not fucking in love with her, Caleb. Calm down. I find her *entertaining*."

"Uh-huh. Enough that you brought her to Vesper and left after like ninety minutes last night?"

"How did you—"

"I heard from Johnny. I have my spies, too. He said you came in with a redhead last night. Look, just admit it. She's got you over a barrel. Don't fight it. Lean into it. Get your dad off your back. She's a bloody actress. She could sell it. She also seems like the type to want to play the game."

Caleb made an excellent point and she *did* owe me.

CHAPTER 13
Normal Expectations

LANIE

I WAS HEADED to bed when I got the text I never wanted at a time I was tucking into bed and feeling lazy. With Chloe and Dora in Paris, I turned in early after freezing on the roadside until Baz's driver came. I knew what a privileged statement that was, but just wanted to start the day all over again tomorrow.

Baz texted.

BAZ

You up still?

I rolled my eyes.

ME

I am not taking drunken booty calls.

BAZ

I'm not drunk

ME

Uh huh

I ignored my phone for a minute as I tossed my pajamas on the bed. It vibrated. He was calling.

"Yes?" I answered.

"I'm not pissed," Baz said. "I figured it was easier to say it than to type it and have you not believe me."

"Then why are you booty-calling me?" I asked.

"I'm… not?" Baz sounded confused.

"Oh," I backed off.

"I had a favor to ask."

"Uh… okay?"

"Well, you owe me. As you said, Lanie—"

I set my jaw. "Just say it, Baz. I don't like playing games."

"I disagree very much with that statement," Baz said. "I think you enjoy our games. We have that in common, Lanie. In fact, I think you relish it so much you will want to go to hell with me in another way."

I massaged my temples. "What, Baz?"

"My father assumes I should be married by now."

"Baz, how old are you?"

"Forty-six. How old are you?"

"Almost twenty-nine," I answered. "Do you feel old? Because you are and most men your age *are* married."

"Ouch. Why are you being so combative, darling? Also, wow. I thought you were younger."

"How young?"

"About twenty-five?"

"And you *still* slept with me?"

"You're fit and clever. We're both adults. I wanted you. You wanted me. I feel no guilt."

I shrugged. "Alright, that's fair. My point stands that he has normal expectations, Baz. Why *aren't* you married?"

"What do you mean?"

"Well… can I be frank?"

"Aren't you always, Lanie?"

I smiled. I pictured his cheeky grin.

"Fine. You know me better than I thought. Well, you're tall, handsome, rich, well hung, and you fuck like a man half your age. What is wrong with you that you aren't married? And don't say it's because you work all the time because that's no excuse. My parents made it work even with my father's career until he died a few years ago."

"I'm sorry to hear that," Baz said. "I lost my mother when I was very young. Losing a parent is hard."

"It is, but don't sidestep the question, Baz."

"I adore your persistence. You really put a man's balls in a vice."

"You fucking love it."

Baz chuckled. "I do… to a degree. There are many reasons. The number one being that I've never fallen in love with a woman who wouldn't demand I do a fucking 180 on everything I believe in. And if I settled for someone I could tolerate, I would never be the man she needed and I'd break her heart. Also, I'm morally opposed to cheating."

"Same," I said.

"Then we get each other?"

"Sure, I suppose. But what does this have to do with me?"

"My father demands I come home for a visit. He plans to dress me down over being completely unserious since he threatened me over not trying to find a wife. I need a wife and heir or he's going to disinherit me."

There it was. That was the admission I needed to know he *was* under fire. He confirmed I had an "in" with my scheme.

"So, you want me to… marry you?" I laughed.

"No. God! He'll be dead soon. I just want you to *pretend* to be my prospective partner to placate him. This wasn't my idea. It was Caleb's, but I don't think it is awful."

"You talked about me to Caleb?" My jaw dropped.

"Yes, but stop worrying. Long story. He's not upset. He was mostly relieved I didn't ditch our match to fuck you—not that I didn't debate it."

I shook my head. "I am in no mood, Baz. For the first time in months, my libido is shot and requires some time to reboot. My sister's stupid fucking car scared me. Now it's at the shop and needs a new transmission. It's like a $100,000 car.

Granted, it's older and hasn't been driven in ages but... it should work."

"Yes, it's not as if it is an Audi."

I smiled. "No. I will figure it out. I probably shouldn't drive but I had a bad experience in a taxi back home a few years ago and I don't like to take them. I realize how privileged that sounds."

"Did someone hurt you?"

"I jumped out before anything happened," I said. "But I don't take taxis alone anymore."

"I understand." Baz unexpectedly didn't make fun of or call me spoiled. "I'd never want anything to happen to you, Lanie."

I didn't answer.

His voice took on a sudden sweetness, then doubled back. "Will you come with me? You just need to keep up the ruse for a few days. We're talking rural Scotland on the sea. It's beautiful at the very least."

I couldn't say no. If I did, I would break our bargain. If I didn't go, I would never learn about my family history. Going with Baz would not only allow me to stare down the person who stole things from us but also see a place my mother had never been able to take me. I'd do it for her if nothing else.

"Fine. We had an agreement and you've been otherwise a gentleman."

"No one has *ever* said such a thing, but thank you, Lanie."

"Anytime."

CHAPTER 14

365 Gift Horses

LANIE

I WOKE to our doorbell ringing. Still in pajamas, I raced downstairs to a black suited man with a clipboard. Assuming he was here to convert me to a religion, I opened the door mostly annoyed.

"I'm Catholic, definitely not interested in being saved, and not worth your time, honestly," I said.

Confused, he cocked his head. "What? Is Lanie Day here?"

"That is my stage name, yes," I said.

"I am here to deliver a gift," the man said.

"Oh… okay?" I looked around but saw nothing. "Where is it?"

He stared like I had two heads, "Were you expecting us to put the bow on it? Because that's just for the Christmas commercials. I swear, women always expect the bow!"

"I don't know what you're talking about," I said. "I really don't."

"The RX?"

He turned.

"What is an RX?"

"The Lexus?"

"A car?" I asked, confused.

He stared.

"This is from my sister, right?"

"IF your sister is Basil Osgoode, then yes," he snickered.

Basil? It took me a moment. *Baz* was short for *Basil*. Weird. Basil didn't fit the man in the slightest.

"Baz… sent me a car," I said.

"Per him, it's a lease that can be converted. He wasn't sure if you were choosing to stay in the UK long. He also wanted you to verify that you like the blue. He thought it would look nice with your hair."

I snickered. "Are you fucking serious?"

"I have a set of notes I must read from. That was on there."

"People embarrass you with this stuff, huh?"

"Sometimes. Can you sign here, please, ma'am?"

I took the clipboard and signed, granting his request. "Thanks."

He handed me the keys. Astounded, I went outside barefoot and looked in the windows of the beautiful new car. Baz was insane, but I had wheels! It was time to get out in the world. I wasn't sure how I would explain to everyone that a billionaire bought me a car, but wouldn't turn down hundreds of gift horses in the form of a high-powered engine.

I changed, put on some eyelashes, and got ready before taking my new chariot out to the races. Or, rather, as far as getting to Victoria station to find a car park. Growing up in a *very* public way made life weird for me. Trips on transit were forbidden, and we always flew private. As a result, I never learned to read a transit map and feared crowded spaces. Cars were freedom for me the minute I got my license. Of course, working in Hollywood and traveling ended that. Baz had no idea the achievement he unlocked.

After finding a valet, I bought admission to the National Gallery and asked a docent for help.

"I'm looking for the Countess of Dwyfor. Lady Ruth Morgan," I said.

"Oh, yes. I've had people looking. She's a character in that television show, they say."

"I play her," I said. "The director and showrunner told me there was a painting of her and I'm dying to see it."

"Really?" The older woman's face lit up. "You're an actress? Oh, how fabulous!"

"Can be," I laughed. "Sometimes."

"I'll bring you to see it."

I followed the peppy woman across the place until I stood looking at the portrait. Lady Ruth sat looking off into the distance, painted profile, sitting in her wedding dress and tiara. I couldn't see a family resemblance with Leah, but I almost saw one with myself. Her alabaster skin, blue eyes, and gorgeous auburn hair did make her very visible. Her slightly round cheeks and high cheekbones made her look possessed of a warm, happy heart.

"She was beautiful," I said.

"She was. Tortured, they say. Married off to man she didn't love for a title. And for what? So her mother could gloat."

"They didn't have an altogether unhappy marriage, though," I said. "Eventually, they fell for one another. It turns out the Earl was a misunderstood, awkward man with some demons—largely caused by his unstable home life growing up—and with a little love and support, they were there for one another. They both experienced loss and an odd start in life, but grew up together a bit. It's a beautiful story, but I agree. Fuck her parents."

The woman snickered, probably embarrassed by my frankness. "I am glad it had a happy ending. Did they have children?"

"She went on to give him six children. Sadly, the last was only a few months old when he fell ill and died of pneumonia. He was much older. I'm one of six, so somehow, I relate to her."

"That's so sad."

"It is, but in her diaries, she reflected that she would

rather have loved and lost than never met him and that he taught her to trust in someone other than herself. It's a lovely story for certain."

"Do you need anything else from me?" The docent asked.

"No," I said. "I'm going to look around. Thank you for your help."

The woman stepped away, leaving me to stare at the face of a woman whose fate could have ended so much worse— the fate my mother would have had if she wed Baz's father many years before.

***

BAZ

I was in a business meeting on a development in Southwark when my mobile buzzed several times. At first, I ignored it, then I saw it was Lanie. Given that I was still in some sort of punch-drunk situation where I thought about her at least every few minutes, I wanted to hear what she would say. I hated how much I wanted her and how much space in my mind she occupied.

LANIE

You're not going to say anything about leasing a car for me?

Daddy Vibes, what have I done to you?

Also, thank you.

I cringed at *Daddy Vibes*—something she no doubt knew and exploited. She pushed every button and knew how to make me squirm. I hated it, but willingly took on Daddy Vibes if it meant I'd get access to her more readily. She was usually *very* giving.

ME

Lanie, I couldn't have you stranded again.

LANIE

Do you think I am more indebted to
you now?

ME

If you were, what would I get?

She typed. I focused too much on the bubbles flashing, I longed to see what sort of lurid non-answer she'd give me.

"Baz, are you with us?"

I turned back to Jeremy whose face showed confusion.

"Apologies. An issue," I said. "What do you need?"

"Council requirements. Do you have concerns?"

"Not unless you do," I said.

"I suppose not," Jeremy said. "Well, that's it for now on my agenda. Are there any other worries?"

My mobile buzzed.

LANIE

I'd let you eat me out on your dining table.

That response should *not* have made me get hard like a hormonal teen thinking about his crush in class. I shouldn't have contemplated making Jeremy reorganize my afternoon to run back to mine and eat Lanie out like it was my fucking life's work. I tried to think about anything but wanting to taste her, but came up short. I managed to get rid of my previous level of rallying excitement for long enough to tell Jeremy I had a thing come up and needed him to bump my 2PM.

He did, grudgingly, as I texted Lanie.

ME

Meet me in 20.

LANIE

Okay. I'm at Harrods, so you're in luck. Will
stop by and leave my car here with the valet.

ME

Technically, it is my car. You're borrowing it.

LANIE

Possession is 9/10ths of the law, baby

ME

Not quite. Door code for the day is 12879.
Type it in and then press 7. Let yourself in if
you get there first.

My driver drove me home all too slowly. When I arrived, the house was silent. It was a buzzkill as I wanted so badly to come home to her looking spectacular. I didn't have to wait long though. When I arrived in my dining room, Lanie was naked, poised on the edge of the long table with her legs kicking casually.

I slowly approached, playing it cool, and pulled her even closer to the edge.

"This is what you do?" I asked, playing with her nipple.

"You said you wanted me. I told you what I was willing to do."

I placed my jacket on the chair next to her and tried to feign calm even if my palms sweated with anticipation. I tortured her with a kiss on the neck, running my hand up her thigh slowly but I stopped short of her pussy.

She whined, "What are you doing?"

"Nothing. You didn't say anything about fingering you," I protested. "That wasn't part of our hedonistic bargain."

She pouted. "Make me cum. Don't tease me, Baz."

"I am doing expressly what was agreed upon, Lanie."

I didn't know how *she* had already estimated the distance of my face from the floor if I knelt, but she nailed it. I dropped to my knees and came face-to-face with her pink pussy. I kissed her thighs playfully. She was unsatisfied with that, giving off an impatient, greedy gaze as I took in the bit of her I'd not yet tasted. I kissed the small bit of red hair above her clit, then slowly made my way down. As I gently licked her wetness, the release and relaxation within her hit. She rolled her hips towards me and grabbed my hair.

I pulled back, pushing her hands away.

"Patience is a virtue, Lanie."

"Who said I was virtuous, Baz?"

Good point.

I sucked her clit slowly, taking in the full taste of her. She was sweet and soft. She met everything I'd imagined, but the unexpected low moan I elicited felt even better than before. I'd assumed she played up her reactions for me with other people—to torture me. Instead, she was even more willing. Like putty in my hands, I brought Lanie closer. I pushed both her legs back over my shoulders, pressing my palms into the tops of her thighs to steady myself. She held onto the table for dear life. Every time I looked over to see her white knuckles, I grew harder still. She was undeniably sexy—wanton, impulsive, greedy. She was everything I could have asked for in a woman. I reveled in how she smelled, tasted, and sounded as she ground against my face, desperate for a release.

Quicker than I expected and with more force than I anticipated, she broke my rules, grabbing my hair and pressing me against her pussy as she came.

"Oh, Baz, fuck!" Lanie screamed.

She dripped down my chin, leaving me satisfied. I'd done everything to get her here.

"Fuck me," Lanie pleaded

I pulled away, pinning her to the table. "That is all you get. I will not fuck you. You're too badly behaved."

I'd do anything to torture her now. I only knew it would whip her up more. Even if I delayed my own gratification, I held all the cards. Lanie Day was mine to own, torture, and please. And while we were never exclusive, keeping her satisfied also drew her back every time. She was loyal so long as I continued to work her over so well.

CHAPTER 15

Braemoor House

LANIE

On a Wednesday, Baz and I flew up to Braemoor House. I was still unsure if this was the right approach. I loved our game. I longed to be doted on, but fought the nagging feeling I lived a lie. With every interlude and enraptured look, I became more invested in Baz. Whatever began as harmless fun turned to me torturing him took on a new life.

If I told myself I was only going to Braemoor House to dig into family history and potentially put the screws on the Osgoode Family, I'd be lying. I *was* curious and called to take this opportunity to see a place my mother longed to revisit, but I didn't want to hurt Baz. I knew there was a very real opportunity he might discover my true identity. I expected him to do so with a quick Google before this, but I sensed he neither cared who I was nor wanted the real story. If we never talked about anything too weighty, there was no risk of hurt feelings.

As we rode forty minutes from the airfield to Braemoor, Baz gave me a rundown of expectations.

"I apologize for my family in advance. Father may look over you like someone does a horse they look to buy. Well, I suppose that assumes you understand horses."

"I understand," I agreed. "Dora Elizabeth rides competitively. We all rode growing up."

"Good. Apologies. He is a frightening person when it comes to potential wives. He put Alex's wife through the wringer even if she is the most inoffensive sort of person."

"What is her name?"

"Nessa. They have a son, B.C."

"B.C."

"It's short for his first two initials. He's twelve and loud."

"I have five siblings. I am used to loud."

"Five? Jesus, Lanie!"

"I'm Catholic," I shrugged.

"Are *you* Catholic?"

I snickered. "A very bad one. But I did all the things. No one in our generation was married in the church to my mother's horror."

"We are *technically* Catholic, but I believe in nothing."

"Would your prospective wife have to convert if she wasn't? I'm asking so I nail this role."

"Not necessarily. It's a big bonus and something I hadn't thought about. However, my heir *must* be raised Catholic. That's part of the terms of the estate and how father inherited it. He was so far down the list and the lone Catholic. An heir —per the title holder's directive and that of five hundred years of tradition—must be male, of noble or royal blood, and Catholic."

"I'm just an American," I lied.

"Uh-huh," Baz said. "Well, you tick the other boxes, and we can excuse that because of me. Would it help if I gave you a synopsis of what he expects?"

"Yes, please," I said.

"Be demure. Properly address people. Can you do that?"

I nodded.

"Be your clever self, but not too forward."

I rolled my eyes.

"Americans generally get a pass because people find it

charming, but Father will not. And try to make nice with my sister."

"Who is she?"

"Eleanor. She's the baby. She's technically my half-sister."

"Oh, so your father remarried after your mother died?"

Baz cocked his head. "How did you know that?"

I flushed. *I knew it because my mother told us about Basil the Elder's wife dying.*

I shrugged, "I gathered it. I got a vibe."

"You're perceptive. Yes, after father remarried, they quickly had Eleanor. Unfortunately, by the time she was three, she had a freak stroke. She's very beloved in the family, but Father often talks down to her. I hate that. She's the peacemaker and would be an ally for a prospective wife. If this was real, I'd rely heavily on my sister's opinion of you."

"So, charm the sister-in-law? Can do."

"Yes. And don't bring up my mother. It… it bothers him."

"Oh? Was their marriage unhappy or—"

"If anything, I think he did love Mum. He just never had the emotional ability to process grief. He took it out on us that she died—especially my brother because she died in childbirth. Thankfully, he loves Eleanor and blamed her less for the death of her mother."

"How could you blame a child for that?" I gasped.

"Dad is… likely a narcissist. Mum was barely in the ground when the previous Baron called Father up and… basically proposed a relationship to the Baron's daughter. She was a girl still in uni, and Dad was in his mid-forties by then. She didn't love him, but she agreed to it."

My heart stopped. Was he speaking of my mother? I knew the match was *floated,* but I didn't realize anyone took it so seriously. The story she told us was very vague and Daddy was already in the picture. I used every bit of my acting chops not to react to this story told from his perspective.

Baz continued, "I'm sure it makes no sense to an American, but the pairing would have kept the estate in her family. The Baron had many daughters but no sons. It was *practical,* she could still produce children, and she was of acceptable breeding and background. For my father to approve of this match, my opinion or love for you would matter not. You simply must please him on paper, not openly offend him, and be willing to wed me and give me a male heir in theory."

"What happened with the girl?" I asked.

"Uh… she spurned him if you ask my father. My memories of that time are now so fuzzy as I wasn't yet five. I do remember thinking she was kind and that if we had to have a new Mummy, she would do. Our stepmother never took to us, so I always wondered how it could have been different. In the end, the almost-wife married some rich American and moved away. I certainly don't blame her now."

I played it off. "Why, because you find American accents irresistible?"

He rubbed his chin stubble. "Something like that, yeah."

I couldn't manage words, trying to think about the math. Mum had *accepted* his proposal, but she'd still run off with Dad? I assumed the cruelty Baz implied was the reason she ended things with him and ended up with Dad. My heart hurt for my mother to be passed off like that. She was brave, in the end. I tried not to transfer my feelings to Baz about how much this had damaged her. After all, if his father was the cruel bastard he implied, Baz was also a victim.

"It sounds brutish," I said.

"It is life. All of us are objects in his game of chess. If you can funnel all of that into a character who would be willing to marry me not *despite* that but *due to* that, then you'll be the best woman for the job."

"I can do that," I said. "It's a role of a lifetime."

It was. Part of me wanted to play the game all weekend, then drop the gauntlet. The other prayed I'd never have to speak the truth. Eventually, Baz would tire of me as Caleb had. I'd tire of him, too. We'd be spent. I'd have fulfilled the purpose and allowed someone I thought was good enough to take over the estate. What was done with his father was finished. I couldn't fix it. I could touch it for a moment if I played the game. But what good did it do to hurt Baz? He'd never been unkind to me or anyone else in my presence. I didn't want to hurt him, so I'd play on. Then, we'd slow fade. I'd go back to my work, and he'd return to his. The old bastard would die none the wiser.

———

BAZ

Lanie was better at this than I predicted. I'd saved the choicest bits for once we arrived in Scotland. Half of that was because I'd thought up what to say for days. The other was due to a fear she might run when she heard about my awful family. Instead, she asked me to direct her into being wife material. I worried that her American-ness would turn the old bastard off, but she'd meet every other stipulation. In the end, I vastly underestimated Lanie's performance.

Upon arrival, the staff led us to the drawing room for tea. My father was in his usual chair, looking paler than before. To my surprise, he did not stand. My heart leapt with joy. After all, if I could fool him this time, he'd be assured I changed my ways and never update the will. Even I had a pang of guilt and remorse for feeling glee at the prospect of his passing, but he'd never been good to me. To him, I was a worthless fuckup until I wed a desirable girl.

Lanie gave a little bow as I introduced her.

"This is Lanie Day. I met her through Caleb," I said. I wasn't about to tell that story in full.

"Nice to meet you, Lord Osgoode," Lanie said sweetly.

"And what are you doing in London?" Father asked. "You are American?"

"I am. I'm an actress, actually."

"An actress?" He was displeased.

I should have known that wouldn't fly.

Though off to a rough start, we sat for tea. Lanie

impressed with her ability to not only *pour* tea properly, but to sip with grace.

"Miss Day, how long have you lived in Britain?" Father asked.

"Off and on for about a year. I am filming a period piece. I was a small player in last season, but the director just informed me I am playing the lead for this series."

That was news to me. She said she was renewed but I never knew she was a *lead* actress on a show Leah Roughy put together. I felt something similar to pride now.

"And yet, you are adept at tea," Father said.

"My mother grew up in Britain," Lanie said. "I am adept at many things and familiar with societal expectations. She didn't raise me in a barn."

"That is good to hear," Father said.

Lanie confounded him as much as she did me. But while I lived for the unexpected, Father loathed it. This wasn't a feature, but a bug.

My sister entered. I rose to hug her and Lanie followed suit. Introductions began anew and Lanie bowed slightly once more with great poise. I suspected whatever work she did on her series paid off.

Eleanor lit up like a Christmas tree. She gave me an excited hug, then turned to Lanie.

"Well, you are... not at all what I expected." My sister beamed wide.

"She's American," Father said flatly.

The words may have hurt, but Lanie didn't respond.

"She's lovely," Eleanor said. "Lanie, how do you find Scotland? And how did you end up here?"

"Scotland is beautiful, Lady Osgoode. This house is wonderful. I cannot wait to tour it."

"She's an actress," I said. "Here filming."

"Very curious," Father muttered. "Odd that you would chase after an actress."

"Call me Ellie," Eleanor offered. "Please. And Pa, be kind.

She seems like a very nice girl compared to what he usually runs around with. She has *manners*."

Lanie stifled a laugh. The little smirk made me want to touch her. I refrained, but the impulse remained.

"Are you aware of my son's history as well as his obligations, Miss Day?"

Lanie looked to me. "I know that Baz lives a colorful life—after all, he has lived a *slightly* longer one than I have."

Ouch, Lanie!

"But it doesn't bother me." She squeezed my knee, playing the role of doting girlfriend perfectly.

I melted a little—in a much more genuine way than I anticipated.

She played dumb. "What do you mean by obligations?"

I didn't know why she didn't just say "yeah, sure, fine."

"Obligations to the family. Before he gets too old, he must marry and produce an heir—something he always sacrifices for his harebrained schemes."

"I think they are hardly harebrained given the results," I pushed back.

Father didn't address that. "Four is always up to something, which I think makes him unappealing. Now, given your bountiful youth, I think the part about heirs should put all else to rest."

Ah, the nickname I loathed was back!

"Can we not speak about her fecundity as if she is simply a commodity?" I asked.

Lanie furrowed her eyebrows at me as if I made her job harder—not easier.

"Four, you must be realistic. Darling, how old are you?" Father asked as if he might a child.

"In two weeks, I will be twenty-nine," she said, almost adorably, but not with an ounce of trepidation.

"Young, healthy, beautiful. Well, those are odds in your favor."

"I would say charming and clever are better qualities—both of which she appears to be," Ellie said, sweetly.

Lanie beamed at her. I felt a genuine exchange between them. With Lanie, though, I couldn't distinguish the game from reality. The lines suddenly blurred. I realized my feelings for Lanie grew stronger and went far beyond a desire to have her or—more specifically—have her *to myself*. Instead of winning her, my goal focused on *pleasing* her across the board. I found myself protective and adoring in a way I never had been before. Lanie was different. I read her responses as genuine, but were they? She was an actress. I worried this was all for show. Could I trust her?

"Come," Eleanor said. "I will take you for a tour."

She reached out her hand to Lanie. They left like school-girls on a trip. I'd never understand the uncanny bond of womanhood. And, after seeing Lanie with her sisters, I knew she gravitated towards crowds of other women. It relieved me she had my sister's endorsement.

Father said what he wanted. "I do not like that she is American *or* an actress."

I took a deep breath. "She is a very nice woman, Father. She is charming and clever—as Ellie said. She is also family oriented. Her family is big—and Catholic—and she is a doting aunt. I am not sure how I will find another prospect— raised in a Catholic family—in all of Britain who would meet those criteria. In real estate, you must choose two of three— size, location, and price. What will give? With Lanie, it may be her nationality."

"But if she is an actress, will she not always be gone? Do you expect her to retire?"

"I have only experienced the genuine desire for her to be career-minded in a good way. She is driven and proud of what she does. She ticks all boxes—especially one quality."

"Which is?"

"Bloody independent. I cannot handle someone who needs to be micromanaged. I know she is young. It worries me as well. She is also shrewd and knows what she wants. She may ask for me to assist her, but does *not* require me to fix every crisis. She is her own woman. I need someone like that."

I spoke the truth and realized how much I needed independence in a partner. Up until now, I felt suffocated. Maybe it was the game or maybe I could tolerate the idea of commitment to someone if they were as much their own person as Lanie was? Maybe it wasn't impossible for me to eventually find someone? Certainly, if Lanie existed, there were other girls who could meet that bar?

"Well, is she *too* independent?"

"Father, the estate needs a diplomatic woman who can manage affairs while I am busy with my own. You have devoted your life to this place—alone. I cannot continue to work and do such a thing. I need a woman willing to pitch. I know I can lean on Ellie some, but she has a life, too. And— not to throw her under the bus—she would crumble under that pressure. She is so quiet that I worry she couldn't even handle dealing with tenant matters."

"Having a woman focused on family isn't a problem. It is a benefit when you have children. Your mother was very good at it. Without her, I struggled."

"I understand," I said. "I do not want to marry a woman who is opposed to home life. What I am saying is Lanie loves her family. I think she could be good at that. She's never mentioned it bothered her."

"I will think about it. She certainly has *some* redeeming qualities. I do like her."

But…

"But, there is something off about her that unsettles me. And if you are asking me, the fact that she is an outsider without noble blood *is* a problem. This house has been proudly unimpacted by the rather unseemly democratization of the aristocracy. Nessa is of noble blood."

I forced myself not to roll my eyes at the mention of my brother's wife.

"An American—especially one seeking out fortunes— could tank the place, Four."

"She's not a fortune hunter," I responded. "She lives in a grand house and grew up well-off. While this thing is new to her, Lanie is not interested in my money. She's never asked for anything."

"Does she know about your inheritance and how this hangs in the balance?"

Play the game.

"No," I lied. "She is in it because she cares for me. That is all."

CHAPTER 16

The Dark Fairytale

LANIE

Braemoor House looked like a sweet fairytale home from afar, but presented a darker retelling up close. As my mother said, it was cavernous, a bit drafty, and slightly dark—especially in older parts. It also had beautiful tartan charm, massive fireplaces, and character everywhere you looked. As I followed Ellie down the luxurious halls, I tried to picture my mother here. The sheer scale blew my mind away. I couldn't imagine her just lounging on a couch or skipping down the halls.

When we reached the ballroom, I had to hold myself back. I thought about my parents' wedding photos here. The church in town hosted the wedding, but its reception followed at the castle. I remembered smiling pictures of my parents swept up in a fairytale—so in love, so happy. I wouldn't come about for more than a decade, but I smiled as I thought about what they must have felt.

"The house is beautiful," I said. "So much history, I'm sure."

"They oldest part of it is about 600 years old," Ellie said. "The prettiest parts—like this room—were built in the late 1700s. It became a showplace then. And the house was improved upon until the early 1900s when it reached its crowning glory and repeatedly hosted the royal couple. To think about those parties!"

"Are you much for parties?" I asked.

"I would be if they were here. I know my brother loves London—as do you, apparently—but it's not my style. It's too loud. If Baz ever gets married, I hope we can have a big celebration and host everyone. With lots of people, the house feels wild enough for me."

Her face then lit up as she took my hands. "Come, I want to show you my favorite room!"

We moved into a massive hall deep within the castle's original walls. Fireplaces sprung up on opposite ends. These were hearths big enough to cook a feast. In the center was a massive dining table that must have seated twenty.

"We don't eat in the hall often," Ellie said. "When we host an event, it is nice to have the space. What I love about it is all the art and portraits."

I looked around. For some reason, upper-class Brits loved to cover every inch of the walls with photos. It was like going to a kitschy American chain restaurant, except the kitsch was very expensive and old. I ranged, looking at photos of my history. These were *my* relatives—the people who made my mother and, by-proxy me.

I settled on a portrait that took me by surprise. It was my mother, wearing a beautiful tiara, staring out a window. Her profile was unmistakable. It struck me how much she looked like Lady Ruth in her portrait.

"Why are there so many paintings like this of women in this country?" I laughed.

"It's a common pose for debutantes who were presented at court," Ellie said. "I never was. I'm not much for that sort of thing and it fell out of fashion by the time I was of age. This is the Late Baron George Carlisle's daughter, Danna. She was so gorgeous here."

"She was, yes," I prayed she did not see the striking

resemblance everyone else did. "So, she was presented at court?"

"Yes. Note the white dress. She was a tremendous beauty—per my father—but she wanted nothing to do with him. After all, he was a widower with young children. I do not blame her. The way her aunts talked, she loved this place."

It hit me in the feels.

I moved along, settling now on a painting of a beautiful woman in a red ballgown. It wasn't the look of her or the bright dress that caught my eye. Instead, it was her mischievous expression. I placed the nose immediately.

"This is Baz's mum, right?" I asked.

"How did you know?" Ellie laughed.

"She looks like him, of course. He has the same nose. She was stunning. People must have been completely wrapped up in her."

"Yeah. From what I heard she was charming. It's a shame I didn't get any of her charisma like my brothers. My mother was rather quiet, I am told."

"Nonsense!"

I turned as Baz entered. "You ladies are both plenty charming. Has she been all around now?"

"I did not take her to the library or conservatory yet," Ellie said.

"I'll do it," Baz offered. "Thanks, Ellie."

"Anytime. If you need anything, Lanie, let me know."

"Thanks," I said.

Baz walked up behind me, wrapping his arms around me. I leaned back, comforted by him. He was big, imposing, but softened with me. I melted as he gave me an affectionate kiss on the cheek. I sensed it was for show, but adored it.

"Did I pass any test?" I asked.

"It is up for debate," Baz answered. "But you didn't fail. He is hung up on the American, non-noble bit."

"But he buys it?"

"He does. And, to be honest, I'd buy it, too. You're an excellent actress. I owe you."

The words hurt somehow. Yes, I was play acting and this was the game. However, I realized it was more than that. As he draped his arms around me and held me close, I realized there were some feelings. I spun, staring in his eyes.

"Baz... I... I honestly don't mind. It's not hard to pretend I might want all of this. You're charming, you take care of the people around you, and you've been good to me. It's not much work."

Baz thumbed my chin. He gave me a long, sweet kiss. My knees weakened and, for a moment, I felt like I might fall for him.

BAZ

"Four!"

I stopped dead in my tracks and turned, balancing a glass in both hands—one for me and one for Lanie. Upstairs, Lanie waited for me to return and settle in for the night. If I made a break for it, I'd be a very happy man. I hedged my bets on getting to the butler's pantry unseen and lost. If I ignored him, he'd grow angrier and ring my room until I came back. Either way, all hopes of getting hard while he demanded my attention were gone.

"Yes?" I went to the doorway.

"Sit, son. Sit."

My father's voice was nearly tender. Confused, I lowered the glasses and sat on the couch opposite his chair.

"You buried the lede with her," my father said. "Why did you not tell me who her parents were?"

"I don't know them," I said.

"Well, you've impressed me. I am dying, Four. I will die and leave this Earth, but I am delighted it will be knowing that somehow Danna Delphine's life has gone full circle. She may have turned me down, but now she's going to have to watch you raise her grandchildren here. It will probably torture her. Or, alternatively, never invite her to visit. She doesn't deserve it."

"I don't follow—"

"Delanie Delphine is Lanie's legal name. Danna Delphine —born Danna Carlisle—is her mother. She's the daughter of David Delphine and an heiress to the Delphine retail fortune. Way to bury the lede!"

I swam in my thoughts, confused. I contemplated. It was feasible Delanie was her legal name, as I thought her sister referred to her that way. However, now, I started putting together the familiar face with a woman I didn't know but knew *of*. There were pictures of Danna in the house. My sneaking suspicion was that they would confirm what my father thought he knew. Lanie had played me! But why? Did she know who I was? Had her mother just never told her any of this?

As I grasped at straws, I noted my father's chipper mood. Was he *excited*? Why!?

"Well, never mind that. I'm just happy you found someone who will fit in."

I stammered, "I'm… I'm sorry. What?"

"Now that I know her provenance, I can confirm her suitability in all ways."

"You say Danna Carlisle spurned you. You said—"

"She did. However, her family is of good breeding and she's young. I cannot leave the house to no one. If the girl is plucky enough to storm in here and want to take it back, well, who could stop her?" A sly smile crossed his face. "Yes. A woman like her is *exactly* what you need."

"How so?" I could barely breathe. My chest tightened and the room felt overly small.

"Well, she's what you deserve. I personally love the idea that you will have to put up with someone so conniving for the rest of your life."

He got off on watching me be bested by a vindictive little actress.

I set my jaw. "I refuse to!"

"Oh, Basil, it's okay to admit when you've lost," Father sighed. "And if you want me to keep you on the inheritance and give you this place when I go—it is only a matter of weeks, you'll propose to her and marry her."

"Dad, that is *madness!*"

"Love is madness."

I couldn't *love* Lanie—especially if she had *lied* to me about her identity all this time!

I stood, pacing. "Love! Love? You haven't felt it—"

My father's voice grew sharp. "I did for your mother! She was the only woman I'd ever loved. She may have trapped me with you, but I only had wonderful memories."

"Jesus Christ!" I pulled a face at the mere mention of my conception. "I cannot just commit to something so ridiculous!"

"And that's the problem. You say you would like the estate and are willing to run it, but I see none of that. I see a man obsessed with London and its many women. Alexander has a plan—"

I cut him off, voice hot. "Alexander's plan is to turn this into a tourist trap and call it a bloody day! Right now, we limit tours. This house—our family home—would become open to the world twenty-four seven. And you know how distressing that would be to Eleanor. She loves this place. She wants to keep the horses here. She must have that stability and—"

"Well, I know she and Alexander don't see eye-to-eye on this but... you leave me no choice. Someone must care for this place. And leaving it to you will turn it into ruin. I cannot say many nice things about Danna Delphine. She embarrassed me in front of everyone by ending our engagement and marrying that American weeks later. However, if she's anything like *her* mother, she's an overbearing cow and would do anything to take care of the place and keep her daughter in line. Let that work to your advantage. If the girl agrees to wed you and oversee it—as well as take care of your sister—I will grant it.

Besides, the mere mention of who is marrying her daughter will be punishment enough for the old bat!"

"You told me I had a year!"

"They told me I had two, Four. I don't. I have two months now. Things are going badly. I cannot walk across the house. Your sister follows me everywhere and it wears on her. For Eleanor's sake, I hope I go soon."

I didn't know what to say. I didn't want to marry Lanie. She'd only agree to it if she had something in mind—a scheme. However, losing the estate wasn't right. My sister would lose her mind if we lost it and she had to move to London with me. I shook my head.

"No. I need more time."

"You have drug your feet. You have a woman young enough to give you children, attractive enough not to leave you too bored, and tied to this place by blood. What more could you want?"

I groaned and stood. "I will think about it."

I marched out, headed to the great hall to see the picture of Danna Carlisle. As I approached, staring in the low light of the fire and moonlight, I couldn't deny the resemblance. All I could see was Lanie's eyes, lips, and hair. I couldn't ignore it now. What were her motives? Did she seek me out for some sort of revenge game? Was I only a pawn? I needed answers.

CHAPTER 17
Confronting

LANIE

I LAY IN BED, annoyed and sucked into in a see-through, useless garment, attempting to seduce a man who disappeared twenty minutes ago. Where was Baz? And why did I bother? All he would do was pull off these pointless panties and fuck me. The see through chemise didn't hide anything, anyhow. I was beyond annoyed when he flung open the door and entered in a huff.

At first, I suspected this was some stupid machismo bit, then I realized it wasn't. He was *livid* about something and pacing.

"Here's your drink. It's not poisoned. Although, perhaps it should be?" Baz slammed my drink on the nightstand.

"Excuse me?" I scoffed. "Baz, what is wrong?"

"Do you want to be honest about the lies? Or the betrayal? Or anything?" Baz demanded, pacing.

Genuinely confused, I said, "What do you mean?"

"I know your identity because my *father* knows who you are. And thanks to whatever this is, now my father is committed to *marrying* you, as if I could ever manage such a thing! In fact, I am packing my things and moving down the hall. I cannot even *look* at you!"

I understood the anger, but not those words. He couldn't *look* at me. That much hurt.

Baz rifled through his wardrobe and tucked into what I assumed was a stack of linens.

"It's fine. I will go sleep elsewhere," I said.

"What? Dressed like that?" Baz sneered. "So, the entire house can marvel at just how incredibly tactless you are? Have you already not embarrassed me enough? Does everyone need to know about how little self-control you have —and how you throw yourself at anything with a dick that moves and is willing to spend money on you? You're good. I will grant you that. Very, very good. I worried I might have feelings for you, but those, Delanie Delphine, are *long* gone."

His diatribe cut through me until tears welled. "Baz, I am sorry. I don't know how you found out."

"Father did the research. And while he loathes your mother, he finds you a good match who will tie me here. He thinks you will be a stone to punish me—and by proxy my mere existence will punish your god damn mother. Lanie, you had several weeks to *tell* me, didn't you? And yet, you didn't."

"First, Baz, we barely know one another. Second, I didn't know at first. Once I found out, I did have a period of—"

"I don't care," Baz shouted. "I do not fucking care."

He threw pillows on the bed.

"Baz, please."

"Oh, don't cry your god damn crocodile tears, Lanie! I hate that you got under my skin, but I will not have it. And sadly, I *must* marry you! If I do not, I will be disinherited. He's made up his mind, so we must all fall in line or risk losing the place. Bully for you! You're now stuck with me!"

He climbed into bed.

"Aren't you going?" I sobbed.

"After considering all of those options, I suppose I am stuck here lest I let everyone know how much I truly hate you."

"Hate me?" I sobbed. "Why do you *hate* me? I came here

to help you Baz. Please let me explain! It's not some massive scheme to hurt you. At first, I did want to torture you because your father stole my mother's estate. However, I have since come to appreciate you."

"Yes, because I spoil you and you like nice things."

"Baz, I can buy myself nice things! Is that what you think this is?"

"You never turn down a gift."

"I deserve to be doted on," I said. "Because I am worth it. I do not need expensive gifts, but I do deserve affection and the lavishing of attention. *That* is what I crave—not cars and expensive jewelry. Sadly, you've made up your fucking mind already and I'm nothing but a jezebel out to get you!"

Baz turned away.

"Baz, I cannot fake this with you. I cannot pretend everything is fine."

"You're an actress. It's your job," Baz said, voice low and monotone.

"Baz, this isn't an acting job. This is my *actual* life. It's my reality. Marriage is no joke. It involves a lot of liabilities."

"Yes, because you are the type of girl who wants to play happy families, aren't you?" The words dripped sarcasm. "Lanie, this is all a game to you and you're only sad you lost."

"No. These are my real feelings, Baz—feelings I suspect you have for me, too. And… I don't want to be shackled to a man that hates me. Especially one who no doubt is bright enough to design an iron-clad prenup that will leave me reeling when you desire to leave me for someone else."

"You go right for the money. That is all you care about, clearly!"

"That is not true. The truth is, I want to be happy. I want to be free to love a person who loves me. And I want to have children with that person when the time comes. I crave that, in fact. You can tell yourself I'm in inconsequential, soulless whore but I am a person, Baz. A person you pretended to care about until now!"

My voice vibrated. I flipped onto my side and closed my

eyes. I wanted to be sick. I needed to scream. Instead, all I could do was sob and move far to the edge of the bed. I was only half an inch from falling. He had a right to be angry with me, but he had *no* right to reduce me to this low status. I'd not meant to hurt him this time. I wanted to help. And here he was casting aspersions. It was all too much. I wanted to go home to London once morning hit.

PART TWO

Marriage of Convenience

CHAPTER 18
Another Scheme

LANIE

I COULDN'T SLEEP, so after tossing and turning, I left my room to walk the grounds wrapped in my robe and contemplate what life might be like if I decided to marry him. A day before, I'd still been playing the game. I still wanted to twist the knife. Why now, did this frighten me?

I thought through what happened in the time since my arrival. My thoughts landed on first my disdain for Baz's father, but soon turned to Baz's sweet sister and the beauty of this place. I easily understood why my mother had never gotten over it all. As I wandered the gardens before the house came to life, I imagined what life was like growing up here. I listened to the sea and smelled salt in the air.

This would have been a beautiful place in the summer, I thought. I walked through the rows of rosebushes and wondered if this place had once been filled with the laughter of children and barking dogs. Dora Elizabeth would have gotten her dog if we lived up here—maybe a Scottie named Angus? As the sun rose, I smiled and thought about its warmth and how lovely it would be to pace these rows with a baby on my hip. I thought about the appointment the following week I made with the fertility clinic my sister recommended—the one I insisted I needed to ensure my eggs wouldn't go to waste.

But no matter what my imagination spit out, I couldn't shake what I could have if I agreed to some stupid hare-brained scheme. I could have this slice of heaven. I could give these moments back to my mother. After losing my father, I knew how fleeting life was. But what did I get out of it beyond the house? I never entered this to saddle myself with a man who had no desire to wed me.

"It was just a game to wound him... until it wasn't," I whispered, standing in the walled garden.

Now that the game was over, what did I do? He hurt me. I should have felt self-satisfied, but I couldn't. Yes, his outburst was unacceptable, but that was raw emotion. When he felt betrayed, it guilted me.

Returning to the room in the still early-hours, I found Baz awake. He looked at me expectantly. I expected him to be gone or yell at me. Instead, his face spelled concern, then relief.

"Are you... you're alright?" Baz asked.

I shook my head. "I don't know."

"I worried... I thought you'd run off."

He missed me? It wasn't the response I expected.

"I'm fine. I... I want to go home, but I wouldn't do that. I wouldn't just run off without letting you know."

Baz massaged his greying temples and let out a low groan. I had never seen him shirtless and still in bed in the morning. It was as if he always just appeared in a suit out of nowhere. I assumed he simply blinked and was fully clothed. I found him sexy like this, even if I still wanted to throttle him.

"So... what now?" He sighed. "You just run back to London?"

"Baz, what else do you expect me to do? Marry you?"

His face went from worry to anger. "Isn't that what you wanted? Didn't you engineer this—"

"No. Baz, it is true that I knew something you didn't. It's

true I wanted to hurt you, but... once I accomplished my mission... I didn't want to. It's not that."

"Then you just want to torture me?" His voice grew stronger.

"No more, Baz. I... I don't want that," I promised, tears welling. "Can you please not yell at me right now? I'm trying so hard to not be angry with you, Baz."

———

BAZ

Normally, tears didn't affect me the way Lanie's did. I labeled such things as hyperbole and moved on. Instead, even hung over, Lanie's tears cut me down. I began to doubt my worries about her. I questioned whether I should have given her a chance to explain. Racked with sobs, Lanie's tiny body shook the bed. I'd been harsh, I supposed, but her reaction came out of left field. She cried herself to sleep. When I woke, she was gone. I panicked, but here she was, back and hanging her robe over a chair. She went to the wardrobe and began sorting.

"Lanie, please. Just come and talk," I called.

In the tiniest voice she repeated, "I want to go home. I want you to call a plane for me or I will walk."

I sighed. "Lanie, I cannot do that for you."

"Are you holding me hostage now?" She stood before me, face puffy from crying all night.

She looked pitiful. I felt like a monster.

"I... I need you to just play along. You agreed—"

"No. I was willing to play along and *help* you because I assumed your father was a fucking asshole who probably tortured you and your siblings. He stole this place from us. I wanted to get you back at first. I played the game and tortured you until I realized you were not that much of an asshole. If anything, you are misunderstood—just like I am."

I reached out my hand to take hers. "Then… just sit and we'll talk."

She held my hand. "And so you can apologize?"

"For what?" I asked.

She pulled her hand back, her face flashing to rage. "Of course not! You know, I feel like an idiot that I felt guilty for what I did! But after what you said last night? No. You think I am some sort of whore. You are no different than the others! They all want to cage me and shame me. I am not staying here. You can lose your inheritance for all I care! Maybe your brother will care for this place. Maybe—unlike you—he has a motherfucking soul!"

She stood—mostly naked in some sort of lingerie she put on for me last night. It was hard to concentrate with her nipples visible and a thong barely covering anything underneath the netting of the top. She was perfection and I ruined everything.

"Alex isn't going to take care of the place, Lanie. He's going to hand it over to someone else to run as a museum."

"Well, maybe that is what needs to happen. You don't care about this place. You just want the money. You *live* for money." Lanie blessedly folded her arms over her breasts.

"That's not entirely unfair," I granted her. "And perhaps I am not over-the-moon about this place, but my sister is. She has some very bad social anxiety and struggles with people."

"What do you mean?"

"She's easily overstimulated. She's the sweetest person, but she needs routine and places to escape. Here, she has her horses, her garden, and a volunteership in the village at a creche. She's happy. This is her home. If she loses it, she'll be crushed."

"Eleanor is lovely. I had no idea. She said she wasn't a city girl."

She softened and stepped closer, once more exposing the nipples that would have been mine if I'd just gone along with it.

"She's autistic. She's wonderful, but she struggles with

change and can meltdown in certain situations. I don't want her living alone in a new house somewhere. That won't help her anxiety or stability long-term. She survived university, but it wore her down. I won't have her go through that again."

Lanie crossed her arms over her chest, giving me a brief reprieve from her nipples. "But you don't want her moving in with you?"

"No. If I was around more in a place she could call home, I'd be glad to have her live with me."

Lanie sighed. "Why didn't you say that she was autistic, and this was part of the deal?"

I did a double-take. "Well, because I didn't want it to color your first meeting and, clearly, that impulse was right because—"

"I'm not dragging your sister's autism. Jesus!" She threw her hands up, then balled them. "It's just… you should have told me more about this. You're claiming I knew all these things like I stalked your social media or targeted you."

"And you didn't?"

"First of all, your web presence is non-existent. I suspect you don't even have social media on your phone."

"I don't," I admitted. "I do not live perpetually online like some people."

"That is *so* unnecessary—"

"It was. You're right. I'm just upset." I tried to save what little face I had left.

"So, yeah, there was nothing there to find. I didn't stalk you. Caleb brought me to the party after a hookup. I was bored, he asked me to go, he was hung, I went. Is that what you want to hear?"

"When did you find it out?"

"When he told me your entire title. I decided to seduce you and torture you by not letting you have me, which was fun for… a minute."

"Then why did you agree to this?"

"Because once I let you have me, I was…" She looked

down, her words fading. "Because I was into you. I liked you. Okay, I craved you. But... then I felt bad because I knew something you didn't, and you seemed genuinely tortured by this thing."

"Oh, so you're just benevolent?"

"No, Basil!" She rubbed her temples. "Neither of us is all that benevolent. I did care about you. I did feel bad. I also wanted to see this place for myself."

She appeared honest, shifting her weight and expecting me to respond with kindness. Still livid, I wasn't there yet.

"I don't know how to help you, but I cannot marry you, Baz. I won't marry a man who tells me he hates me. I put up with a lukewarm man who gaslit me for years."

"I don't hate you, darling," I sighed. "I said those words—"

"You cannot just go around screaming at people and snapping your fingers, Baz. You can't just buy me off, either, which I suspect bothers you."

I shrugged. "Perhaps, it changes the power balance. Regardless, If I lose my inheritance, there will be no one to look after Ellie. Alex loathes her and despises that she never married. He will put her up in some godforsaken place or force her to move south. So, it's not just me. It's all of us, okay? And... I am sorry."

Lanie slowly deescalated. She kept her arms folded, but her face softened. "For what?"

"Talking to you as I did. It was unacceptable. I can explain it away because I was drunk, but... the words I said were inexcusable. The fact of the matter is that seeing you is like lightning in a bottle. I hated myself for allowing my heart to feel something for someone I assumed was trying to take advantage of me and my inheritance."

"I don't need your money. My mother inherited a great deal of her family's wealth, and my father was a billionaire, so..."

"How was that?"

"Normal... for me. I suspect like you, I know nothing

different, but I'm not a country bumpkin or suburban kid with stars in her eyes, Baz. I'm not here to steal your family's money."

I looked at my hands. "I'm sorry I assumed that."

She sat. "Thank you. Selfishly, I've always wondered about this place. My mother still laments it. She refuses to talk about it much because it makes her homesick. You can do many things, but not villainize my mum. She would have told me *not* to do this. And to know we'd been together would enrage her. Your father is right about that."

I chuckled.

"I don't know how to explain it, but I do know you'll never speak to me that way again if you want all your parts.

"Lanie, I'm sorry. Truly."

"I should have told you sooner," Lanie admitted. "But, Baz, I figured you'd tire of me long before we had that conversation. Or, like… you'd google me and see it at the top of the search results."

"I am a clever man only when I am not thinking with my trousers," I admitted.

"You get pussy blind," Lanie snickered. "I understand. And while I did *initially* intend to fully seduce and torture you because of your family origins, I know you are a victim of your father's machinations and your sister is sweet. I think it is good you care about her. However, I cannot marry you, Baz."

A mixture of relief and worry came with her words. If she'd agreed, it would have shown she had no common sense and was wrong for me. However, now, there was no way forward. I felt despair. I needed to find another way. I was *so* close, yet so far. And what she didn't understand was that my father would wear us both down in the process.

"Lanie, can we just… talk about it? Is it because you don't love me?"

"Oh, sweetheart, of *course* I don't love you. I didn't think I needed to say it. No, it's not that."

"Is it because I don't love you? Because, maybe I could learn to, Lanie. Is that what you need to hear?"

It was my weakest attempt at argument, and she saw right through it.

Lanie giggled. "Don't be ridiculous, Baz! This is so stupid! You don't love me. I don't love you. We have incredible sexual chemistry and your kinks and mine sort of align, but… that's where it ends. I'm not fucking marrying you."

I gave up on love and convincing her, cutting to the chase. The obvious appeal lay before me. She drove a hard bargain.

I quipped, "What is your price?"

"What?" Lanie scoffed. "I am not a commodity. We played a game, but marriage isn't—"

"What would it take to convince you I could make you happy so you could help me through this, Lanie? What would I owe you? I'd give you anything I could—in writing if you demanded."

She stared, confused. "What?"

"Tell me what your terms are. I will tell you if I can meet them. What would you want—other than love. I may not be able to give you love, but I can promise you security and—despite yesterday's drunken outburst—respect. I truly am *so* embarrassed about that. I rarely drink that much."

"I know. We were both upset. It was not okay and it won't happen again."

"Agreed," I promised.

"I dunno."

"You worry if you lay the cards on the table I have the upper hand, huh?"

Lanie shrugged.

"You're clever, Lanie. I'll grant you that."

She blushed. Flattery worked, but only if there was substance in my sweet words.

"Let me put it this way. I am the one in the bind. You actually hold the cards, Lanie. If we were to wed, my liabilities would outpace yours. No matter how wealthy you are, Lanie, let me be clear. I would stand to lose a company valued at more than a billion dollars. You do not."

"There are prenups."

"The UK doesn't view them like the States does," I explained. "They'd stay to the terms of our properties and such, but the company? It's likely they would cut you in no matter what a piece of paper says."

"I don't want your company, Baz."

"I am aware. But divorce makes people go mad. I must trust *you*, Lanie."

She looked forward at the wall. I let her sit with her thoughts.

She turned back with a determined look on her pretty face. "I want children and I want those children to keep all of this. If you can promise me that any heir we produce would inherit this place, I will think about it. And I want to continue working. I do not want you controlling me or telling me I cannot go on shoots."

"I wouldn't do that, Lanie. I'm not even asking for strict monogamy, okay?"

"Nor am I," she said. "But... I want those things. And a decent settlement."

I chuckled. "That's all?"

"If I am helping you secure your inheritance, you owe me that much!"

I couldn't believe her. "What... what changed?"

"I didn't want to freeze my eggs."

I cocked my head.

"I was done waiting for children—to the point I was going to put my eggs on ice. Now, I don't have to do that and shoot a television show all at once."

I furrowed my brow. "That was in your calculus?"

Cooly, she said, "Everything is in my calculus, Baz. Don't underestimate me."

I shook my head. "Of course not. I shan't. Give me some time to call my solicitor and iron out the details."

"And when he does, I will call mine—my sister's divorce

attorney—and have her redline the hell out of it. So don't try anything stupid."

"Who is she?"

"Bridget Callaway," she said.

"Oof. Well, I wasn't planning on anything, but I will mention that to him. She's tough."

"Tough enough to help bring down an entire government, yes. So don't fuck with me. There may come a day when I will let you fuck me again, but no fucking *with* me. Understand?"

"I do."

"And I'm serious about children." She sat taller and flared her nostrils. "Do not make me drag you through the shit for putting me off for years. Obviously, I'm working right now and busy, but... someday soon—"

"I don't think we'd struggle with the mechanics," I assured. "I cannot promise I will be the world's greatest father, but I'll support you and any children we have. That is ingrained in me. I may not be home every night, but I will be there."

Lanie thought a moment. "I spent the early morning trying to figure out under what it would take. In all honesty, I'm a bleeding heart falling in love with this place. My biological clock ticks. I don't want a husband who hovers. I need someone who is sexually compatible and..."

"Emotionally distant?" I joked.

She giggled. "Not distant... not pushy. Someone who fucks me like he can't imagine the world without me when he's around and otherwise leaves me to my own devices. Someone who doesn't try to make himself the center of my world and isn't intimidated by my success."

I squeezed her knee. "Lanie, I cannot think of a single thing that is sexier in a woman than success."

She did a double-take.

"What? I'm not allowed to fancy a strong woman?"

"It just... it doesn't track with your tough guy persona."

I pulled her chin towards mine. "You are altogether terrifying in your sheer persistence and cleverness, Lanie, but that doesn't mean I don't find it dead sexy."

I wanted to kiss her, but she pulled back.

"Well, maybe you've just met your intellectual match, Lord Osgoode? It had to happen sooner or later." She stood. "Look, we can talk about ironing out details later. I need to get dressed for breakfast. I cannot go down in a negligee."

———

LANIE

"Can we do this?" Baz sought assurance.

"Do I have a choice?" I murmured, straightening my dress and turning from him.

Before I could even ask him to zip me into my dress, he finished the task.

"Lanie, I'm not forcing you to do this. You must do it freely or else… I don't want it."

"I just need time to adjust," I said. "It's going to keep the place in the family. I will adjust."

He rubbed his temples and paced. "Lanie, I want to make you happy. I feel like all I bring you is incredible grief."

He was talking himself out of it, even after just talking me *into* it. I didn't find his waffling attractive. The push-pull of this annoyed me more than the ridiculous idea of our arrangement.

I sighed. "Fine, don't then. Would your brother not *sell* you the estate? Could you not just buy it off him? Problem solved."

"If he sells it, he pays tax. If he keeps it and donates it in part to Scottish Heritage, he pays none. And he has plans for some god-awful holiday village on the property. Some sort of gauche thing—to make the everyman feel fancy. It will be hideous, not match the place, and be poorly put together. He won't sell."

"My family," I said. "It has been in *my* family."

Baz nodded. "Yes, I suppose."

"I remember my mother tried to buy it back and your father wouldn't sell."

"Not to her, no. It's a matter of pride with him. Still, as I consider it again, I think I'm asking too much of you."

"Baz, you're not asking me to give up my job or my life. You're not even asking for exclusivity. I think I can manage it based on the terms of our agreement—the estate and a child in return for my some method acting."

"Well, it's on your timeline—that bit," Baz said. "I am in no rush. And you don't... we don't..."

I cocked my head. "What? Now you have me and you suddenly find me repulsive?"

"No! Lanie, I never could!"

"Last night you were."

"Last night, I was drunk and feeling like a caged animal," Baz explained. "I had it all wrong. I don't find you repulsive."

"You can barely look at me."

He met my gaze and stepped towards me, his expression intimidating.

"You don't have to lie, Baz. I'm a big girl. And if you feel like that, we shouldn't do this. I'm not settling. I don't need to love the man I marry, but I do deserve someone who is fucking addicted to me." As he knelt before me, my words slowed, "If we do this.. neither of us should feel like we're trapped—as you said."

His brown eyes met mine, suddenly sweet and soft. "Lanie, You're magnetic. You make me laugh. You torture me, but I love that. I cannot ever completely figure you out, which is why you continue to impress me. I spent twenty-five million dollars just to watch you fuck someone else. If that is not addicted, I don't know what is."

I fobbed his words off, unable to accept his kindness or deference. "You never mentioned I was beautiful or fit."

"Those are implied given that I cannot keep my hands off you."

"Or mouth," I snickered.

"That, too."

Instinctively, I stroked his cheek. "Do you really think you could just... deal with me? And maybe what we both need is... a timeframe."

"What do you mean?"

"Treat it like a business partnership with a term. I stay with you three years and then, if at the end of it, we've met our objectives, we can part amicably. Alternatively, three years or until I produce an heir?"

"That's wise, Lanie," I said. "I will speak to my solicitor this afternoon."

I prevailed. Never did I think I'd feel as though I had the upper hand while also saving someone. And the man before me on his knees? The one who never settled for anything but a win? It was a total chef's kiss. I was never the type to appreciate a man who hovered. I wanted a man to dote when *I* wanted him to and then go back to his own turf.

I wanted children, but was this really the *best* way to get them? Perhaps not, but it was the only surefire way to get what our family deserved—this beautiful place and all the memories within. It was also the only way to help Baz and his lovely sister. I may have experienced slight moral bankruptcy, but I wasn't completely heartless. If it were Dora Elizabeth facing eviction the way my mother and her family had, I'd never have forgiven myself. Baz's father may have been evil, but I had scruples.

CHAPTER 19

Out of my Hands

LANIE

BAZ and I arrived at breakfast late. I was sure everyone thought we'd been involved in carnal pursuits. While I wished we had that excuse, I couldn't have wanted anything less. I wasn't ready to give myself to him in anything other than a business agreement in this moment. We were *cordial,* but gone was that lust we felt. I worried that the days of him eating me out on his dining table were over. If he was only interested in the chase, finally having me would bore him.

I entered the room and bowed slightly to my host, even if I just wanted to stab him in the fucking eyeball. The Baron's smug look conveyed he had Baz under his boot heel. Ellie smiled pleasantly. There, as well, were four new faces. One was a priest. The other two I guessed were Baz's brother, nephew, and sister-in-law. Why a priest was at breakfast, I didn't know. The look of confusion on Baz's face signaled I wasn't the only one. A footman rushed over with a fry up, but I wasn't hungry.

"Four, are you going to introduce the lady to your brother and Nessa?" The Baron asked Baz.

Why does he call him that?

"Apologies. This is Delanie Delphine. But her *stage* name

is the one you might recognize… Lanie Day," Baz said. "Lanie, this is my brother, Alexander. And this is his wife, Nessa, and son his, B.C."

I nodded a polite hello.

"And I shall introduce you to Father Merill," Baz's father said. "Father, Miss Delphine is the granddaughter of the previous Baron. I can assure you the two of them are only *distantly* related. And it is all very above-board."

Baz turned, his expression almost sending me into a fit of laughter. Nothing about us was above board. This whole thing was ridiculous. *Were we the only sane ones?*

"I don't know why you didn't tell me that yesterday, Lanie," Ellie said. "No wonder you were so taken with that photo of Lady Danna."

"I felt it might be a little awkward," I lied, not sure what to say.

"Miss Delphine's family are quite good practicing Catholics, Father."

It was a weird flex, but not untrue. Well, true for my *mother* but never my father. Daddy had never been religious. He went along with it for Mum. We all sort of went through the motions due to guilt, but Mum was very outspoken about her own spirituality. That included her own desire to wait until marriage—something she tortured us *all* with growing up. Maybe Dad loved her enough to refrain but I'd never buy a car without driving it first. Unless, of course, a billionaire bought it *for* me.

"That is lovely to hear, given that we do not hear or see much of you, Lord Osgoode," the priest leveled at Basil.

"Well, I am in London. There aren't many parishes there."

That seemed incredulous at best.

"Basil, would you like to offer up the good news?" Baz's father said.

What news? I couldn't seriously believe the old man was about to announce an engagement that hadn't happened in attempt to force us together, but I expected very little of what I'd seen here over the past twenty-four hours.

Baz, just as confused, asked, "Which news?"

"Don't play coy. We're all quite invested in this. It's been probably twenty years now I've waited to hear this news from you. He's engaged. He and Miss Delphine are set to be wed. And, it cannot come fast enough for I... I am unwell."

My jaw dropped. Baz and I stared nervously at one another. I had to take the lead.

"How did you know?" I played along. "Did he tell you he asked me last night?"

"Well, he did this morning when I rang his line and pestered him. Yes, indeed."

"It was... unexpected," Baz said.

To my knowledge, no such call was made.

"I'll say as you didn't even do the bare minimum to buy her a ring," Alex said. "Jesus Christ, Baz!"

Nessa smacked him, aware of the priest.

"That is quite alright, darling. Our jeweler is on his way up from London. I am flying him up with some options for you," The Baron declared.

"I'd rather Baz choose me something and surprise me," I wanted to torture Baz just a bit. "I mean, given his unconventional proposal. It's the least he could do."

"I could do that," Baz coughed. "Really, Father, that was unnecessary."

"Will you be wed in the church then?" Father Merrill asked.

"They will," Baz's father said. "And hopefully quite soon. I have only a few months left. I am already housebound."

"He is very fragile," Ellie said. "It will be complicated to have a wedding."

"Well, then there is a rush," the priest nodded. "I could waive the premarital counseling, but such things usually take at least six months. I would need the archdiocese to agree."

"Could you please check, Father?" The Baron asked. "It would mean the world to me to see my boy wed his bride. And they both feel strongly that their future children should be baptized in the church."

"The church might catch fire at the very thought of it," Alex murmured.

Baz shot him a death stare.

Here we were—tired, somewhat miserable, and full speed ahead on a sham wedding that even the church would sign off on. Baz's father played puppet master with our fate. I could only hope he was near death and would *actually* expire soon. We could pray for that alone.

———

BAZ

"Is there a *reason* she doesn't want to choose the ring?" Jonathan the Jeweler asked.

That wasn't his *legal* name. I had no idea as to what his given surname was, but I imagined it had a nice *ring* to it.

"I don't know. She says she wants to be surprised."

"Women say that," Jonathan sighed. "But they do not *mean* it. That is just women for you. Can you ring her?"

"She's here," I said. "But she's not the type who minces words. If she says she wants a surprise, that is her expectation."

"What is she like?"

I didn't know where to begin. I was marrying a woman I met only a couple of weeks ago. I didn't know her favorite color. I wasn't sure what stones she liked. I only found out who she *actually* was about sixteen hours ago. I wasn't even planning on marrying *anyone*—let alone a girl who came to my country house with a friend. What did you get the girl who had impeccable taste and came from money? She knew good jewelry and wouldn't be satisfied just because something cost money.

"She's very fashionable. Vivacious," I said. "She likes to be spoiled. She's American, if that matters."

"Oh, interesting," Jonathan said, not finding it interesting as much as confounding. "Well, is her taste very… subdued or is it a little more 'wow'?"

Old money or new money?

"She's not the type to draw attention to herself unduly." *Well, unless she's feeling like an exhibitionist.*

"I think a simple and classic is good. I would recommend a solitaire. Halos are very popular."

Jonathan passed me a ring with a find row of diamonds around one central round stone.

"I don't much like that," I said. "It cheapens the look of the main stone. What is the point?"

"To enhance the size of the ring."

"I don't need that," I pointed to an emerald-cut stone. "I like this one. It's classic. Simple."

"3 carats. Will that be enough?"

"Yes," I said. "She would like that."

He handed me the ring. I rotated the brilliant stone around in the light. I was no expert in gems, but this would more than do.

"Yes. I think this is good," I confirmed. "It's simple, but it makes a statement."

"That was easy. And her band size?"

"She said it was four-and-three-quarters… whatever that means."

"It's an American size. I can translate that. We can send the rings back by courier if you'd prefer to have them delivered here."

"We must go back to London, so I can pick them up in a couple of days," I said.

"Excellent. Well, what sort of band would you like?"

"For her?"

"And for yourself, obviously!"

"I don't want a band," I said. "I won't wear the thing. I will ask her if she has a preference. For now, let's assume it's something simple. Something to match the engagement ring."

"Alright," Jonathan said, but that did not satisfy him. "Do

you want to *show* her the ring? I can settle matters with your account in the interim."

I dropped my credit card on the table. "That should do it."

No doubt I'd just dropped a couple hundred grand on a ring I didn't even expect for a woman who didn't want it.

I took the ring down the hall to the library where my unlikely fiancée sat in the window seat with a copy of *Jane Eyre*.

She looked at me.

I handed her the box reluctantly. "I have a ring. I did my best. I hope you don't hate it."

"I don't even care, Baz. It's not like I am deeply invested in this beyond what we agreed."

"I want you to love it, though. You must wear it for at least a couple of years."

She sat the book down and peeled back the box. Judging by Lanie's pretty, happy face, it thrilled her. She slipped it on just for a look, holding out her hand for full effect.

"Yeah. I could manage it. You really are not too bad of a gifter, Baz."

"Lanie, I have nailed every single gift I've given you!" I scoffed.

"You lack humility, so I must humble you. What are you doing about the wedding bands?"

"I said to keep it simple."

"And yours?"

"I didn't think about it."

"Well, get yourself something you don't mind wearing."

"I wasn't planning on wearing one," I said.

"What? No. If I am marked, so are you, Baz."

I winced.

"Baz, do you want a wife or not? I'm not asking you for anything beyond what we've discussed. I don't even expect fidelity, but I do expect you to try not to embarrass me too much."

"Okay," I agreed, rolling over on my first hill to die on.

This wasn't the place to fight with her. I could wear it when she was around or I was in public, at least.

"It's beautiful, Baz. You did well," Lanie said.

Her genuine and appreciative tone relaxed, but also reminded me. I craved her approval too much. I didn't love her. I didn't know what to do with her, even! However, I longed to get a smile out of her—a sweet grin. The sides of her mouth curled slightly. It was better than I'd expected six hours ago.

"I'm still so sorry, darling," I said.

"I know. I am, too," Lanie said. "It's a hot fucking mess, but this ring isn't. And you were so sweet to play along."

"For you, anything," I said. And I meant it.

She gave a cheeky grin. "Well, I will remember that."

The way she looked at me was uncomfortable. She added to it by slightly biting her lip. I wanted to think about anything but that right now.

I cleared my throat. "I need it back, though, because he must resize it. I'm sure you will get it back soon."

"Okay," Lanie handed it back. "Well done."

I smiled, then left her, unsure how to tell her that I did it because I cared about her. I didn't want things to feel like this. I also couldn't imagine what things would feel like if she wasn't here with me. Without her agreement, I'd have lost a great deal—we all would have. She did this for my family as well as hers. I owed her the world.

I returned to the drawing room and handed the ring back.

"Was the lady satisfied?"

"Very," I answered. "And my ring... I uh... make mine match hers—a thicker band, keep it simple. Platinum is fine. I don't have a preference beyond that."

"Good choice. They may tell you they don't care *before* the wedding, but they do. Men who say they won't bother always come back in a panic days before the wedding needing a quick fix. Don't be like that."

"I think this is a rush job," I sighed. "My father is dying. He wishes to see us wed. So, it's all happening very fast."

CHAPTER 20
Face the Music

LANIE

BAZ and I went through the motions, but I remained a zombie. I wanted to stay in this house since childhood. I longed to feel connected to people I never met and places I never went. Now rooted here, it all felt so hollow. Not only was this a ruse, but it was also almost shameful. My siblings and mother didn't know about this scheme. And as we returned to London, I didn't know how to handle it.

When we left Scotland, I felt physically ill. How would I begin to explain this? I wanted to run home, but could not. Nothing felt right. Everything made me uneasy.

"You look nervous," Baz said. "If you're having second thoughts—"

"No," I said. "It's not second thoughts. It's… how do you explain to your family that you're up to something like this?"

"You could tell them and then the ones who could come quickly for a small wedding can," Baz shrugged.

"I don't want that," I said. "That's the thing. If I tell anyone, they might come for you. Hell, my brother lives in London and would love to kick your ass! My mother has a quick temper and an even faster tongue."

"I figured you got it from somewhere," Baz chuckled.

"I cannot tell them. And yet, it all seems so bizarre."

"It's just a business decision, Lanie. It's as you said."

"Well, that's right. And that's all I want right now. Without my father to give me away…"

My voice trailed off as I fought a very vulnerable part of me. I didn't know Baz well. I wasn't sure he even cared about my emotional side. I worried he'd find me too messy. However, talking about Dad always sent me spiraling.

Baz put his computer away and turned, his eyes settling on me compassionately.

I continued cautiously. "When Daphne married Cal, my brother-in-law, they did it in front of the entire world. Cal and the sisters basically surprised Daphne with a wedding in a spot she knew well. The Cultural Center is iconic to Chicagoans. Daphne and Cal are like the prince and princess, you know? And Dad always loved the idea of them ending up together. So, to have him *not* be there and to miss it… I struggled to get through the day, Baz."

"I imagine losing your father that late in your life feels altogether difficult than losing a parent at a young age."

I reflected on his own loss. "I'm sure it is. I am sorry you lost your mother."

"I don't remember much of her beyond how lovely she always was. Sweet, compassionate, and everything my father is not. She was an ideal match, but…"

His words faded.

"What happened?" I asked.

"He changed. Her death broke him. Maybe he was no saint before, but he was nothing but cruel after," Baz said. "It got worse after he remarried, even if our lives stabilized a bit. Everything about my father's lifestyle—his love of showy things, his desire to constantly travel and leave our step-mother home with us, his affairs—they all wore on her. After she had Ellie, she was very sick, but everyone just pushed it aside It was as if marriage made him worse. He married again out of obligation, but it made him angry. I do not want that."

"So, my fears are about weddings and yours are about you

becoming a monster because of a marriage of convenience? Baz, should we really be doing this?"

Baz shook his head. "I barely know you, Lanie. I don't think I am capable of that cruelty, but unlike me, I *know* you are a good person. I would never want to hurt you."

"I love that you think that, but… I am not a saint. After all, I was the one who tried to manipulate you first. I'll remind you of how angry that made you only days ago," I warned.

Baz paused in thought. "In retrospect, I now respect the hustle. You and I live for negotiation and winning games. We're both motivated by never standing still and possess unacceptable amounts of bravado. Lanie, we're both adequately independent. We value family, but don't need obsessive handholding. And while the age difference *should* give me pause, I need to produce kids and—"

"You're a billionaire who isn't going to settle for less than a hot piece of tail?" I asked.

It was a half-truth.

"I don't like that," Baz groaned.

"What?"

"You reducing yourself to that. Lanie, you are gorgeous. I'd be oblivious if I didn't tell you that the sheer look of you excited me. And watching you come unglued is the most rewarding experience. I love undoing you. It's not that. You aren't a piece of tail. You're much more than that—even to me. Don't ever make yourself seem petty or small. I'm a little cross you didn't tell me about your big break. Offended, even."

I grinned. "I will tell you over dinner sometime."

"Good. I would like that very much. Lanie, I can push back on the wedding date. If we're lucky, we can buy ourselves a few week and the old bastard is in the sod before we even choose a cake flavor or whatever."

I snickered. "No. While I hope he does for your sake—for all of ours—I don't want that. I find the idea of a big wedding painful. If we ever manage to properly make this work and want to renew our vows, we can throw a big party. By then, my family will adore you and Mum will want to host it at Braemoor. We could have a lovely late summer blow out. But I don't want that. Even with the idea we could get a church wedding—"

"About that," Baz said. "Father is quite angry, but our priest couldn't accomplish that. He'd offer us something to legitimate our marriage so we could baptize our children, but that's all he could give us. I found out this morning. I was worried it would only add to your stress—"

"A convalidation is the word you seek. Baz, how do you not know *any* of this?"

"How do you?"

"My mother is a devout Catholic. Braemoor's history is storied because it was a Catholic stronghold. I was drug to mass regularly and went to parochial school."

"I only went to parochial school when I was very young, then switched to a public school where I only attended mass as needed."

"Wild," I said. "My mother would have a heart attack hearing that. Her father is rolling in the grave. I do not give a shit, but I know it's a requirement for the title. And it's history and all that shit. But I don't feel right exchanging such vows if I don't mean them."

"Says the actress."

"It's acting. It's fiction," I said.

"Let's just go to registrar and get married, then," Baz said. "Keep it simple. We already have the documentation to file for the special license. So, we should be able to wed quickly. What's done is done, right? They can complain, but it's done."

"And if your dad doesn't agree?"

"He'll be dead soon. We can tell him we were trying to fall pregnant and couldn't wait any longer. He doesn't care about having a big wedding—clearly. He just wants this all to fall apart spectacularly so he can take me down a peg or give his favorite child carte blanche to destroy the place. But what he doesn't realize is that the second option would destroy the life of the only person who ever cared about him."

"You and Ellie deserve better," I said. "Let's not give him that satisfaction. Let's play the game. Tell me where and when to meet you at the registry office and I will be there."

"Why don't we meet there tomorrow and then I can take you out for a glorious lunch after?"

"I'd be down, but I have to be done by three," I said. "I have costume fittings."

"Fine."

I turned back to him with one last question. "Why does the old bastard call you Four, Baz?"

Baz sighed. "Uh… I'm the fourth of my name. I am merely an extension of him."

My heart sank for Baz.

"Oh's he's a bastard, as you said. Ignoring him is the best way forward."

CHAPTER 21

LANIE

I ONLY TOLD my sister and Chloe that Baz took me on an adventure. I didn't inform them who he really was or that I visited our ancestral home. I didn't explain our plot or the lies we told. I kept it simple and wrote it off as the lurid affair I wanted them to assume it was. Mission accomplished, right?

But, I had to tell *someone* as the day grew closer and that someone was Chloe. I could trust her. I wanted to let all of this out to someone. So, when I had a moment alone with her, I climbed into bed next to her to break all the news. She was curled up watching a cheesy tv movie with a bowl of popcorn. It was the best possible circumstance I could expect.

"So, about Daddy Vibes," I sighed.

"Yeah?" Chloe asked. "Is this some sort of wild sex story?"

Given that since our forced engagement, we had exactly *zero* sex, it was not.

"No," I said. "No sex clubs, no exhibitionism, no table fucking. It's quite boring."

"Then why do you look so nervous?"

"Can I tell you something you cannot tell Dora or Cal or *anyone*? And I mean *anyone*?"

"Sure," Chloe said.

I trusted her. She held my secrets close to her heart.

"Baz is the son of the man who stole my mother's family's estate. His father was supposed to marry my mother, but she turned him down to wed my dad."

"Holy shit! You just found this out!?"

"Not exactly. I initially planned to seduce and torture Baz for his family's sins. And because men are stupid and don't think to google their dates, he never looked up who I was. I gave him my stage name only. So, he didn't find out who *I* was until we were in Scotland, and his dad confronted him about it."

"How?"

"I look like Mum," I sighed, "and he's a schemer. Baz had on rose colored glasses because he was into me, I guess? I dunno. Sometimes very smart men only think with their dicks."

"True. Very true," Chloe sipped seltzer. "So, what now? Are you guys done?"

I chuckled nervously. "No. His father basically forced us to get engaged."

"What the fuck, how?"

"It's all kind of hazy, but Baz needs to marry *quickly*. She must be of noble blood or better, be able to give him a male heir, and be Catholic. I meet all those markers on paper. He basically forced it on us in front for a fucking priest!"

"This dude is psycho. And Baz didn't think to be like 'fuck off?' and plans to... what... imprison you?"

"No, no. He's not like that. His dad is a fucking monster, but he isn't. If Baz doesn't marry me, his father will disinherit him before he dies—which looks like it will be in the *very* near future."

"So, fuck them! His family stole the estate from your Mum, right? Why do you even care?"

I took a deep breath, knowing none of this computed. "His brother will take over the family estate and destroy it. Baz doesn't want to see that happen and his sister has some struggles socially, and it would rock her world. She is really the sweetest soul, Chloe. She's very much like Dora. They would be so close. No, it's... I agreed to it."

"Why? Why the fuck would you be so stupid?" Chloe hopped from bed. "No, Lanie! No!"

I winced and shielded my face with a pillow. "Because, I think Baz is actually sort of ideal."

"How on Earth do you figure? Yes, he's rich and hot, but like... what about this sounds like a good idea?"

"He doesn't expect me to fall in love with him in five minutes, he doesn't even care if I fuck other people, and he needs children. You know how desperate—"

"Lanie, you cannot let yourself be trapped in a sham marriage because you're desperate to be a mom. That's silly!"

"Time flies by, Chloe. This urge is too much. I need to have a baby. So badly! And here, I can do it. I can keep working and remain independent. He will be there when I need him. We can have great sex, but we aren't stuck. Plus, we're about to have a lock-tight prenup that favors me."

"What? Why? How?"

"Daphne's attorney is reviewing the agreement his solicitor sent over. Basically, I marry him and stay with him for three years or until I produce a male heir. If I want to terminate our agreement at that point, I will receive $100 million and the deed to Braemoor will pass to our child upon my husband's death. I will be permitted to stay at Braemoor indefinitely. I don't know how much easier a marriage could be."

"Until he decides not to let you work or starts being a controlling shithead."

"He's not," I said. "Trust me. I've seen him pushed to his limits, Chlo. He's not like that."

"So, when is this sham marriage happening? And when should I prepare for Danna Delphine's angry arrival?"

"We're going to wed in secret soon—here in London—at the registry office. We're filling out the paperwork tomorrow. I have a ring, too. It's being sized. It's massive and gorgeous. He picked it out."

"Why the fuck are you doing this, Delanie? It's so unlike you."

"I waited years to have someone tell me they loved me. I uprooted my entire life, moved to LA, and gave up everything. Then, when his career blew up, he wanted nothing to do with the reality of settling down with me. I worked everything around that and almost ruined everything. I almost didn't come back for this season because he wanted me to stay in LA. Baz can give me everything and will stay out of my hair. And he can give me children if I want them. I know it sounds insane, but I can have all of it and get our family back what was stolen. That's so satisfying. And while I do not love him, I do care about him and his sister. They're the victims of that man, too."

"I love you," Chloe said. "But this is fucking nuts—even for me. Daddy Vibes does not deserve your charity."

"I hope you will give him a chance, Chloe. I really do."

"When am I going to this sham wedding?" Chloe sighed.

"What do you mean?"

"Lanie, you are my best friend. You're basically my sister. I am not about to let you get married without being there to hold your bouquet."

"Who says I will have a bouquet?"

"You need one."

"I'm not buying a wedding gown."

"That's fine. We can get you something else, but you need flowers, okay? I will get you some. I won't tell a soul about this unless you exclude me. You need a witness. Who better than me?"

I smiled, resting my head on her shoulder. "Okay. I will tell Baz I have someone who wants to be my witness tomorrow."

————

BAZ

"Jeremy!" I called for my assistant from my office door.

Jeremy appeared holding a printed paper.

"Yes, Baz?"

"I need to speak with you about some important developments," I said.

Jeremy entered my office.

"Close the door, please," I said.

"Alright?"

"Today, I have an appointment with the registry office."

"For what?"

"I am to marry a woman I've been seeing," I said, as if this were a normal statement.

"I'm sorry, Baz, but what?" Jeremy laughed, assuming my remark was a jest.

"It's not a joke. If I do not wed, I will lose my inheritance. Father finds this woman acceptable, she is more than good to me, and I want to make it official."

"This is the one I've been building your diary around, but you won't tell me she's in the picture?"

"Yes," I sighed.

"And who is she?"

"Her name is Delanie Delphine. Her father was David Delphine—the retail magnate. She's an actress."

"Ah," Jeremy said. "Alright. So, the girl *Caleb* brought to the shooting weekend? This is madness, right? You know—"

I'd forgotten he'd been there the first night and met her. *Fuck!*

"It is. It's a play of desperation on my part and act of charity for her. I need you to also ensure a courier delivers my rings from the jeweler today. Please keep them safe. There should be three."

"So, this is really happening? In a week, you're getting married?"

"Yes. It will be sometime soon. Today, I will meet her at the registry, take her to lunch and then pad for time before my driver delivers her at the studio for wardrobe fittings. She's filming a big role for a tv series."

"When will you be getting married?"

"As soon as they can make it work," I said. "Oh, and one more thing, can you schedule a birthday dinner for Friday? It's her birthday."

"What year?" Jeremy wanted to torture me—clearly.

He knew she'd not be within ten years of me, but the actual answer would lead to ridicule.

"She'll be twenty-nine," I winced.

"Seems about right," Jeremy said. "That poor girl."

"She's no girl. She's formidable and feisty. I promise when you get to know her, you'll like her."

"Are you sure you're alright? Do you need to see a physician?"

"No, I'm fine," I said. "It's… complicated… but I haven't completely lost it."

"I only mean that she appeared to have a brain—more than Caleb deserved and more than you've ever dated in the past. Good on you for finding someone more your intellectual equal!"

I rolled my eyes. "I've dated clever girls before."

He shot me a disapproving look. "Uh-huh. Well, I will have Leslie schedule a reservation for you somewhere wonderful and get her a nice present."

"I will do that," I said. "I have an idea for a gift."

"Suit yourself. You must really like her—regardless of what you say—to plan all of this. It's been at least five years since I've seen you plan something for a birthday. And I don't believe that was for a woman."

"No. It was Caleb," I said.

At some point I needed to call Caleb and explain this. I could only hope it did not burn a bridge with my mate, but I knew there would be some who would never understand.

"Well, she's a lucky girl, then."

I nodded. "I hope you will come to respect her, Jeremy. I

do think she is good for me. And I think she will impress you."

"I will respect her, I am certain," Jeremy said. "I just worry about her dealings with your family."

"My father's heart is failing," I said. "It's the end, Jeremy. It's over."

CHAPTER 22

Bramble

BAZ

"How can I help you?" An old woman behind the desk asked.

"I'm here to enquire about an exemption to the twenty-eight-day waiting period," I answered. "My girlfriend…"

I realized I already fucked up.

"My fiancée," I said. "She is meeting me here. My father is dying. I have documentation, but my solicitor's office said I must file the request in person."

"Ah. It's new. And this is a pressing health condition?"

I sorted through my briefcase and pulled out the file I brought from Braemoor. Ellie asked the doctor to fax proof. She'd been an angel to go behind dad's back so we could apply for the special license in London. She was sad to know she wouldn't be there, but happy for me, too. I felt bad lying about how I loved Lanie and that this was all romantic and exciting. I didn't love her. I respected and adored her, but did not love her.

I handed off the folder. "You will find everything in here, ma'am."

She sorted through it when Lanie burst through the waiting room doors looking altogether different. Her hair was piled high atop her head. She was dressed in a full face of makeup.

"Oh, my god! I got stuck in a hair and makeup consult for about 2 hours longer than they promised it would take," she said. "I'm so sorry, Baz. And as for my appearance, I know you cannot take me out in public like this."

"It's alright. I just got here myself," I said. "You're fine. We'll figure it out, Lanie."

"Oh, are you ready to begin the paperwork, then?" The woman asked, still head down.

She put her glasses on and turned back, then gasped, "Oh, you're Annie! Are you Annie?"

Lanie pointed at herself. "Me? That's my character but—"

"You're little Annie! I love her to bits! Do you do the accent for fun or... are you going all method?"

"She's American. It's how she talks." I assumed Annie was the character. I reminded myself I should probably watch the damn show.

The woman looked at me, then Lanie.

"I shouldn't judge. I really shouldn't. And it's none of my business but... you're old enough to be her father," the woman said.

I wanted to call her out, but Lanie's deep cackle made it alright.

"Oh, God. No. I'm not Annie's age," Lanie assured, throwing her passport on the desk.

"I'm two days from twenty-nine. So, was it physically possible? Yes? Was it likely?" Lanie turned to me. "Depends on his level of sheer stupidity in his mid-teens. Although, my best friend calls him 'Daddy Vibes' so, there's that."

"Good God, Lanie," I groaned.

"What, Baz, it's all in good fun."

I wanted to expire or fade into the wall paneling.

The woman snorted and looked over Lanie's identification. "Very posh. An American passport."

"Any American would assume yours are *truly* posh," Lanie said.

"So, are you shooting again? Can you tell me *anything*?"

Lanie blushed, her apple cheeks rose. "Oh, I'm sworn to secrecy, but would you like an autograph?"

"Oh, my goodness! I would die and go to heaven! Could I have a photo?"

That was how I ended up taking the photo of a mid-sixties woman with my forced fiancée. The woman handed her a wedding brochure.

"Who do I make this out to?" Lanie held a pen.

"Caroline Bramble."

"I like that name," Lanie said. "Very British."

I snickered. She was so cute when she said things like that.

"What?" Lanie asked.

"Nothing. You're adorable. That's all."

"I finally got a smile out of you. I'll take it, Baz."

Had I really been so steely lately she felt I was upset with her?

"For you, anything, darling."

"Okay, so I will ring my supervisor," Mrs. Bramble said. "He must review this and sign off on the application. It will then go to *his* supervisor for final approval with the council."

"And how long will that take?" Lanie asked.

"It comes back usually within three days. I assume that by Monday you will get your authorization. In fact, if you'd like to book something in the afternoon, we can begin thinking about venues."

Venues. It made my palms sweat. No matter what happened, this wasn't abstract. I would be married within the week to a woman I *barely* knew but so admired. Even smelling heavily of hairspray and decorated with enough makeup to outfit a troupe of stage performers, I couldn't quit Lanie Day. The woman had me in a spell.

———

LANIE

"I think given your needs, this is the best option," Mrs. Bramble said. "You will find it is well-appointed."

I turned to Baz, who shrugged in back of the room. It was neither a ringing endorsement nor opposition, but Baz wasn't emotive even on his best day. The room was well-appointed with nice chairs and a lovely fireplace, so he couldn't hate it *that* much, could he?

"Could we say our vows here?" I asked. "It would be best for photos."

"Are we hiring a photographer?" Baz asked nervously.

"I told Chloe our plans—and only Chloe. She will take photos and hold my bouquet. She promised," I said. "She is great with a camera."

"Oh… okay. I just didn't realize we were getting sentimental, darling."

"Well, we should have *something* for posterity."

"Fine, fine. Jeremy, my right hand will be our other witness," I said. "He insists on attending."

"Is he single, attractive, and okay with headstrong blondes?" I asked. "Could be a match made in heaven?"

"Darling, this is Jeremy… *my* Jeremy. He's gay, into men with very impressive beards, and probably isn't the best match," Baz chuckled. "But he will like her as she seems intense."

I thought a moment, then recalled a man who lived for lobster who I only met briefly. I realized if I didn't pretend to know him, it would look quite odd.

I facepalmed. "Sorry, wedding brain!"

Thankfully, Caroline ignored my bobble, "Now, I will need a downpayment for the venue. It's only two hundred quid. Is that alright."

"It's a steal." I filed through my purse.

"What are you doing?" Baz stopped me. "No. You will not be footing this bill, Lanie."

"Baz, I—"

"Stop. I will be glad to pay it in full," Baz said.

We proceeded to the room where we'd begun. A short man with a bun held our paperwork.

"I think we will have this approved by Friday afternoon. The documentation is very good. I am sorry to hear about your father's health, Mr. Osgoode. And, I suppose, my apologies as well, future Mrs. Osgoode."

Future Mrs. Osgoode? Fuck no! I'd have to nip that in the bud. For now, I played along.

"Well, I appreciate that. And thank you," Baz said. "We really are grateful."

"And your father will attend of course? That would be a happy moment," Mrs. Bramble said.

"My father is bed-bound so he cannot make it but just knowing we were able to sign on the line will make him so happy."

She and the supervisor exchanged glances.

"He's very invested in Baz finally settling down." I played it up, trying to walk this back.

Baz was *bad* at this game. He froze and forgot himself.

"Yes. He's in Scotland. We're here. We thought he would come down," Baz agreed. "But the situation got more dire over the past week. We plan to go there shortly after we are done."

I nudged him playfully. "Another reason we need good photos."

"Yes. He will appreciate them, for certain." Baz was wooden, unfeeling, but thankfully they interpreted that as normal.

"Perhaps it will put him at rest, dear," Mrs. Bramble said sweetly. "Oh, that is difficult. A weak heart is hard to fix."

"Yes. There is not much fixing to do." Baz rubbed my back, finally showing a degree of emotion. I couldn't determine if it was a desire for connection or just going through the motions.

I longed for this unexpected feeling—one not of possession but of investment. I felt so disconnected when I broke down and told him about my feelings on the plane the day before. I'd not felt much other than we were friends aiming for the same goal. I looked at him, a slight smile on my face, to telegraph my gratitude for his acknowledgement.

"Well, given that we have everything for now, you may go," the supervisor returned our documents. "We will ring you when the time comes. Who would be the primary contact?"

"I will," Baz said. "She's very busy with work the next few days. My assistant will always answer a call."

Mrs. Bramble noted that. I reached for Baz's hand—not thinking. He squeezed it. I realized it was the first time we'd held hands in public like a proper couple. While this simple gesture still felt slightly awkward, I couldn't help but enjoy the newness. We waited for the elevator.

"So, it's… feeling real," I nervously added words to the mix.

"We don't have to panic over it, darling. It's not like that."

I nodded.

"What is all of this? I feel a little dense. I know I should watch the show—clearly people love it."

"I was only in an episode here or there after the first one," I said.

"And even then people fell in love with you, so that's even more impressive."

I blushed and looked at my shoes. "I feel so ridiculous. I got in the chair at the asscrack of dawn this morning only to wait forty minutes. It meant I had no time to take this all off. I look ridiculous."

Baz pulled my chin up, observing me. "It's different, but you're still beautiful. I am concerned, however, that your face lacks any natural pores."

I giggled. "On purpose. I am supposed to look flawlessly dewy. I need to play a seventeen-year-old until episode two."

"Oh, fuck! No wonder she gave me trouble!" Baz said as the doors opened. "You could have told me, Lanie."

"Yeah, well, I didn't think it was your type of show."

"And I don't care if you're in it. I feel like the world's worst partner to not even know what my… my fiancée is up to."

We were both struggling with *that* f-word. All other f-words were appreciated and noted. Fiancé was a complicated word, and Baz and I were cart-before-horse since day one.

"Catch up on Sky," I snickered. "And if you don't have Sky—"

"I have Sky. I cannot watch half of my team's away matches without it. Speaking of which, how do you feel about football? Do you have allegiances?"

I snickered. "I've paid it no mind, but I have a sneaking suspicion I'm about to gain a new team."

"I do hope you will manage it. Now, about lunch—"

"Can I just go home? I can order in—"

"Lanie, it's not that bad. Your hair looks lovely, I think."

"No, it's not that," I whispered as we stepped onto the ground floor.

"What then?" He raised his eyebrows.

"They shoved me into this corset this morning because they needed to do adjustments to something I'm trying on later. I had no idea what they planned on, and I was running so late I had to just get in the car and come back from Ealing. I need to get out of it. Can we just go round yours and—"

"Well, I'd be glad to be of service getting you *out* of it," Baz agreed. "And I can plan for lunch. I'll send the driver to get whatever you want."

I bit my lip and shook my head. "Only you would turn this inconvenience into such debauchery."

"I never look a gift horse in the mouth, Delanie."

CHAPTER 23
Pet Names

LANIE

I tossed my trench coat, unveiling the unflattering way my sweater hung over a tight-laced corset. I was used to the look and feel of it, but it didn't lay well under thin, modern garments without attracting the wrong type of attention. Baz's curious, investigative side took over as a cheeky grin crossed his face. It wasn't thirst as much as interest in the way I looked. Suddenly, I felt shaken out of whatever funk I fell into. I loved that look.

Baz approached, pulling me towards him forcefully by the hips. I kissed him—slowly and almost delicately. The more it continued, the hungrier I got. Baz's hands lowered until they held my ass firmly, holding my body tightly to his. He pulled away, taking in my face.

"And you have to wear this all the time—without me around to bother you?"

"I'd get nothing done like this," I said.

"No, I suppose not."

"You wouldn't either."

"I don't care to right now. I'd rather devour you," Baz said.

I started to pull off my top, only to have him assist me by

whipping it off and tossing it to the floor with a sense of finality. He backed me against the wall, pinning my arms behind my head. As his lips grazed my ear, then my neck, I shivered and pressed my pelvis into him—needy and desperate for him to have me.

"Fuck me," I moaned.

"Why should I?"

"Because you cannot resist watching me cum."

Gaze locked, Baz said, "You're too greedy, darling. I don't want to spoil you."

"You love spoiling me." I bit my lip.

In response, Baz flipped me around, pinning me to the wall. I moaned.

He spanked my ass and held my head against the wall. "I don't want this to be about you. I am enjoying you right now."

Baz separated my legs and pressed his erection against my ass.

He ran his hand over my leggings and whispered in my ear with hot breath, "Take these off. Take it all off—everything but the corset."

"That's not everything then," I argued, fighting his hand on my head.

He pressed me against the wall with force. "Do as I say or you won't get off."

Fuck! My whole body vibrated as he released me, stepping back to watch me disrobe in the entryway. I played coy, both because I liked the reaction I got and because I was overwhelmed. I liked being roughed up—something he knew a little about. He unlocked more of my urge to be subordinated. I loved that he could have such self-control and restrain himself when he watched me play with others, but now he could ratchet it up to eleven and be the steely, demanding alpha who wanted to use me like a plaything.

"Satisfied?" I asked, standing half-naked.

I felt a little silly in this period-accurate garment, but thirsted for his approval.

"Touch yourself," Baz said. "I want to watch you get yourself off first. Cum for me and I will make you cum again."

"Oh... okay," I said.

The request threw me. I'd never had a man ask me to pleasure myself like this—out in the open and for seemingly *his* benefit. If anyone else had asked, I'd be worried I was walking into a trap, but if I could trust him to watch his good friend fuck me and not misbehave, I could trust him now.

I was already wet, so I dipped my fingers inside my center. Now lubricated, I rubbed them over my clit, slowly. As I did, I met Baz's gaze. He perched on the sofa arm, arms crossed defiantly. It was as if he were my teacher and I was a naughty student turning in a makeup assignment. My urge to please him was almost as great as my need to get off. I pressed my ass against the wall harder, spreading my legs more. My fingers sped up, my clit more swollen now. I was close, but I rarely got off without penetration.

I slipped two fingers inside myself, shuddering with the pleasure that it brought. My head rolled back a moment, then came forward once more. I stared at Baz who now tossed his trousers aside and freed his cock from his boxers just enough to be useful. He played with himself as I moved my fingers in, my thumb slamming into my clit. The sight of his cock only added to the fun. My nostrils flared and the heat crept up my chest, neck, and finally my face as I began to seize and tighten.

"Oh, fuck. Oh, God!" I moaned, moving faster. "Fuck! Oh yes!"

And then, I came—panting and letting out a high squeal. My fingers felt my pulsing orgasm. Wetness ran down my hand. I wasn't satisfied yet, but I was quite happy. I wanted him to fuck me so badly.

"Does that... please you?" I asked.

"Does it please *you?*" Baz asked.

"I don't know. Maybe I faked it?"

"No, you didn't. You came—and you came hard." Baz leaned to grab his wallet.

He found a condom and popped back up, still staring as I tried hard to compose myself. I tried to wipe the wetness from my hands on my hips.

"No. I want you to lick it off," Baz demanded. "I want to look at you as you taste yourself."

It could have been humiliating, but I gave him what he wanted—face defiant.

Baz approached with a condom and took my face in his free hand forcefully. "Don't try me, Lanie."

He dropped his hand and sheathed himself.

"Are you going to leave these boxers on?"

"I want to know I had you for the rest of the day," Baz said.

My nostrils flared. Baz flipped me against the wall, pressing his cock into my back. He pressed my head against it, thoroughly destroying my hair. It pulled—hard—but all I could do was moan in sheer pleasure at the feeling.

"You and I should get tested," Baz said. "So, I don't have to do this anymore."

"Who says I'll let you stop doing that?"

"Well, you'll be my wife, Lanie, so I think it's fitting."

My wife. In this moment, that sounded hot. We played the game. He owned me for a few minutes, and I let him have that much. Outside this space and moment, the idea of being someone's wife under these circumstances felt odd. Here, though, I lusted after the thought of having him bare inside me.

"Oh… okay," I said.

Baz released me from his grasp.

I turned, but he pointed. "Go. Get on the table. Lean over it so I can fuck you from behind. I want to punish you for all your naughty behavior."

I couldn't have raced faster. Baz pressed me over it, again smashing my face down with one hand and pulling my hair. He parted my legs, played with my clit for a minute, then thrust inside so hard that the table moved. His demands and hunger made me want to lose myself. Baz thrust slow at first, ensuring I was okay. As moans of pleasure, then pleas for release overtook me, he sped up.

"I want to cum, Baz. Please."

"Cum for me, then, baby," Baz said.

Each thrust got me closer to the inevitable pleasure of the moment. I was out of breath—the corset *not* helping—and desperate. The roll of pleasure finally won out as I dug my nails into the table runner and shouted.

"Baz, oh, fuck me! Own me!" I screamed.

Baz thrust harder and faster until finally, he gripped my hips and came with a loud, hungry growl. He let my head go, but I remained on the table as he collected himself, then pulled out. I turned, staring at him as he tucked his still-hard cock away, condom in his hand. He tossed it in the kitchen trash, then returned, staring at me. This, time, though, he looked nervous.

"Are you alright? Or was that… too much. You could always say no or tell me to stop something—"

"No," I said. "I'm just catching my breath. That was… so hot. I'm… spent. Never apologize for that. I may be your wife someday soon, but I needed that—and I probably always will. I'm not a demure flower, Baz. I'm a demanding woman."

Baz pulled his trousers on and zipped them with some finality. "You are. I admire that about you, Miss Delphine. Or is it Miss Day when we're in here?"

"I think when we're here and completely beside ourselves, I want you to call me Mrs. Osgoode—and only when we are here."

"You will not be Lady Osgoode, then?" Baz asked. "Because that would be your correct title, darling."

I pulled back, "Really?"

"Yes. Unless you are opposed. I'm not asking you to do it unless you *want* to, love. It's just that when the old fucker dies, you'll be Baroness Oban and you already have the courtesy title of Lady. It will anger Alex and Nessa to no end, and I'm dying to see that as well. I'm not asking you to legally change your name if you do not want to. Nor am I asking you to drop your stage name."

"Oh," I said. "I will think about it."

I hadn't considered that I would have a *title*. My mother would have slapped me upside the head over it. I always said I wouldn't change my name. Even my own sister and Cal had chosen to hyphenate *both* their names to Delphine-Markham. They were a political brand. And, in due course, I thought maybe Baz and I would be our own brand of power couple—at least for our public face.

"Where did Day even come from? Lanie makes sense. Day doesn't. It works, but where is that from?"

"I liked the sound of it. I wanted to give a nod back to my dad since he supported my idiotic insistence that I be an actress. Mum has *never* liked it. But Lanie Davina or Lanie David didn't *quite* work. I ended up with Day because I love Doris Day and Day is what my Mum sometimes called my dad. They had all these embarrassing pet names for one another. I found them cringe at the time, but now I miss them so much. They grew old together—but not as old as any of us wanted. I'm glad I included that bit in my stage name, though. It means even more now."

"I'm not much for pet names," Baz admitted. "I won't promise you any of that."

"You already call me darling. You just called me love."

"Nothing inventive, I mean. I've never been that way."

"Nor have I," I admitted. "But I think when you're with someone for forty years, things change."

Baz wrapped his arms around my waist. "That is entirely possible. And if we can follow through with this, almost anything is?"

I grinned. "Yeah, I guess."

He kissed my forehead tenderly, before stepping back. "I will drop you off at work. I just saw my mobile. The driver has the food and should be here any minute."

"Great," I said. "Before then, can you free me from my

stays? I'm pretty used to wearing one of these by now, but my tits are begging for mercy, Baz."

"I was only marveling at how lovely they looked pushed clear up to your chin," Baz chuckled. "You're even more precious when you're so prim and proper like that."

I smacked him on the arm. "Get me out of this thing."

———

BAZ

"I'm giving up on this," Lanie sighed, trying to straighten herself in the reflection of the kitchen's double-hob.

"What do you mean?" I asked.

"My bra is back at the studio. And this sweater is a disaster without one."

I snickered. "Is it? Or is it just right?"

Lanie rolled her eyes. Hands on hips, she said, "I don't want to walk around with my boobs so obvious. It's clinging in the worst way."

"I disagree. It's a gift."

"One you didn't earn, Baz."

"I also disagree. I think I proved my worth several times there."

She strode out of the kitchen with a torturous sway in her hips. The more I invested my time in her, the more I enjoyed Lanie. She didn't care if she offended me.

"Lanie, what are you doing?"

"Solving my own fucking problem!"

The door buzzer rang. I saw my driver waiting below. I buzzed him up to deliver our lunch—Thai food from Lanie's preferred place.

"The food has arrived!" I called as the driver handed it over.

I remained befuddled as I portioned it out on the counter-top. Lanie finally emerged in one of my shirts—one I very much liked. The light blue pinstripe was well-worn until perfectly soft. I debated telling her to choose another.

Lanie explained, "It's baggy. I blame you for the corset issue, and I can wear it when I am stuck getting in and out of things all afternoon. After all, I won't always have you there to undress me."

"If only I could," I murmured. "But of all my shirts… that one?"

"What? I cannot have this one?"

"It is perhaps my favorite shirt, Lanie."

"Well, than you should be so lucky for it to grace *my* body." Lanie opened the plastic cutlery pouch.

"You think you're quite special, Lanie."

"I *am*. And the shirt will come back to you—I promise. You owe me for what you just pulled."

"What was that?"

"I've never just gone along with anyone telling me to get myself off in front of them."

"Why not?" I asked.

"Why does that do it for you, Baz? Honestly?"

"Why wouldn't it?"

"You don't seem like a man who would take second place in any competition. So, why wait for me to pleasure myself first —or let someone pleasure me? What does that do for you?"

I cocked my head. "You think I am losing? Or coming in second?"

"You let Caleb fuck me—for a while. You let that rando go down on me—"

"The verb you use tells you all you need to know, Lanie."

"What?"

"I *let* you. I *let* him. I controlled the whole thing through *my* rules."

She bit her noodles, mulling it.

"Lanie, it works because what I get off on—what I crave— is a woman getting off. And I get the pride and satisfaction of knowing you never cum harder than you do with me."

Lanie coughed, choking. "And how do you know that?"

"Because you scream my name and you enjoy it. You like performing *for* me. I encourage you, yes, but you are desperate to get off for my benefit. I live for that. You're such a good little performer."

Lanie bit her lip.

"And I wanted to watch you get yourself off for my own selfish reasons," I said.

"Why?"

"So, I could more effectively do it," I said. "And in hopes that maybe I'd find a way to make you squirt, since you haven't done that for me yet."

"I hate to break it to you, baby, but that isn't something I do."

"Maybe you just haven't had the right partner?" I raised my eyebrows. "You should never say never."

Lanie smiled slightly. "Fine. Again, I'd never done with anyone. It's a little odd. Most men even get offended to know you own a fucking vibrator—and *everyone* owns a vibe. I'm a lot more efficient with one. Who isn't?"

"If I was intimidated by a sex toy, I should hang up my boots," I said.

Lanie smiled. "It bothers you I'm wearing this shirt, doesn't it?"

"A little, but you look damn good in it," I said. "You can steal my clothes, Lanie, as long as you come back to me and play the game."

CHAPTER 24
Birthday Girl

BAZ

I KNOCKED on Lanie's door. Chloe answered, looking me over.

"I'm here to take Lanie out," I said.

"I'm aware." Her glare only intensified.

I shook my head. "I know I must do some sort of penance and you are aware—"

"I want to not hate you," Chloe said. "Lanie is my best friend. Her sister is married to my brother. She should basically *be* my sister. But after what your family did to her mother… I struggle to see how this works out for her."

"I understand your concern, but we are on the same side of shite my father did," I said. "And we are united in our utter disdain for him."

"Be that as it may, I am still watching you. I am fucking on you like stank on shit, Daddy Vibes. Don't think I don't know everything."

She held power not usually associated with someone so small.

"You are a striking sort of woman. Where did you learn to talk so authoritatively?"

"My mother was a boss bitch and could still kick your

whiny little British ass," Chloe said. "I will find a way to crush you if you hurt Lanie."

"Chlo, down girl!" Lanie's voice hit atop the stairs.

As I looked up, she descended them in a beautiful gold dress, holding a pair of red heels.

"I was just *warning* Daddy Vibes."

"Daddy Vibes is aware," Lanie bent to put on her heels.

I resisted the urge to look down her dress as she did.

"Where are you taking her then?" Chloe asked.

"Cliffside," I answered.

"That place in Soho?" Lanie's face lit up. "The one with the duck?"

"You said you liked duck," I said. "And it seemed a good fit. Does it suit?"

"It's great," Lanie agreed.

Mission accomplished. I'd given Jeremy almost no parameters, but it was the best option. He was a bloody genius and let me win the night.

"Well, we're going now," Lanie said. "So, we'll leave you."

"Fine, whatever," Chloe said. "Don't murder her or my minions will murder you."

"Aye-aye, captain," I said as Lanie stepped out ahead of me.

"She's very protective," Lanie explained.

I closed the door.

"I get it," I agreed. "If I were in her shoes, I'd feel the same. It's good to have someone like that in your corner."

We hopped in the car, headed for SoHo to a spot that had been nothing only six months before. Now, it teemed with the theatre crowd hoping to get a sitting on an impossible list. I strode by with Lanie, listening as people recognized her and whispered. She ignored them.

A hostess sat us at a nice table on the second-floor balcony. We could see the bar below and out the massive two-floor windows onto the street. The refinished building was cozy and modern. I appreciated all the openness. It made the place feel alive.

"People were gossiping about you," I said. "Should I worry?"

"Only if it bothers you." Lanie shrugged. "They are ramping up the PR on the app and have been planting stories. People hear about me all over. I ignore it. Don't worry, I'm still mostly a nobody."

"I disagree," I said. "I watched the show."

"And?"

"It's not my thing," I admitted. "And watching you inhabit the role of a seventeen-year-old is rather disturbing."

She giggled, "Welcome to Hollywood."

"But you do a fine job playing a character who is everything you are not."

"And you mean?"

"She's naive, sweet, and obsessed with the way men view her. She's very immature."

"And I'm not?"

"No. You are confident, somewhat jaded, a realist, and anything but immature, Lanie. If you were like Annie, I'd have no interest in you."

"Then why date someone my age? Why..." Lanie lowered her voice. "Why *marry* someone my age?"

"Because you are young, but not inexperienced. You may be lithe, but you are an old soul who can handle me."

Lanie bit her lip. "Can I?"

"Yes."

The server took our drink order. Lanie confidently ordered a *very* expensive bottle of red wine without asking for the right to do it. It may have read presumptuous to some, but felt right for her.

"Thank you for taking me out," Lanie said. "I really do like that you tried to make it feel all offish."

I chuckled. "I've never minded taking you out and treating you to anything, Lanie."

Lanie threw her hair over a shoulder. "Fine. Then take me to the club after this."

Her unexpected pass threw me off course. I didn't want to

share her tonight. Something about going through the motions of properly treating her to dinner made something sordid like that seem inappropriate. I should have jumped for joy, but I couldn't bring myself to do it. I didn't want to let anyone else touch her tonight.

"No," I said. "I don't want that. I want to take you home and be greedy after this."

Lanie cocked her head. "This is one of your last minutes of freedom, you know?"

"We both know that was not the bargain we struck," I said. "And right now, I want to play the good boyfriend. Then, I will get you home and put you through your paces."

Lanie pouted. "Even for a minute? What if only you touched me?"

"Have I created a monster, Lanie?"

The wine arrived.

She took a long sip, setting the glass down and smoothing the tablecloth. "Don't act as though my wild side is a fucking inconvenience for you, Baz. It's not like you don't get off on it."

She was correct. I also found myself strangely jealous of anyone else who would have her. The thought of it made me dig in.

"What good is the membership if you never use it?"

I sighed. "Lanie, I didn't use it *all* the time. It's a nice fringe sort of benefit of being me."

"And me... by proxy if you're about to marry me. Do the benefits transfer or am I just SOL?"

I rolled my eyes. "Lanie, I—"

"Baz, are you being greedy?"

I took a very long drink, confused as to what I could say. Of *course* I was greedy. She stole my favorite shirt. She's slept at my place a couple of times. She got me to sign a marriage license—something I never thought I'd do. I was somewhat entitled, wasn't I?

"You are," Lanie said. "Unbelievable. And what do you want from me?"

She wasn't cross. Her face showed sick satisfaction to know I got caught up in it.

"Given that I have a clean bill of health, I'm hoping you can say the same and I will get to take full advantage of it," I said.

She feigned surprise. "Lord Osgoode, what are you implying?"

"That I am going to get to do the thing I've been wanting to do since we first discussed this matter."

The sides of Lanie's full lips curled. "I'm good to go. But I want to finish this duck first."

LANIE

"Well, well, well, if it isn't Lanie Day."

I looked from my steak as Caleb approached. Baz had run to the bathroom, leaving me alone, trying to figure out how to navigate this. He had no idea who I really was or what Baz and I agreed to. Had he seen me here with Baz? And would there be beef over it?

"Hello, Caleb," I tried to be neither too warm nor too icy.

He looked at Baz's lamb chops and the glass of wine. "You busy?"

"Having dinner, yes," I answered.

"Well, I was surprised to see you here. You're still in the UK then?"

"They have made me the big story of series two," I answered. "So, I am around for a bit."

Caleb's gaze trained somewhere behind me. I panicked as I realized he spotted Baz.

"Well, well, well, if it isn't you," Caleb chuckled.

Baz approached, not looking the least bit worried.

"What is the occasion to get you out to dinner before ten? And a proper dinner at that, mate!"

Baz sat, as if reminding Caleb of his place in this bizarre hierarchy. Even here, Baz was the man on top of the pyramid.

"It is Lanie's birthday," Baz said. "I figured the least I could do was gather her up for a good meal. And given that her friend gave me such grief for not properly taking her out, I couldn't ignore that I'd neglected her much longer. That girl is terrifying."

"Chloe is like her mother," I said.

"What was her mother?" Caleb asked. "Was she a drill sergeant?"

"She started from nothing and built a cosmetics empire," I said. "So, yeah. All-around badass."

Caleb's jaw dropped. "You know powerful Americans."

"I'd hazard she *is* one, Caleb."

Caleb was sweet and good in bed but lacked Baz's wit or intellect. Comparing them side-by-side was perhaps perverse, but they'd sort of done it to themselves. Baz's strategy, his determined work ethic, and his overall intelligence turned me on more than Caleb's young, hot, sweet aesthetic.

"Well, either way. I shouldn't be rude and… bother you," Caleb said. "I've also got a dining partner. It was nice catching up, Lanie. See you next week, Baz."

He left, as if having seen a ghost.

"What was that about?" I asked.

"What?"

"He just put his tail in between his legs. Is it because of you? Or is some woman flagging him down."

"He's here with a business associate," Baz noted. "Not a date. He wants to chase you, Lanie, because you're a fun actress. You weren't *serious*. He got to be the serious one. Now that he realizes you are rolling with powerful people—even if he has *no* idea who your father was—he's turned off."

"What? Over that?" I snickered. "So, he's a misogynist?"

"No. I wouldn't go *that* far."

I rolled my eyes. "What do you call a man intimidated by women so much he couldn't get it up?"

"Well, I don't know. That's *not* my problem. If you were

boring and simple, I'd have long ago tired of you. Meanwhile, that is what Caleb prefers—young, fun, uncomplicated, and impressed by flash."

"And I'm not any of those things?"

"We can lie and act like you don't have the manners of a debutante received by Her Majesty at court or that you didn't grow up or that your family hasn't amassed tons of wealth. I could bloody well ignore most of that and play along. What I cannot ignore—and what he never could—is you're clever. And now he knows not only are you that, but you don't need him to save you or bankroll you. So, what do you need him for?"

I furrowed my brow. "What does anyone need anyone for? Isn't it love?"

Baz snickered, "That's fucking adorable, darling."

His phone buzzed. He looked at it, grimaced, then turned it over.

"You can get it," I said.

"It's just work. I am sure Jeremy has it covered."

I rolled the duck around in my potatoes as he stared into the distance. His mind was elsewhere. Suddenly, the thought of him fucking me against the wall that graced my mind earlier no longer did.

"I don't want you if you're unavailable," I said. "I do not mind spending time with you and boosting your image—"

"Boosting my image?"

"Baz, I'm a young, pretty actress from a good family. You are going to get told that you're *the man* because you ensnared me. Don't lie. I don't want you here if you're really needed elsewhere."

"Lanie, it's your birthday," Baz said.

"I'll call Chloe. We'll go out," I said.

The phone buzzed again.

"I do have to take this," Baz said. "I'm so sorry, Lanie."

"It's okay," I watched him wander off.

He stood on the railing down the way, talking business. I

had no right to be upset. We weren't a real couple. Business came first for us. He returned in a minute.

"I'm going to meet Jeremy at Heathrow," Baz sighed. "There is a problem with a project in Berlin and I must run. I am so sorry, Lanie."

"It's okay," I tried not to let his quick departure hurt.

Baz's genuine dismay telegraphed as I stood. He gave me a soft kiss as if he needed to take a bit of me with him—but not too much—then left. I sat back down and resisted the urge to call Chloe. I'd have to hear "I told you so."

CHAPTER 25
Wedding Bells

LANIE

"You ready?"

I appeared in Chloe's doorway sporting my outfit of choice—a white and pink tweed Balmain dress with a low-but-tasteful neckline.

"I am… wow. You look amazing," Chloe stopped, looking me over. "Sorry. I was just getting my camera and good portrait lens."

She flipped through her wardrobe and tossed a couple of things in a camera bag.

"You went full va-va-va-vintage," Chloe said. "And you're bringing the hat?"

"We'll pin it on when we get there," I answered. "We're not *trying* to draw attention to ourselves."

"He's actually going to be there, then?" Chloe asked.

"If he stands me up, it's his fault. He would be the one who stands to lose."

"True."

A Bentley waited before our house. I climbed in quickly, setting my hat box down. Chloe followed with her camera bag in one hand, and my bouquet in the other. I reached out for the bundle of beautiful pink peonies I'd chosen to match my dress. Chloe grabbed my free hand as the car drove away and squeezed it tight.

"This is all insane, and your mother will lose her shit. However, I am always here for you, babes. No one is going to take that away."

I smiled. "Thanks, Chlo. I promise it will be okay."

I honestly had no clue. When I spoke to Baz early this morning, he'd missed his connection in Paris and was chartering a flight into London City. I didn't know if the groom would show, if we'd go through with it, or what life held. It was stupid and ridiculous and yet I couldn't get out. To leave would mean admitting my harebrained scheme was a silly idea, and I acted impulsively.

At the Old Town Hall, we departed. We rushed the steps and fled to the bridal holding pen. Mrs. Bramble met us. I listened to her directions as Chloe pinned the bright pink pillbox to my head.

"You look so lovely, Miss Delphine," Mrs. Bramble said. "Soon to be Mrs. Osgoode."

"Lady Osgoode," I said, "before I know it."

Chloe pulled the small birdcage veil down over my face and positioned the mesh to frame my face.

"Oh, yes. Lady Osgoode. Well, you are very lucky. Where is the groom waiting?"

"He is still on his way," I said. "He got stuck... in traffic. He will be here."

"Well, given that he's running late, I'll come get you when he's ready in the room."

"Or you can just take me up there?" I said.

"Well, but that would throw off the reveal."

"I'm not walking down an aisle. I'd like to just assemble, do our vows, and then sign things," I said.

"Oh, well, if you and your future husband don't mind, I can take you up. This dress is *lovely* on you with the pink shoes and hat. How darling!"

We went up one more floor to find the small room where the ceremony was slated to occur in only five minutes. The officiant waited patiently. Introductions were made, but they couldn't slow my pulse. I found myself sweating, worried he might have planned to miss this. I'd be mortified.

"I just need some air," I whispered to Chloe as she attached the flash to her camera.

"Gotcha," Chloe said. "Don't run without me."

"I'm not."

I stepped outside and paced, wondering what my future held. As I stood against the wall, I looked down. I heard feet approaching. Baz appeared, face pulled in stress. Despite his cross-continental trip, he looked handsome as ever in a dark grey suit. I worried he was about to tell me the worst news. I wanted him to smile. I needed that affirmation.

Instead of a smile, he swept me up in a kiss—the type that ran from my lips down to my toes. I wrapped my arms around his neck and leaned into him. I couldn't think about anything else. As quickly as he disappeared Friday, he was now back. I felt comfortable as ever in his arms. I'd somehow taken on the role of Lady Osgoode in more than just appearances.

Baz pulled back, holding my face in his hands. "I am so fucking sorry. The whole thing was a nasty mess but I'm here now. And you… you look absolutely beautiful."

I smiled, unable to hold back. "Thank you."

"Are you sure this is okay?"

"Yeah," I said. "Let's do it."

I turned to pull him back in and found Chloe holding her camera.

"Are you ready now?" She called.

"As ever," I answered. "Let's get this show on the road."

———

BAZ

As I held Lanie's hand, I was dazed. I was sleep-deprived, but also confused. Lanie looked like she'd taken the assignment seriously. In her own way, she looked pitch perfect. While a short dress didn't usually strike me as wedding attire, she did it her way. Lanie never did anything half-assed and never doubted herself.

Lanie declared without hesitation, "I, Delanie Beth Carlisle-Delphine, take you, Basil Callan Osgoode, to be my wedded husband."

I followed. "I, Basil Callan Osgoode, take you, Delanie Beth Carlisle-Delphine to be my wedded wife."

The statement wasn't a lie. Lanie *was* my wife. But the symbols of fidelity, love, and devotion I slid onto her tiny ring finger was a farce. A pang of guilt hit. Women wanted grand gestures and beautiful weddings, and I only granted her scraps. As I took in her beautiful smile, I winced. She deserved the world. Unfortunately, by the point I had regrets, it was done.

The officiant announced, "It therefore gives me great pleasure, to pronounce you are now husband and wife. You may now kiss!"

So, we did. Or rather, Lanie kissed *me*. And it was a hell of a kiss. She had thrown all of herself into being the head-over-heels bride. The least I could do was match a bit of her enthusiasm.

"Lanie, let the man go," Chloe said.

"I figured it was worth it for the picture. Can you confirm you at least got a photo?" Lanie asked.

I fought laughter.

"I've got your fucking photo," Chloe confirmed.

Jeremy stared at Chloe with confusion. He did not understand these Americans.

We signed the register and were free.

"That's it?" Lanie asked.

Our officiant beamed. "That is it, Mrs. Osgoode. Congratulations!"

"Lady Osgoode." She *swiftly* corrected.

"Correct," I added, rubbing her back for assurance.

"Well, may you have many happy years," Mrs. Bramble swooned.

She was moved to tears at some point. Lanie had asked her to please stay. That was Lanie for you. She'd go out of her way to make other people happy.

"I do have your engagement ring here, too, Lady Osgoode," Jeremy was altogether formal, and unsure how to address her.

"Oh, Lanie is fine," Lanie insisted. "And shit! I totally forgot about it."

Jeremy shot me a look of uncertainty.

Jeremy handed her the second ring. It occurred to me it was the first time she'd seen it fitted for her hand. She grinned and held it out.

"That will do, I guess," Lanie said.

We filed into the hall where Chloe began to disassemble Lanie's hat., which took some doing. It seemed unnecessary but from a standpoint of the press finding out, it made sense.

"She is… a cyclone," Jeremy remarked. "Just… not at all as I expected."

"I said that, Jer. I told you."

"Well, she holds her own, but is also a child."

"She's not. I promise," I said.

"Well, if you think you can manage, I will get out of your hair. Your reservation should be good. I will go back to the office."

I winced. "I get the feeling she will be cross when she finds out I leave again in the morning."

"She doesn't know, Basil?" Jeremy's jaw dropped. "You married her, and you didn't tell her. But also, you haven't offered to bring her."

"What? So, I could dump her in a hotel room and spend hours unfucking what Karl did?" I scoffed. "She's better off here with her family and friends. Besides, she must work, too."

Jeremy's face didn't show confidence, but it was the truth.

Lanie, finally sans-hat, asked, "Alright. Where to?"

"The world's most sorry honeymoon," Jeremy whispered.

CHAPTER 26

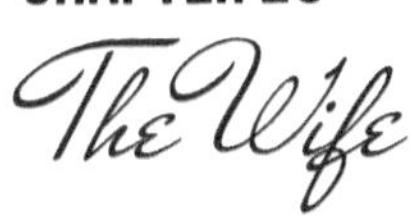

LANIE

"You're not going to carry me over the threshold, then?" I demanded as we stood before the hotel suite.

"And if I were to drop you…"

"Well, you'd damage your own investment. And I'd never believe you could fuck me against a wall properly."

Baz looked up, fighting the urge to say something spicy as two old biddies passed. With a flash, instead of a delicate hoist, he threw me over his shoulders like a sack of potatoes. I squealed nervously, then giggled so much it hurt. Baz, seemingly unbothered by the women, smacked my ass hard. I giggled more.

"Miss, are you alright?" One called from the elevator.

"We're newlyweds. It's fine," I replied.

"Oh, congratulations and best wishes!" The other said.

Baz opened the door and strode in with me over his shoulder. He unceremoniously dropped me onto the bed.

"Why is it that when married couples go at it, it's fine? But, God, the same awful acts done by unmarried people is *the worst*?" I asked.

"God has sanctioned it. Although, in our case, he hasn't." Baz tore his tie off and fiddled with his cufflinks.

I kicked my shoes off, staring at him like he was a divine meal.

"You're very cheeky, Lanie."

"And you're the asshole who spanked his wife in public."

"You like hearing that word, don't you?"

"No. But I like how uncomfortable it makes you, dear husband."

He shook his head. "It doesn't. I live for the game, as do you. I'd rather let *everyone* know you are my wife in due time."

"Why? So, men will stop bothering me as you show ownership."

"I don't mind the idea of men bothering you sometimes," Baz said. "I rather like it. However, right now, I realize I've never had you properly and so freely, and I want to make you cum and feel every bit of you."

"I'd have let you have me again and again this weekend, but you were too busy in Germany."

Baz changed the subject, "How did you like my gift?"

He removed his shirt and pants. Then, he tossed off his boxers to reveal how badly he wanted me. I appreciated the view, but wanted him inside me. I did torture him a bit first.

"I prefer your cock," I said. "But the gift was appreciated."

Baz sent me a very expensive vibrator to make up for his absence. It was good, but he was better.

"Did you use it like I asked you to?"

Baz climbed onto the bed, parting my legs with his body. I leaned into the delectable way it felt when he pressed against me.

"Yes, naughty boy, I did," I said.

"And?" He kissed my neck

I sighed, "I got off a few times."

"Did you think of me?" Baz rubbed the head of his cock against my entrance.

The feeling of his hard, hungry cock against my swollen, desperate pussy sent a shiver down my spine. I gasped, then moaned. I didn't have to tell him who I thought about or what after that. The answer was yes.

"Yeah, you like that. You *did* think of me."

"Uh-huh," I said as he again kissed my neck.

Baz could be simultaneously rough and tender. While his body pressing me into the mattress was strong and demanding, his kisses were soft and gentle.

"What did you think about?" Baz whispered. "When you touched yourself?"

His cock continued to torture me. I could feel the wetness of his precum. He wanted to be inside me but denied himself for his own sick satisfaction.

"Fuck me, Baz, please."

Baz pinned my arms behind my head. "Tell me. I want to hear you say it."

"I wanted you to watch me. So, I thought about that."

"You're very bad, Lanie."

"I know." I bit my lip, staring defiantly.

Baz slowly pushed himself back, then pressed into me, his cock slowly parting me and soaking up my wetness. It was torturously slow but felt *so* good. I moaned and grasped my right breast for dear life.

"Oh, you're quite pleased then?" Baz asked.

I nodded, my breath quickening as he thrust slow and deep.

"You feel so good, Lanie. Fuck! It's better than I imagined," Baz moaned.

"Fuck me harder," I growled. "Don't stop until I cum."

Baz slowly picked up speed, giving me what I wanted. He placed my legs on his shoulders again, pounding me harder. It felt so good as he went deeper, touching a spot within me that swelled with each thrust.

"You're hitting my… G-spot," I panted. "S-s-so good."

Baz moved his hand from my knee to my clit. The sensation threw my head back. It was almost too much. I thought I might have to pee and remembered that was a symptom of a squirting orgasm.

"If you keep.. doing that.. I might squirt," I warned.

Baz kissed my ankle. "Oh, that's too bad. We'd not want that."

He got sweet satisfaction thinking he might be the first to do this. I could tell just by his words. But as he stroked my clit and pressed into me deeper, I grew too close. I went over the edge, losing myself to the biggest, most whole-body orgasm I'd ever had. I screamed—nothing intelligible—and writhed. Then, I lay there, spent and unable to think.

"We're going to need another duvet," Baz smirked, quite proud of himself. "But you are beautiful when you cum like that."

"Uh... Uh-huh," I panted. "Fuck."

Baz had slowed to give me time to recover but once more picked up speed.

"You're amazing," I moaned. "God, Baz, don't stop. I'll cum again."

"Cum for me, then," Baz said.

I sensed even he—the glutton for delayed gratification— couldn't avoid the inevitable much longer.

I didn't have to work hard. As easily as he pumped me and as sensitive as I remained, I came again. This orgasm was less of an out-of-body experience but still lovely. And listening to him meet his own glorious end didn't hurt.

"Oh, fuck, Lanie," Baz growled before falling forward.

Still pulsing inside me, he kissed my lips sweetly. I laced my fingers through his hair. It felt like something real happened between us even if it was still just a game. I wanted him to give me more of himself.

Baz pulled back. "I don't want to leave you. You feel so good."

"I am sure you say that to every girl," I giggled.

Baz hopped up, entering the bathroom. He returned with a towel.

"I generally don't do that, so you're a divine treat," Baz said. "For many, many reasons. Here, you'll want this. I will tell housekeeping we need another duvet. Next time, we should put a towel down."

"Did you know what you were doing?" I cleaned up the mess we made.

"Darling, I wasn't born yesterday. Yes. I wanted to wreck you."

"Was it worth it?"

"Every bit of it. Forgive me if I get greedy and do it again. Was it worth it for you?"

"It was fucking amazing!" I laughed. "Yes, of course. I felt like I was on another planet in the best way."

Baz settled in by me, running a finger from my clavicle to my pubic bone. I shivered again.

"Baz, what do we do if we are with other people? We should have some ground rules. I'm fine with *us* losing the condoms, but I don't like the risk—"

"We always use protection with anyone else—doesn't matter who," Baz said. "But I'd like to have unfettered access to all of you just like this."

I could have melted. He made me feel *so* good.

———

BAZ

"Why did you insist on a hotel?" Lanie asked.

"What do you mean? We'd just gotten married," I said.

"It's not real, though. And your house is even nicer than this suite."

"You know the way to my heart by complementing my house," I said. "But even if it feels fake, I wanted to make it wonderful for you. And I figured I'd get much more of you this way—along with room service."

"Can we do room service then? And can I do this thing we used to do where we ordered every single dessert on the menu?"

"Eat to your heart's content, Lady Osgoode," I chuckled. "You know how to torture one's bank account."

"Happy wife, happy life," Lanie joked.

"Correct."

"Is there a tub?" Lanie asked.

"Yes."

"Ugh. I want to take full advantage of it," Lanie said. "Decisions, decisions. I am going to take a bath. Then, I will return, and we can order room service."

"As you wish," I said.

I watched Lanie pad to the bathroom naked. I'd probably never regret that sight. Fake wife or not, Lanie was more than I could have asked for. I couldn't keep my hands off her. It was a terrible thing to be so wrapped up in her—in my *wife*.

I rolled over, searching for my mobile in the trousers I threw down. After dangling off the bed, I secured the device and sat up. Climbing under the covers, I dialed my father.

"Four," he sounded breathless.

"Father, I wanted to tell you that I married Lanie," I said. "Here. Because we very much wanted to make sure it was official before you passed away and didn't want to cause you more stress."

"You wed her? Already?" Father coughed.

"Yes. Today. We requested a special license back home, too, but got denied. And… given you are unwell, I thought you might want to hear that from me."

"I did, thank you," Father said. "Really? You went through with it? And she did, too?"

"It is very much legally binding. We signed the prenup last week. Don't worry. We're protected."

"Good girl," Father said. "Ellie will be heartbroken."

She knows. "I think she will get over it as soon as we come home. She'll be happy to spend more time with Lanie."

"Well, when *will* you be home?"

"As planned, next week," I said. "The gamekeeper will come up with the dogs Thursday."

"I cannot go out. Maybe I can sit and watch from a car," Father said. "But I will not be able to shoot."

"Yes, I know," I said. "We will figure it out. B.C. Can join us."

"That would be best. That way the girls could all get to know one another better."

"I think Lanie will come with," I said. "She's a dynamite shot. I doubt she'd be too encouraged to stay home."

"She is your *wife*, Four. Her job is to sit quietly and look pretty, not shoot pheasant."

"Well, I thought her job was to produce an heir and make us look good. Do we not want to keep Lanie happy?"

"Fine," Father agreed. "But I don't like a woman out shooting."

I rolled my eyes. "I am not dying on this hill. I refuse to regulate where and when Lanie can move about the property. It is now her home, too."

"Don't fuck this up, Baz. You don't have much time before you do. Get her pregnant, produce an heir, and then whatever you do, just fly below the radar. She's tied to you once you've succeeded in that. Before, if you anger her, she'll leave. She's like her mother—she's flighty."

I didn't agree. Lanie was carefree and wild, but she wasn't flighty. No one would agree to this arrangement under *that* designation. Instead, she was just her own person. My father would never understand my disinterest in any wife who would prefer to lounge around the house eating bonbons when she could be out enjoying the poor Scottish weather in real time. That sort of "no fucks given" attitude was what I loved about her. Yes, I *loved* something about her. It shook me for a moment before I considered if you could love something about someone without loving *them*.

CHAPTER 27
Reality Check

LANIE

I woke to Baz rustling through a bag. The light was breaking through the slight holes in the shades. Rolling over, I spied him packing luggage on the floor.

Confused, I murmured, "Baz, it's so early. Are we already going? I need to rest."

"No, darling. I must go back to Germany. We're still in the thick of unfucking something. I'm so sorry," Baz said.

I sat up. "Baz, you are running away like eighteen hours into whatever this is."

"It's a partnership. I'm still a partner. Trust me when I say I would much rather be in bed with you right now. I will be back at the weekend. Promise. Stay. The room is paid for through tomorrow. You can stay another night."

"Baz," I groaned.

"What? I tried, Lanie."

"So, you're never coming back?"

"God, no! I will be back here ASAP. Promise. Wait..." A mischievous grin crossed Baz's face in the low bathroom light that streamed in. "Are you going to... miss me?"

"Maybe. Am I not allowed to miss you?"

"No. I will miss you as well. And when I get back, I will

go down on you endlessly to make up for it. But, I have a job. I must *do* my job."

I'd be lying if I didn't say I was disappointed. The evening before had felt other-worldly. He left every inch of me quivering and wanting more. I had never had a man treat me quite so well in bed. I knew he didn't love me. I didn't love him, either, but I didn't *care*. I only wanted him to lust for me and demand I cum. So, I'd lean into missing him if it meant he was even more giving the next time.

"Okay," I pouted.

"Oh, stop it, Lanie. You know when you do that it wounds me."

I smiled slyly. "You don't have time to go again?"

"No," Baz said. "Nor does any man on this floating rock have the stamina to match your libido right now."

"No man? You sure of it."

"No man that could make you see heaven as I did last night," Baz said. "I'm worth the wait. I know that for a fact."

"As am I. But I still want you here. We just got *married*, Baz."

He sighed and then sat on the bed. "You are the most utterly infuriating women I've ever slept with."

"And yet every time you rub one out you think about cumming inside me."

"Or on your ass. Or on your tits. Even better, your face."

I grimaced.

"I can entertain those thoughts even if you're not into it."

"True, but why?"

"No clue. I just think you'd make that face and it would be altogether satisfying to watch. Anyhow, Lanie, I must go."

He leaned over and kissed me gently. His hand brushed my cheek. Then, he was gone. I curled in a ball and tried to drift off. I knew Baz cared. If he didn't, he wouldn't have shown up for anything. But *damn* I realized now that being Baz's *priority* wasn't easy. And suddenly, I was no longer just his hot hookup. I was full-on method acting my way into matrimony. What was it doing to my brain?

CHAPTER 28

Breaking News

LANIE

On Friday, I woke to someone banging the back door. I knew it wasn't my ride to the studio because it was too early.

"Dora!" I called for my younger sister who was always up at the asscrack of dawn.

No response.

So, I pulled myself up and raced down the steps to stop the banging. Still in a nightgown, I encountered two men in suits standing before a black Land Rover. I worried I'd slipped into one of Chloe's spicy mafia romances. What if Baz was *actually* the son of a mafia king?

"What are you, the mob?" I scoffed.

"Miss Delphine, Lady Danna would like to speak with you."

"Really? Mum sent goons for me?" I groaned. "What is it now? And where is she?"

"Ma'am, your presence has been requested," one answered, not explaining.

"Fine," I said. "I will change, but I am *not* dressing up for tea."

I stomped back upstairs, cursing that Chloe jetted to Bali with some guy the day before. I was all alone. No one could save me. I quickly pulled on leggings, an Air Force sweatshirt I stole from my father a decade before, and a pair of running shoes. Then, I left for wherever they were taking me.

"Why are we going all over god's green earth?" I asked, annoyed.

"Ma'am, I don't know if you're aware," a goon replied from the front seat, "but you're a public figure. The press are crawling all over the place. We are just trying to protect you."

"Why?" I asked.

The two men made eye contact in the front seat. I shifted nervously, confused that I was about to be taken to a warehouse in north London or forced into the backroom of a Wetherspoon's to eat a full English with one of my ex-brother-in-law's MP cronies. The last time I'd been involved with those fuckers was when I used my tits to help Daphne convince a cabinet secretary to rat out her asshole ex. It wasn't fun, but it was worth it.

"Are you going to kill me?" I asked, annoyed, as the car continued in no particular way.

"No," the other goon answered. "We are here to take you to meet your mother. We were given the orders to deliver you safely."

"Again, I would ask from what are you protecting me? Moreover, are you ex-military or something?"

"We're private security," the passenger seat goon said. "And you really have—"

I ignored him as my phone buzzed. It was my publicist in Hollywood. There, it was still late evening.

"Yes, Melissa?" I groaned.

"Are you aware of what was published on *The Times* webpage last night?"

"No," I answered. "What is—"

"That paper ran a story about how you wed the son of the Baron something or something."

"Oh, that," I laughed nervously.

"Did you get married to a Brit without telling me?"

"Well, I didn't expect someone to *blab* about it."

"Did you marry him?"

"Yes," I said. "But it wasn't like a big wedding. It was… a minor thing."

"Promise me there was a prenup."

"There was. A good one."

"So, I need to come up with an announcement. Jesus Christ! Lanie, stay off social and tell Chloe to do the same. She's bound to get in trouble."

"Yep," I sighed. "Accurate. No worries. I am mostly a zombie from pre-production tasks."

"Good. Stay safe and keep your nose clean."

I turned back to the goons. "Sure thing."

I groaned and threw my phone in my purse. The goons said nothing. After a few minutes, I realized we were headed for Davey's house in Canary Wharf. *Why* was my mother here? And *why* had I been summoned? Was this because she knew?

The housekeeper brought me to see Davey. He sipped coffee, looking like a nervous kicked puppy, as his two-year-old twin boys screeched and ran down the hall from their bedroom. Mum, however, did not sit. She stood, ignoring me, while looking out the window.

I ignored her mood, turning to my nephew, who ran in with a shopping cart and a massive baking potato.

"Are you about to start cooking?" I asked.

"Po-TAY-to!" He said.

"Yes. Are you going to cook it?"

Davey sighed. "If only. The thing is about to grow eyes, but dear Max has decided it is his best friend. He carries it everywhere like Robbie carries his lamb."

"You want?" Max asked.

I held out my hands as he gently tucked the potato into them.

"Hold it!" He demanded.

I tucked the potato in my arms like one would a tiny infant. Though I felt ridiculous, it lit up his little face.

"Now, you'll have to hold it for hours," Davey warned.

"I am hoping I will not be here so long." I flicked my eyes towards Mum who still refused to look at me. "Where is Eva?"

"She's in Paris," Davey said. "And our nanny is out sick, so I'm home with these little distractions. I gave up on work."

Davey's wife, Eva, was his former employee. Now, she was the family company's chief information security person—its CISO—but he wasn't CEO anymore. He'd stepped down to be president of a greenwashed startup that filled his cup and let him be home for the boys. Eva was the more ambitious of the two. If it seemed like he was complaining, it was probably just lack of sleep. The oldest Delphine loved being a dad more than anything.

"Have you missed me, Lanie?" Mum asked as Robbie plopped by me.

Once more, she refused to even face me.

"Yes, Mum? I didn't *miss* you. I was very distracted with the boys and this… potato."

"Delanie, you may not use a potato as an excuse!"

While her voice was strong, her commitment to the act of making a potato a serious matter sent my brother and I into a fit of laughter. Mum became enraged.

"Do you think it's funny?"

I snickered, "Well, I am holding a potato as a human shield and that angers you, so, yes."

She threw her hands up, "Enough with the bloody potato! Delanie Beth, did you get married this week?"

My mouth dropped. Clearly, she had read *The Times*. I momentarily panicked, realizing I was wearing my wedding band and engagement ring. I tried to hide it, but my mother stepped forward to grab it.

"That is… impressive and incriminating."

"So, you found out?" I pulled my hand back.

"It was in the *Times* wedding announcements. Apparently Lord Osgoode cannot help but announce the happy marriage of his son Basil Callan Osgoode IV to one Delanie Delphine."

"Not my name, but okay," I said.

"He dropped the Carlisle as it *pains* him to say it. What is going on, Delanie? And why have you married the son of the man who would have been glad to ruin my life? This is ridiculous! Did you mean to wound me?"

"Mum, I warned you about being calm," Davey said.

Yeah, that's going to work.

"God damn it, Delanie! What were you thinking? If your father were here—"

"I am saving the estate!" I shouted.

"How?"

"It's complicated but the long and short of it was Baz was about to be disinherited as he was unwed and had no child. It's a business agreement. I help him keep the inheritance and he will guarantee me the estate."

"So, it's like... a business relationship?" Davey looked appalled.

"Sure. We got married at the courthouse. It was NBD. His dad is a total prick."

"So, you aren't sleeping with him?" Mum asked. "Please promise me you will never sleep with him."

Davey looked ready to die of embarrassment.

"Why not?" I snickered. "We're married. Isn't that what is supposed to happen."

"Not like this! He's a monster!"

My brother's saintly, yet brave, housekeeper checked on us. "Mr. Delphine, would you take more tea? Or would Ms. Delphine prefer some coffee?"

"I'll have a really strong coffee," I said. "No tea. And can I get some whiskey in it?"

"Yes ma'am." Like any good Brit, she didn't blush at my whole consuming-hard-liquor-before-noon thing.

Mum continued to pace while I cradled a potato, watched Robbie assemble a block structure, and sipped whiskey in coffee. I chocked it up to frayed nerves and Scottish blood.

"Why on Earth would you think he'd give you the estate? His father hates me," Mum said.

"Baz isn't like his dad. He's a scoundrel, yes, but he's not a prick."

"He's definitely not ugly," Davey looked at his phone. "You know, I recognized the name, but I've seen him around. He comes by the club occasionally."

I tried not to think about *which* club and told myself it was the social club in Mayfair where my family retained a membership—a place wealthy men went to drink and escape their wives. Davey was *far* too vanilla for The Vesper Room.

"I hate that," Mum said. "Do not defend him, David."

"What? I can't even make jokes now, Mother?" Davey scoffed.

"I mean, he's hot. Chloe calls him Daddy Vibes, and she's not wrong." I added fuel to the fire.

If I couldn't convince my mother, I'd just annoy her until she gave up and flew back across the Atlantic on the broom she arrived on.

"No. Just… he's your husband. It's *ridiculous!*"

"Yes. But, as I said, it was a pragmatic deal. I don't want to explain this. We didn't really intend for anyone to find out."

"What, until your high-profile divorce?"

I groaned. "Look, as I said, I am well taken care of. I am getting the estate back for all of us."

"How exactly *will* you do that?" Daphne asked. "And why would he agree to it?"

"Because he knows it means a lot to our family," I answered.

"That's not enough, though. It's worth real money, Delanie. I know he probably lusts for you. You're too young for him and you're some rising star, but that's not enough. Unless he loves you endlessly and is willing to start a war, I'm not buying it."

"Maybe there is more to it, Mum," Davey said. "You don't know he doesn't love her. You and Dad fell instantly in love and married before you even knew one another, so should you really judge?"

I patted Davey's knee, comforted that at least my oldest

brother had faith I wasn't a total fuck up. I prayed the fact that he was Mum's favorite would help.

She ignored him and strode over to the big window and stared out at the gardens.

"I worry she's done the one thing she knows she needs to and that's the issue."

Davey groaned. "And what is that? Can we *please* stop it with the cryptic talk?"

Mum took a minute. "She does what any aristocratic lady does to cement herself."

"And that is?"

"She produces an heir," Mum said.

I stared at my lap. Mum wasn't wrong.

"I have a prenup," I insisted. "That Bridget put together. I've gotta stay three years or until I have a son. Once either condition is met, the deed will pass onto either myself or my child. And I will walk away with a very large sum of money either way."

"This is madness! Did you learn nothing from your sister's marriage? Why do you chase after powerful men? All of you! At least Daphne learned and settled down with Cal."

"Mum, I'd remind you that you forced Daphne to marry Chandler in the end," Davey said. "Derrick and I tried to spare her, but you brought her back from Paris and told her to go through with it. She's since forgiven you, but that's—"

"And that is exactly why Delanie should know better! I thought you were smarter than this!"

Her words cut deep. When I'd chosen to forgo college, my father had been the only one to support me. Mum felt I was foolish and "lacked direction". Those words hurt then, but felt like daggers now.

"I wasn't forced to do this," I insisted. "I consented to it, just as Baz did. We decided to do it because we are a good match and could accomplish all our objectives. As I said, we're practical people. I'm not getting younger. He's not, either. If you met his brother again as an adult, you would understand why this makes sense. He wants to ruin the place. I engineered this. Please trust I'm not stupid."

She rolled her eyes. "*You* engineered this?"

"Yes. I did."

"How?"

"I seduced him first," I said.

Davey moved awkwardly, but didn't chide me.

"And why would you do that?" Mum demanded.

"Because I could. Then I caught feelings. And now, it just made sense. I don't have to explain anything to you. I don't need you to understand what works for us, but I can assure you I am not a stupid pawn."

"Well, if he loves you so much, bring him to dinner," Mum said.

"Mum, he'll be in Germany until the evening."

"Then I will wait."

I rolled my eyes. "I will speak to him when he gets home."

"Is he living in Daphne's house?"

"No. He lives in his house and—"

I stopped. We never discussed living together or *thought* about it. Now that his idiot father ran his mouth about our marriage, we were going to have to act like a married couple in all ways. I needed to move into his place. We had so many things to discuss—things we willfully ignored.

"I am moving in with him," I said. "To his place in Knightsbridge."

"Bully for you. You can spend all his money at bloody Harrods," Mum said.

"I will still spend plenty of money in the company store, I promise," I groaned. "I am still the same woman."

"No, no you are not. This is not what we raised you to be!"

Tears burned. She didn't see me—not at all.

"Mother! Stop! She wanted to return Braemoor to the family. It's crazy, sure, but she's a grown up. And I won't throw stones because I impregnated a woman during a one-night stand and now she's the love of my life. I'd have it no other way. I've got no space to judge."

Davey squeezed my hand. I suddenly was so glad I came to do this here.

"Why would you care so much?" Mum asked. "Why would you tie yourself to him like that? And force yourself to have a baby—"

"I am falling for him," I told a white lie that maybe someday *would* be true. "And the place is so beautiful. It's not just special to you and me, it is dear to his sister who is a doll."

"She was the one born just before that bastard's second wife died?"

"Yes," I answered. "She's so sweet and happy for us. It's all a hot fucking mess, okay? But also, I don't mind it. I wasted the last portion of my life on a man who swore he wanted the same things until his fortunes changed and he decided he didn't want kids anymore. I wanted babies. I wanted them *badly*. He did not. Longevity isn't promised and I can't change my goals or values. If the worst bit of this is I must have a baby—one I badly want—I am okay with that."

"You should marry a man you love and go from there. Not marry a man who has a house you like and give him a child as payback. I fought the hard fight so none of you had to choose this."

Tears ran. "I'm not a common whore, Mum. I chose this— free and clear."

"You aren't following—"

"If you had listened to what your parents wanted you to do, I'd be Baz's sister, not his wife," I said. "And you'd never have met Daddy. I never follow the rules. I'm always running off. Baz and I are strangely similar. We're a good match. As you and Daddy were a team, we are."

"You have no idea, Delanie!"

I'd never convince her through words. I decided only showing her through experience worked. Just as she'd come around to Daphne and Cal's relationship and embraced

Davey's unconventional start with Eva, she'd settle when she realized Baz and I had a good thing. She'd see me happy and relaxed. If she could accept my sister marrying my father's best friend and put up with Davey's out-of-wedlock babies, she could let this one go.

"At least come to Braemoor sometime," I said. "I'll let you dance on the old fucker's grave. And Baz won't stop you. If he tries, I'll end him."

———

BAZ

"Baz, we have a problem," Jeremy said.

I looked up from the contract our German counsel brought twenty minutes ago. Even in plain English, I had no idea what I read. Our partner going under fucked us. I managed to secure new investment, only to have the German government breathing down my neck. As their countrymen were rather humorless sorts, I never knew if they were just being German or judging me. I did not need *more* problems.

"Yes? Add it to the list," I sighed.

"Sir, did you know that your father told the *Times* you were married?"

"What? No," I said. "Can we stop them from publishing it? I don't even think Lanie's Mum knows and I don't particularly want to tread those waters."

"Well, they may know now. The *Times* printed it yesterday."

"What?" I scoffed, praying this was a sick joke. "How did you know?"

"I have an alert set up for your name. I ring the publicist when things like this happen. Maurice would like to talk to you, by the way."

"Fucking hell," I groaned. "You should have led with that. Put him on the horn, then."

Maurice was my publicist. He managed all the things we

got into—and smoothed things over when something bad happened. I had him dealing with our EU debacle even now. Things were not good. He'd probably want to kill me over this.

The line in the conference room rang.

"Hello?"

"Baz, did you do something very naughty and get married without telling me?"

I groaned. "I did get married. It's no one's business. And I wish my father hadn't squawked. He never told me he would do that."

"Your father is anything but subtle, Baz. And if I didn't like you and your constant flow of business, I wouldn't keep you as a client. You have made my job even *more* difficult."

"I am sorry about that."

"So, you married an heiress? An American princess of sorts?"

"Lanie isn't exactly a princess," I said. "But she is very clever."

"And not bad to look at. She's too young for you."

"So, everyone says."

"Well, what now? We must release a statement. Where is the new Lady Osgoode?"

"She's back in London," I said. "She didn't travel with me."

"Baz, you married her and then flew back to Germany? And she put up with that?"

"Why is *everyone* making me feel dreadful about that? We're going to be married for ages. There will be times I leave. Why is this a different circumstance?"

"Because you are newlyweds! Baz, despite this German disaster, you are still fully capable of dropping some cash on a nice honeymoon."

"My father is ill. It wouldn't look right," I lied.

It wasn't that I didn't want to travel to some exotic location with Lanie. I'd relish seeing her in a tiny bikini. No, it was more that I didn't think it would feel like a proper honeymoon. Moreover, I doubted either of us would be into that.

"Whatever. I won't tell you how to be married. I never figured that out. However, we should coordinate with her people—especially as her sister and mother are very important."

"I'm aware."

"You don't want to tell the Americans to sod off, Baz. They will fuck you."

"I'm well aware."

Jeremy appeared in the doorway looking concerned.

"One second, Mo," I cupped my hand over the receiver, "Yes, Jeremy?"

"The British Ambassador is inviting you for a late dinner."

"Why?"

"I suspect the Germans have something to do with it and he is merely the conduit."

"Great. Just what I needed. Fine. I will go."

"They also invited Lady Osgoode."

It took me a moment to register that mean *Lanie*.

"Your wife, Baz."

"Yes, I… I understand. But I would have to get Lanie here—"

"You've got six hours. It's manageable. Should I hire a charter from City? The jet is still out of commission."

My jet had been in the shop at the worst possible time. I'd flown commercial more than I ever wanted. Lanie wouldn't have time for that—nor did I suspect she would prefer to fly with the public in the middle of a media firestorm.

"Yes," I said. "If I can get her to agree to it. Give me one second."

"Alright."

Jeremy disappeared and I turned to Maurice. "Say nothing. I'm about to fly Lanie out and deal with this in person. We've been invited to the British Ambassador's home for dinner. They want both of us. It will be a charm offensive. She and I will work together on a plan this evening."

"Alright. Well, congratulations. Please start behaving before I dump you."

"You have *no* idea how many times I've heard that," I chuckled.

I hung up and dialed Lanie on my mobile.

"Hello?" She asked.

Two people argued in the background.

"Did I catch you at a bad time?" I asked.

"Yes. But you are a welcome distraction. Things are a disaster here."

"Are you home?"

"No. I am at my brother's. Can I help you, Baz?"

"Yes. Please don't strangle me. Father—"

"I know. That is part of what this argument is about. My mother flew across the Atlantic to inform me of her total disdain for the article."

"Fuck!" I rubbed my temples. "Lanie, I am so sorry. I told Father because—"

"I am not blaming you. I am not upset with you. I'm upset that my mother doesn't trust me to make my own fucking life choices at twenty-nine."

"Lanie, stop being dramatic!" Her mother called.

Her mother's accent struck me.

"Fuck off, Mum! It's been done and dusted, for Christ's sake. Go argue with Davey about the twins!"

"What twins?" I asked.

"Long story," Lanie answered. "What do you need?"

"I uh… I've been asked to the Ambassador's house for dinner. I have a feeling there will be members of the government present who do not like me very much right now. A deal went south and it endangered some German interests. I am pulling it together. Can you help me, darling? Please. They would like us both there. You're so charming—"

"Okay."

I was prepared to list the critical reasons, but she didn't want them. "Really?"

"Yes, I will go. Anything to get me out of here. Get me a

plane, okay? And send me a car. I am trapped here at the mercy of goons my mother hired, and it makes me feel uneasy."

"Yes, of course."

"And I want a car available to me. We can negotiate all those factors, but if I'm your wife, I get that sort of thing."

Was she really having this business discussion now?

"Yes, Lanie, of course."

"Hire me a plane. I will be there with a smile."

We hung up and I called for Jeremy.

"Yes, Baz?"

"She's coming. Hire a plane."

"Alright. Someone's mood has shifted."

I shrugged. "I just want to get all of this over with."

"Oh, you're excited," Jeremy chuckled. "You have a ridiculous grin on your face."

I couldn't deny it. I married someone as competitive and domineering as myself. The respect I had for her only climbed the more we did this dance. Lanie Delphine was a wild woman, and for now, she was in my corner.

CHAPTER 29
Practical Matters

LANIE

"Oh, brilliant. You did make it!"

Baz found me in his hotel suite in a cocktail dress, getting ready before a mirror. I couldn't turn as I placed one of my eyelashes.

"Yes, I did. Are you getting changed?" I asked.

He stared. "Uh… yes… if you feel."

"That grey looks too informal," I said. "Go for black. It's a stronger color on you. It's why I wore red."

Baz cocked his head. "Really?"

"Have I often been wrong, Baz?"

"No." Baz had a strange expression on his face.

"Does it bother you when I'm right?"

"No," Baz said. "It's hot."

"Then why are you staring at me like that?"

"You only have one eyelash," Baz snickered. "It is an odd look."

"Ignore me," I groaned. "Go change."

Baz left me to finishing my eye makeup in peace before returning. "You really do look beautiful, Lanie. And I owe you—"

"Stop. If you owe me, we need to have some practical

discussions about our life together. Let's have this out so I can start feeling a little less precarious."

Baz slung his tie around his shoulders. "Yes, go on."

"You agreed to the car, which I am grateful for. But, if I'm your wife and I'm expected to drop everything to race around the world and be your arm candy, I will need a certain amount of money for the upkeep of what that entails. We need to figure out our finances, Baz. I do have an inheritance, but I don't have access to it until I'm thirty. I get paid well but not   drop-everything-and-go-see-diplomats-every-week money."

"You will, yes. Of course," Baz said. "I never thought about that. You can always ask—"

He still thought this was a negotiation of me coming to him for things. I didn't like it. I needed him to offer solutions.

"Baz, I'm your wife, not your daughter."

"I am well aware, Lanie."

"I need access to accounts as if I am your spouse. Maybe that means we divvy up an allowance? Maybe that means I get unfettered access to your AmEx? I don't care. But I do not want to have to beg you for money. I expect you to keep me comfortable in the lifestyle that *you* have become accustomed to. Either I am your spouse or I'm not. I don't like findom bullshit."

"The fact that you know findom is a thing delights me," Baz grinned, then returned to a serious state. "I can set up an account for you. I don't mean to sound like… I'm a prick. It doesn't come from a place of malice. I don't get off on controlling you like that. Only in bed do I enjoy it. I'd never want to hold finances over your head, Lanie."

I returned to my eyeliner. "Well, we need to sort it out."

"Agreed. When we return to London, we will."

"Where am I to live, Baz?"

"Uh…"

"Baz, have you thought about any of this? We're married!"

"I haven't. I never intended to marry *anyone*, Lanie. I actively avoided it and never gave cohabitation any thought."

I did a double-take. "You have never lived with a woman?"

"Define lived with."

"Has a woman received mail at your house?"

"No," Baz said. "Why would she?"

I scoffed, "Wow! You really surprise me sometimes."

"What? Why? Have *you* received mail at someone else's house?"

Satisfied with my liner, I threw it in my makeup bag and moved onto my eyeshadow.

"Yes, Baz. I lived with my ex-boyfriend before we were even a couple."

"How does that work?"

"We were friends who fell head-over-heels for one another and then we just sort of existed before The Talk."

"What ended it?"

I contemplated for a moment what to say. I had nothing left to risk if I wasn't honest.

"I thought he got me pregnant. I wanted to be pregnant. I… told him. He told me to get an abortion if I was. I sobbed for a day, picked myself up, and then moved out. He'd told me that was what he wanted before. That was, until he became a super famous cinematographer for a big-name series and I just… wasn't big enough. I held him back."

"But you weren't?"

"No. I ended up seeing a negative test and two hours later, my period came. I left him because we were incompatible. I wanted kids, he didn't."

"I'm glad you weren't pregnant," Baz looked at me in the mirror as I finished my eyeshadow.

"Why?"

"Because you don't deserve a man who would do that to you—ask for all the investment and promise you something he never intended to give."

Placing my brushes back in the bag, I looked at Baz. "Isn't that what we both did?"

Baz's gaze on me tore through me like a searing blade. His

hungry eyes stopped my heart. I turned my back to the vanity, but Baz took my face. He brushed my cheeks with his thumbs ever so slightly.

Breath hot on my face, he murmured, "I promised you little, Lanie, other than protection and to keep to my word. I pledge I will give you what you asked for and ensure your every need is met. I may be a wanker, but I'm not a bloody liar."

He moved his right hand until it cupped my chin, then ran a finger over my lip. I shivered.

"You like it when I do that?" Baz growled.

"N… no."

"You lie, Lanie. You do like it."

"I… I do," I admitted.

I loved the way it felt to give over control. I gave him the power to take care of me. It was the way his voice deepened. And it was how his hips felt pressed up against my midsection—authoritative, assertive, and centered. He adored me. I drove him wild. But here, he focused on winding me up. I loved it when he lavished me with attention.

Baz tilted my chin more and bent to kiss me. It started slow—our lips pressed together. His tongue parted my lips and I breathed him in. I gripped his jacket collar, and he pressed me harder into the vanity. Confidently, he picked me up and put me atop it. Pressing his body harder into mine, he parted my legs and pulled me closer to the edge. I gazed at him, nostrils flaring, before he kissed me once more.

Kissing Baz was a whole *thing*. I remembered how long I'd made him wait to even touch me. The wait had been worth it when he'd tenderly given me what I wanted. Now, he had *all* of me. I wanted to tear his clothes off. I began to fumble with his belt, forgetting that we had plans. That was until we heard someone call.

"Baz! Baz! We need to get a move on!"

Baz pulled back and looked over at the doorway. His assistant appeared.

"We're running late," Jeremy said.

"Alright," Baz loosed my hand from his belt.

I'd been too confused to remember what I was up to.

Baz added, "We will be with you in a moment."

"Is he going to constantly interrupt us?" I asked.

"No. He has the key to my room because I have him run things around. I will talk to him about always ringing first if you're here. He isn't used to me having company like this. Are you ready?"

"I just need to finish my lipstick," I hopped down.

I turned back to the mirror, sorting through my belongings.

Baz smacked my ass. "When you're done, come out to the living room."

I let him go, finishing up my look, and took myself in. I was Lady Delanie Osgoode. I could do this. Once I entered the living room, everyone looked ready to leave. Jeremy held the door. I strode past Baz, who followed closely. We climbed on the elevator down to our waiting car. As we stood there, I leaned in and whispered.

"We're going to charm the pants off this asshole. Then, we will come back here. And to make up for me being *such* a good little wife, you're going to go down on me until I squirt."

Baz ran his hand from the small of my back to my ass and squeezed it. "Help me ace this and I will give you anything you want, Lanie."

———

BAZ

"How did the two of you meet?" Ewan Broader, our German Ambassador, asked Lanie. "How does a notable American heiress find herself eye-to-eye with this one here?"

I blanched at the question because the answer was dreadful. I knew she wouldn't say, "Oh when he was watching me fuck his mate in his library." But also, the question was ridiculous! Where does the daughter of a famous, wealthy American retail magnate meet a man of industry? Literally anywhere in posh London!

"Through a mutual friend at a party Baz hosted," Lanie answered.

"And you never let her go, Baz?" Ewan asked.

"No, I did," I said. "But she came back for some reason."

"How do you two know one another?" Lanie asked.

"We went to school together a very long time ago. That is how things work in the UK," Ewan said. "Well, for men like us. We aren't quite so… egalitarian."

"I wish I could say I was raised in some egalitarian educational system, Mr. Ambassador," Lanie said. "Instead, I went to one of the most competitive, elite Catholic schools in the nation. It was so strict, I didn't even get to wear trousers until I was out of high school."

"Ever?" Cate, Ewan's wife, scoffed. "In *high school*?"

"It's a very conservative school. My sister joined a protest once about it—which is saying something as the girl loves rules—and it was the closest she came to detention."

"And you, Lady Osgoode, were you the one always in trouble?" Fritz Becker, the German Interior and Communities Minister, asked.

The way he looked at Lanie bothered me. He might as well as asked if she was a "bad girl".

Lanie's face signaled discomfort for a split second, before she recomposed herself. "I am not much of a rule follower. But, if you ask Baz, I do listen to reason. I just want to smash the patriarchy and ignore arcane rules."

It wasn't the coy answer he expected, but he played along.

"And does your husband know there are rules to doing business in Germany?" Fritz asked.

"Well, he pays a lot of lawyers to ensure he does." Lanie dissected her roast chicken ever-so-delicately.

"Your partner lied, Lord Osgoode," Fritz said. "He lied about the permits."

"I am well aware now," I said. "I realize you are a very

orderly nation. I respect that. We have code in Britain as well."

"Oh, Lord have no fury like a local council on a tear," Ewan sighed. "We painted our house in Berkshire a very similar color of pale green and they came after us for thousands."

"It wasn't even our house," Cate said. "It was our *pool* house. Who even cares about a pool house?"

"I wasn't aware that my German partners were running amok," I followed the script from my attorney. "They cut corners and lied to *me* about it. This will be litigated, I can assure you. However, we have secured new investment and just want to proceed by the book."

"You need us to let you off scot-free as if the rules do not apply," Fritz said under his breath. "That's very British."

"I would say it's very *American*. In America, we'd call that being creative," Lanie joked.

To my surprise, everyone else at the table chuckled at her perfect timing.

"Your father was a good man, Lady Osgoode," Fritz offered. "He may be the last bastion of altruism the US can point to. He was charitable and fair."

"I think there are other good men. My brother-in-law was his protege and certainly embodies those principles. My oldest sister runs the business like a boss and still cares very much for charity. My baby sister is the most benevolent person I know," Lanie said, unafraid to tangle with him.

No one was sure what to say to Lanie. She ate her potatoes in peace and sipped her wine in silence. Her self-control amazed me.

"Did you ever meet my father?" Lanie followed up.

"I did. When he was building out their concept in Munich. I was a young man working for the Chancellor's office."

"Interesting. I don't even remember him building in Munich, other than him being gone a lot. Of course, I'd barely hit puberty," Lanie said.

I snickered, unable to hold back. It wasn't what she said as much as her brilliant delivery that worked. Fritz set his jaw, annoyed, but Lanie merely sat pleased with a sweet, calm look.

"Well, you're grown now. Although, one does question how you ended up with someone old enough to *be* your father," Fritz pointed his butter knife at me rudely. "He is older than I am."

"Well, if Baz was old enough to be my father, I would have been conceived before he could have legally driven in your fair nation, so that seems a stretch," Lanie clapped back. "But even if that *were* the case, I don't think it should bother me."

"People might wonder what you have in common with your husband, Lady Osgoode. He is known to despise politics and diplomacy."

"I am not sure why that matters, Mr. Becker." Lanie said.

"Well, you're family moves in those circles, do you not?"

"I suppose, yes, but my sister openly chides me for being politics averse. I wouldn't say I am apolitical. The next season of my show might scandalize some, but I don't seek out debates. I leave that up to Cal and his sister Chloe. They say enough, but I support them."

"One needs more to make a marriage work, though."

His candor wore on me.

"Lanie and I are aligned on many things. Namely, family and business. She is a shrewd negotiator and ruthless at times. I respect that."

Lanie blushed and sipped wine.

"He is very flattering," Ewan said. "But I thought you'd never marry, Baz."

"I never found the right woman," I said.

In a way, it was no lie. Lanie was perfect for what I needed and accepted what I gave. She asked for little more. Was our union so different from every political or aristocratic marriage on the society pages? Apart from our small, quiet wedding, we were doing what others did—just with fewer rules. Neither of us planned to cheat and lie about it.

"She is remarkable," Fritz salivated over Lanie more than his meal.

By the end of dinner, Lanie had unexpectedly charmed even the most annoying German holdout. He appeared to let bygones be bygones and I was immeasurably grateful. But, as we took to the drawing room for a nightcap, Fritz pulled me aside.

"I will let this go. I will do what I can to ignore your failure and write off this development as a foreign mistake mended quickly."

"Thank you," I said.

"But I don't do it for you. I do it because your pretty wife doesn't deserve to have her newlywed period marked by scandal and regulatory fines," Fritz said. "And don't think I will not think of her moving forward. She may be your saving grace. She's also very stimulating."

The thought of him getting off to Lanie provoked nausea.

"I'd rather not discuss my wife that way," I said. "She is a living, breathing human, not some sort of moving image you'd wank to, Fritz."

"Doesn't mean I cannot do it anyhow. It makes me wonder if I should trade my wife in for a younger model. How do you even manage her?"

I was appalled. "I bet your wife would love to hear that, Fritz. Where is she this evening?"

"Ms. Strauss is busy with her book club. She doesn't enjoy this sort of thing. It's a relief your wife does. She will be your glittering trophy for a few years—well until she is wasted producing children. They all get so bitter. Avoid that as long as you can."

It further angered me, but I held back. The man was even more of a rake than I. His wife didn't deserve that sort of treatment.

"Well, we'll have to agree to disagree on that. Now, I appreciate your willingness to forgive and forget, but as this is interrupting our honeymoon and I owe my wife some time alone with her tonight, I think I must leave you all."

I left him to tell Ewan we were departing.

"Ewan, it was a lovely evening. Thank you for hosting. However, we're off. I haven't given Lanie any of my time today and she'll have my head if we continue on."

Ewan patted my back. "Oh, I'd not want to get in the way of that. I hope it was fruitful."

"It was," I said. "And she appears to have enjoyed meeting Cate."

"Don't be a stranger in London," Ewan said. "Lanie is delightful."

I didn't like his tone, but took it on the chin as I approached the women.

"Lanie, darling, I think I owe you some peace and quiet this evening," I said. "I must be greedy, Cate, and steal her away."

"Of course. You're newlyweds.Very exciting!" Cate brimmed. "It was *so* lovely to meet you, Lanie."

"And you as well," Lanie said.

We departed to the car with Jeremy who had spent cocktail hour on emails in the Ambassador's study.

"We leave tomorrow," Jeremy said. "The jet is back. It should depart at 10, so don't sleep in too late. Lady Osgoode, is that fine with you?"

"Please don't expect an early wake up out of me every Saturday," Lanie sighed. "But yes. I would like to go back to London. My mother and sister are waiting to interrogate Baz."

I winced. "Let's not think of it until tomorrow."

We arrived at the hotel.

In the lift, I whispered to Lanie, "Slip into whatever makes you comfortable. I want to pay you back handsomely for the job you did tonight."

She smiled. "I will."

Lanie strode back into the room, leaving me with Jeremy.

"Jer, I know we've had an agreement about you entering my room and having a key. It doesn't bother either of us, but it bothers Lanie. It is not that she doesn't like you, she simply prefers more privacy. So, I'd kindly request you ring her first or ask me before you assume it is alright."

"I think it is appropriate if I knock and ring the room," Jeremy said. "Someone can let me in. I'm sorry about that. And really, I did not want to see the two of you shagging in the bathroom. I was mortified."

I snickered. "I am sorry. Things… escalated. I haven't seen her in a couple of days."

"You know, Baz, for this being some sort of silly agreement, you certainly do appear enamored of her."

"Everyone is," I sighed.

And I got off on the fact that she was mine alone right now.

"Goodnight."

———

LANIE

Baz appeared in the bedroom, already loosening his tie. He threw his jacket in the corner chair and focused on his cufflinks. He was motivated. Something drove him to want me. Perhaps it was what got interrupted in the bathroom or maybe it was the win I landed for him? Either way, I loved the bravado and wanted him to dominate me.

"I don't want you to demand a goddamn thing until I make you cum," Baz growled, kicking off his pants.

He left his boxers on, as if preventing me from getting anywhere with him.

"What if I don't?" I toyed.

"You always do. Have I ever left you unsatisfied, love?"

"No," I answered.

"Then you'll cum like a good girl—all over my face and until you are spent. Then, I will let you have me, and I will get what I want most."

"Which is?"

"You'll see," Baz forcefully parted my legs.

There was nothing gentle about the way he licked and sucked my clit. I didn't want gentle. Baz knew that. He sensed I wanted to be owned by my behavior alone. I held all the cards this evening, but now I deferred to him. I saved him. He'd *let* me. And now? I was at his mercy.

I pulled his hair, but he batted me away. "No, Lanie. Be a good girl and play with your nipples."

I took the order, but couldn't do so for long before I gripped one breast with my right hand and clung to the bedspread with the other. In an infuriating turn of events, Baz disappeared.

"What the fuck?" I demanded.

"Touch yourself. I need to get something."

I tried to follow that order, but all I wanted was to fuck his face and get off. I'd been so close!

Baz returned with a towel. "I am sorry, but I didn't want a repeat of the debacle last time."

"You really think you're going to make me squirt?" I asked.

"Oh, I will," Baz said. "You begged. I wanted to reward you."

I centered myself on the towel, unsure that he could make this happen so quickly a second time.

Baz focused again on my clit, digging right back into his work. I pulled his hair again—on instinct—and he once more batted me away. In the end, I loved when he got angry.

"I warned you, Lady Osgoode, did I not?"

Oof. His invoking that only made it hotter.

"Sorry." I kept my hands to myself.

Baz didn't go back with his tongue. Instead, he slid two fingers inside to find my swollen G-spot. Slowly, he rubbed that blissful area, tickling it until it grew more desperate for release. I gasped and threw my head back. The response was uncontrollable. I was dying to feel the full-body orgasm once more. I wanted Baz to be right. Once he realized I was near the edge, Baz worked my clit with his tongue and tickled my g-spot with his fingers.

Clinching my pussy around his fingers, I let him know not to stop. I pressed my hips to his face, demanding release. And, with just a few more strokes of his fingers, I came. My climax again overwhelmed me, but now I focused on every feel. I wanted to know exactly where I felt myself go. I wanted to feel every twitch and impulse. As I writhed and screamed Baz's name, I focused on how my center pulsed and my face flushed. I luxuriated in how he made my body tingle. I felt spent, washed clean, and welcomed this elation.

"Don't ever tell me what I can or cannot do, Lanie," Baz said. "I will always send you flying. And you will always come back to me as I get you off like no one else can."

"Yes, baby," I panted. "Yes."

CHAPTER 30

Back to Real Life

BAZ

"Oh fuck!" Lanie groaned, looking out the window to what awaited us in her foyer.

"What?" I tried to pull myself together.

Only Lanie could manage to make a short hop from Berlin to London City so entertaining.

"That's my mother's coat," Lanie nodded at a red coat hanging in the hall.

"I'm sorry. What?"

"She was at my brother's earlier. And now, she's… here."

"Well, hopefully they are here to get *you* and not me, Lanie," I said.

"Oh, we're both in for a ride."

It took me a minute to settle into this. I was disoriented being properly inside her house for the first time. We expected no one to be home. She said she'd swap out one pair of clothing for another. But now, I would have to face her mother? This was *not* good.

Lanie's sister, Dora Elizabeth, arrived, looking concerned.

"Mum is here," she whispered. "But, she's walking the garden with Daphne. So, you have time if you want to flee."

Who is Daphne?

"Why?"

"She wanted to catch you, I suppose?" The girl turned to me, arms crossed. "And you don't have anything to say for yourself?"

"Me?" I pointed to myself

"Is there another person here who married my sister without telling anyone or so much as explaining himself? Lanie, how *could* you?"

"I will explain it all later," Lanie brushed her sister's demands off. "For now, I just need to grab a few things from my closet and leave. Can you stall her?"

"I don't think you will make it. She's bound to come up. Daphne will sniff out trouble."

Who is Daphne?

"Why is Daphne here?"

"Daphne came in on business. Where the hell have you been?"

"Germany."

"Why?"

"Dora Elizabeth, I need to go. Come, Baz. And bring my luggage."

She said it to me like I was a servant, which I resented. However, in a panicked state, I couldn't be *too* picky. My response with all mothers of women I slept with was to run for the hills, and Danna Delphine was no different. I lugged her suitcase upstairs, ever more annoyed with these shenanigans.

"Lanie, what is the plan here? I think I should leave."

What?" Lanie fumbled in her closet and tossed a luxurious overnight bag out.

"I said I think I should leave."

Lanie called from her closet, "You will do no such thing. You do not get to desert me here. I've already gotten a tongue-lashing from her. I'm not doing it again alone. You're half of this."

"And why when it is *your* mother, is it my half?"

Lanie appeared, leaning on her closet doorframe. "Baz, I

need her to go back to Chicago. *You* need the same reprieve. Trust me when I say, if we don't kiss the ring, she's not going home. She will be here—every fucking day—until she breaks me."

I groaned and sat on the bed, head in my hands. "Who is Daphne?"

"My sister. Daphne Delphine. You know of her, Baz. She was married to—"

I remembered. "I'm sorry. I do. She's Chandler's ex. He's a cunt."

"Agreed. She's fine, but pregnant. So, she's moody. But she's a businesswoman and will understand this more than Mum who is just—"

"Irrational?"

"No. Mum isn't irrational. She's *vengeful.*" Delanie approached and put her hands on my shoulders sweetly. "Expect Mum to be rude. Please don't go off on her. It will only be worse for you. She'll come around once she realizes you aren't your dad's carbon copy, Baz. If she can accept Daphne marrying Dad's best friend after he died, she can handle you."

"My parents are nuts," Lanie said. "Sorry… Dad *was* nuts. For the record, I don't want six children. But Daphne is about to be halfway there. I doubt any of us will reach that degree of fecundity, though."

"What?" I asked. "I thought it was just the one."

"She's pregnant with twins. Mum is pissed cuz she didn't tell her that she was even *pregnant.* I'm on the shit list because I accidentally let that slip the last time I saw them."

"Not because you married a dodgy Brit?"

Lanie giggled, "That, too. One who is in a *mood* today. Expect Mum to be rude. Please don't go off on her. It will only be worse for you. She'll come around once she realizes you aren't your dad's carbon copy, Baz."

"I'm just… I am not used to dealing with family."

"And you don't want to be obligated?"

I ruminated. I could blow smoke, and she'd call me on it,

or I could be vulnerable. For the first time, I decided to try the latter approach first.

I stood, taking her hands. "Yes, honestly. I hate this bit. I don't know how to handle parents. I didn't really have any. But also, because I have a feeling she's about to shout at you and anyone shouting at you is bound to set me off."

Lanie's jaw dropped unexpectedly.

"What? Was that too much. Am I *supposed* to let her yell at you? You're a grown woman Lanie and—"

Lanie squeezed my hand, prompting me to stop. "It's fine, if not a bit unexpected. If we're being honest, I love the aggro version of you, Baz. Just know you own me only when I let you. I own the conversation."

A smile crossed my face. "You are so confident, darling."

"I am because I know my place," Lanie said.

I leaned in, unable to resist kissing Lanie. Her defiant streak always did that. I kissed her, gripping her hair firmly. She balled my shirt up in her hands hard. We pawed at one another, snogging like desperate teenagers in a backseat until we heard footsteps. I straightened my tie, and she departed to the vanity. Delanie corrected her lipstick in a mirror she always carried, trying to grasp a shred of respectability. Given all the places her lips had been in the past few hours, my lips were the most benign.

Thankfully, the person who had come up the steps wasn't Danna, it was again the family's sweet, youngest child.

"Mum knows you're here. She saw your shoes. She wants everyone downstairs for tea in the drawing room. I'm sorry, but I tried."

Lanie looked over. "Fine. I know you did, sweetheart. We'll come down."

Downstairs in the well-appointed formal reception room sat a woman I recognized slightly, Daphne, and a man I did not. Her sister and the man I assumed was her brother-in-law stood. Her mother sat, as if holding court.

"Oh, he came, too," Lanie nodded in the man's direction.

"I'm here for an official meeting. She came because *I* came," the man said. "Blame me, I guess?"

"I'll forgive you," Lanie hugged him.

"Everyone, this is Baz. Baz, you know Dora. But, Mum, Daphne, and Cal, this is Baz. Baz, this is my mother, my sister, Daphne, and her husband, Cal Markham. I'd like it if we could be *respectful*."

"Cal is the Mayor of Chicago," Danna said. "He's very busy."

I insinuated all I did for a living was fuck off. She was trying hard already to get under my skin. Sadly, my father painted in back-handed compliments and barbs like that, so she'd have to try harder.

"Well, it's a pleasure to meet you," I said. "All of you."

"For the record, Lanie, I have met your beau before. Except he was a very young child, and his father was there trying to take all my family's wealth and property. Lord Osgoode wanted nothing but to subjugate me."

I cleared my throat and sat. I followed Lanie's advice, even if it pained me. Danna Carlisle was not here to make peace. She intended to throw her weight around. I expected someone demurer. After all, she'd been married to a very powerful man and produced *six* children in that time.

"I will say this," I began, voice calm, "because I want to clear the air. It has never been my intention to subjugate your daughter. In fact, I don't think any man ever *could*. I care for her and respect her. I am sorry for the pain Father caused you, Lady Danna."

She rolled her eyes. "Talk is cheap, darling."

"It is," I agreed. "All I can promise is that I will show you in my actions how much I care. That includes keeping to my word about Braemoor, ma'am."

"We know about your agreement," Danna offered. "I think it's rubbish and exploitative and I'd like you to get an annulment."

I flushed bright red, wondering if this was the feeling

everyone else got when they were supposed to be doing the right thing. *What has Lanie done to me!?*

"Oh, we don't keep secrets, Lord Osgoode," Daphne added. "That is something you will learn about us. Nor is it our job to make you feel warm and fuzzy. We love Delanie to the ends of the Earth. Our obligation is *only* to her."

"It's not an ambush, mother," Daphne groaned.

"Like hell it's not," Lanie crossed her legs neatly.

"And not to be a caveman, but we *do* have concerns," Cal said. "Of course, as I've said, I do want to hear *your* side of the story."

The youngest Delphine chimed, "Yes, I'd like that, too!"

"Can we just all go about our business?" Lanie asked. "We're married. It's done. I'm not getting an annulment. Move on."

"It really makes sense to think about it, and Daphne has looked into it."

Daphne's face pulled, pained. I knew as well as she did an annulment in Britain was nearly impossible. Lanie and I wouldn't qualify. I knew their mother probably knew that deep down as well, but was so disgusted by the idea of us together that she wouldn't hear reason.

"Can I speak?" Lanie said, annoyed.

"Go on," Danna scoffed. "Tell us how lovely this business relationship is. Or is it more than that? Because I do not like either idea, but prefer one to the other."

Lanie looked to me. I knew a response from her wouldn't satisfy the matriarch.

"I adore your daughter. To me, this is not business as usual. I promised to take care of her. I promised to take care of any children we have."

"But that is all it is? It's a box to tick."

Rage took over. I growled, "Lady Danna, look at your daughter, please. Tell me she is little more than a box to tick!"

Danna recoiled, surprised by my voice. For a moment, the room fell silent. As if on cue, another woman entered.

"Ma'am, the baby is awake. Would you like me to bring her down?"

I assumed that was Daphne's nanny.

"I'll grab her," Cal said.

I wished I could follow him. We drank coffee in quiet, no one brave enough to say the next thing as we waited for the child to greet us. In a few minutes, a cherubic, happy toddler arrived. I couldn't help but see Lanie's face light up. It would be no trouble to condition her to the idea of having children—and soon. Meanwhile, it didn't convince me it was a good idea. I regretted how adorable the baby was. This was a losing battle.

Lanie's mother spoke, "Lord Osgoode, you do realize that Lanie is about to leave and shoot a television program for two months in Wales?"

I didn't know that, but couldn't admit my lack of awareness. "We agreed that I wouldn't interfere in her work. She won't interfere in mine."

"So, you won't use her for political gain—like to fly her to Germany to charm their cabinet ministers?" Daphne asked, prickly.

I gathered being a political wife probably made her more attuned to that dance.

"Daphne, that is a ridiculous assumption!" Lanie declared. "Do assume I'm sort of dupe? A pawn?"

"What is *truly* ridiculous is you assuming he cares about you," Danna deflected.

I took a deep breath. "How can I prove to you all that I'm not full of shite? What do you need from me? I am willing to try. Are you?"

There was no time for a response. My mobile rang. It was Alex.

"Apologies. This is my brother. I need to take this."

I could sense the Delphine Delegation shot me daggers as I escaped the assault. It wasn't that I wanted to speak with Alexander. However, I'd take any reason to diffuse the situation.

"Baz," Alexander said. "I need you to come home immediately."

"What now?"

"Dad is dead."

A rush of relief I'd been waiting on for months—if not years—overcame me.

"Oh… okay," I said.

"No apologies? No condolences?"

"What do you want? A sonnet on how I miss him already? Would that be accurate, brother?"

"Well, for someone who just inherited a vast estate despite his true disdain for you, you could be more sympathetic for the people who cared about him."

I rolled my eyes. "Lanie and I will return shortly. We may have guests. Her family are in town. I am certain they would like to pay their respects."

Or to dance on his grave.

CHAPTER 31
The Baron Oban

LANIE

As I READIED to return to Braemoor, several elephants in the room emerged. One, I arrived as the lady of the house. Two, I was now a baroness and clueless about how to *be* a baroness. Three, I returned with the entourage of my mother and sisters. Baz flew ahead, leaving Jeremy and I to pack for him and for myself. I took to my own wardrobe first and packed every black outfit I owned—which wasn't much. That wasn't my power color. Instead, I borrowed from Dora and Chloe's wardrobes. That was the benefit of having two other women of a similar size living in the house. Then, I raced to Baz's place along with the others to pick up Jeremy.

This meant that the entire lot of them came along to see Baz's palatial house.

"You're a princess," Dora murmured. "A real princess. This place is so beautiful."

"Wait until you see Braemoor," Mum said. "If the Osgoodes haven't destroyed it, that is."

"Baz is trying to save it from his brother's planned destruction. The place is beautiful, Mummy. I think you will find it still meets expectations. It's like a dream. This is nothing! You should see Baz's country house."

"*Your* country house," Daphne reminded. "If he puts his money where his mouth is, all of what is his is yours and vice-versa. Trust me when I say, settle for nothing less."

"He's not like that, Daph," I said. "He's rough around the edges but he's not a prick like that."

"Just in other ways," Dora giggled.

"Oh, brilliant," Jeremy carted a suitcase and garment bag. "I didn't realize you'd arrived."

"We did, yes," I said. "Jeremy, this is my family—my mother, Lady Danna Carlisle-Delphine, and my sisters, Mrs. Daphne Delphine-Markham and Ms. Dora Carlisle-Delphine."

"Lovely to meet you all," Jeremy said.

"Jeremy is Baz's right hand," I explained. "He would be lost without him."

"Indeed," Jeremy agreed. "A damn shame we're going north on bad news."

I fought a laugh. Baz practically skipped out the door earlier.

"Yes, it's *such* a shame," Mum said sarcastically.

"Lady Osgoode, are you ready, then?" Jeremy asked.

The mere mention of my title inflamed my mother.

"Yes," I answered. "We're ready."

We left via the alley, finding the motorcade waiting. Cal stood on the phone discussing something with his chief of staff.

"This is… certainly something," Jeremy noted, confused.

"We travel in hordes," I said. "And we had a lot of luggage."

"Luggage?" Jeremy asked.

"You're rolling with a bunch of straight ladies and a man who appreciates a nice suit," I said. "We're annoying as fuck. Just be grateful Chloe couldn't come. She would have brought an entire piece of luggage filled with shoes."

I snickered, sliding by my mother in the second car—behind Cal and Daphne.

"It's odd to ride second," Mum noted. "I suppose it's

telling. You think you're first, but you aren't. You never will be again."

"What do you mean?"

"You think marrying the man at the top empowers you. It doesn't, however."

I furrowed my brow. "Mum, I didn't marry him to be important. I married him to help save Braemoor. I married him because—in some way—it makes sense to me. He lets me be myself. He will give me my independence and a comfortable life."

"That is a farce. Marrying a powerful man is a complicated proposition in ways your young mind cannot understand. It's about sacrifice. It's about putting yourself second always."

"Mum, Daddy always put us first—"

"It's adorable you think that," Mum chuckled. "I picked up the slack. I let him shine. He loved me immensely, but I gave up my nights and weekends to be supermum. Daddy got to shine because I twisted myself into knots many times over."

"We aren't those people."

"You're naive. Wait until you have children and he strays. You'll ask yourself what the point is. You'll feel like nothing more than a nanny. Just wait."

My heart stopped. Was she implying my father *cheated*? I didn't want to believe it.

"Mum, are you saying—"

"It is ancient history. It's also part of the price you pay."

"We have an agreement," I said. "I don't expect you to understand."

"See how he adheres to it. He'll cash in his chips regularly —especially when you're pregnant or nursing a baby. No matter how nice or fair an agreement seems, it will not be worth it. Mark my words."

"Mum, I am sorry you ever felt that way. I never saw it," I said. "But… saying that is gross. I refuse to believe Cal would ever do that to Daphne."

"I don't think he is the type. His mother would castrate him."

I snickered.

"Then why do you assume Baz is out to hurt me? Is it so hard to believe a man could respect me? I am sick of being treated like an object by everyone! Baz seems to be the only one who sees me as a partner. It's pointless to tell you this, of course. You won't believe me, Mummy, but I believe his actions speak loud for what he will give me."

"For now. While you're young and beautiful. Now, you're very convincing. In ten years? You'll see. Have a child and run while you still have your looks."

I fought tears. I couldn't believe what she said! I'd never heard this line from my mother. In my eyes, my parents had a perfect marriage. My father loved her more than anything. My mother adored him. They loved us deeply. They did anything to protect us. I measured the standard of what a husband and father was by my father as a metric. I knew sacrifices were made, but Dad always showed up for us. Was that the truth or was that just me thinking that way since one never spoke ill of the dead?

———

BAZ

I woke the morning of the funeral to Lanie sleeping quietly beside me. The more often I fell asleep by her, the more it normalized her permanence in my life. I never expected to feel this close to anyone that I would sleep *better* with them next to me. I wonder if we'd get to that point. I certainly preferred life with her.

The house remained quiet. Ellie took the dogs for her usual morning walk.

"Sir," the butler said, "Lady Danna has taken breakfast in the dining room. I do hope that is acceptable. And are we to *call* her Lady Danna still?

"She is more than welcome to take breakfast there, and yes. Please continue to do so," I said. "Thank you. I will join her."

It was unorthodox and not the proper use of a title. Others might quibble, but it wasn't a battle I wanted to fight while keeping the peace. I tried to keep an open mind with Lanie's mother. Putting myself in her shoes, I'd not trust me. Daughters were always at-risk. I was the rake whose father had shattered her dreams of this place. Instead of argument, I focused on a charm offensive. My goal was to show the Delphines the best hospitality and to treat Lanie like a queen. The latter was simple. Something about her melted me. She'd broken my brain even if I was loathe to admit it.

"Lady Danna," I sat at the table. "We are the first up this morning."

"I rise early," Danna noted.

"As do I. My clock starts before dawn."

A footman arrived for my order.

"Just a fry up, same as the lady's," I said.

He rushed away.

"Lanie won't ever do a fry-up," her mother noted.

I smiled. "She prefers pancakes or waffles. She's quite American."

"All of them are. Daphne is less so, I suppose. She's lived in London longer than she lived in the States. Life for her is more complicated."

"Lanie fits in, though," I said. "Her manners are impeccable. When she first arrived here, everyone was impressed with her grace. You did well by your daughters."

"My mother had us all presented at court. I raised my girls to do the same I am glad you do not take it for granted, Lord Osgoode."

"Please, Lady Danna, call me Baz."

She looked dubious. I did not expect her to offer the same. Danna was born of a time when one did *not* offer to go without their honorarium or title. To me, it was uncomfortable, but to a woman of her status and age, it was an insult.

"Lanie will sleep late. You'll need to wake her so she can make mass," Danna noted.

"I will. She sleeps in. I usually use the first few hours she's still dozing to work," I said. "Today, I am more focused on the ceremonial bits. I do think everyone should get a proper breakfast, though."

Danna nodded. "Agreed. It was something I always forced David to do. He was so typically American—go, go, go. There is something important about having a nice breakfast. Especially here."

She looked over to the wall where her debutante portrait hung.

"We have been staring at you for years," I said. "And looking at Delanie next to it, ma'am... the resemblance should have been obvious."

"She is the great beauty of the family," Danna declared. "Which you benefit from."

"I benefit from how clever and domineering she is. Beauty is an added benefit. She is formidable, Lady Danna."

"My father would be over the moon to know his granddaughter was Baroness Oban. So, in a way, I am grateful for this turn of events. But, given how young she is—and how little I trust your kin—I worry for her."

"Ma'am, can I speak my mind without fear of retribution?"

Danna gestured to go on.

"You all infantilize her. I'd expect that for the baby of the family. Dora Elizabeth is so young and softhearted. She's precious, but Delanie is the opposite. She's not powerless or a doormat, ma'am. It angers her. She loves you all so much. She always puts family first, which is something I respect. We never had that. Father saw us as pawns in a game. I am grateful you married Mr. Delphine. You deserved a better life. However, Delanie is tough as nails, and I have no intention of harming her. She'd also never put up with it."

"She sees you as a victim of your father," Danna said.

I looked to the ceiling, worrying about how vulnerable to

be. Putting all my cards on the table made me weak, but if I lied and blew it off, she'd always think I *was* my father. The women of this family exhausted me!

"My father treated me with little respect—all of us. He abused us verbally, physically, and emotionally. I suspect you always knew that. Boarding school was an escape in a way I suspect it wouldn't be for children raised in a good household like yours. A girl like Lanie would have her spirit broken by constant abuse. My dear sister became the one I had to protect —always. In a way, she learned to fly under the radar to avoid his ire, but she has more scars than myself and my brother. We got out early. She has terrible social anxiety, so she was educated here her whole life. I don't want to whinge. It's not like I wasn't incredibly privileged, but I suspect all your children had a beautiful—if not unconventional— childhood."

"They had different experiences. To hear Daphne and Davey tell it, they were tortured living in our shadow, but they grew up while their father was still climbing the ranks and courting the press. The younger ones were used to it all. They expected it. But, yes. My children were my calling. It is what has made the empty house so difficult."

"I would imagine it does."

"Your father was a scoundrel, but he kept this place together. I am grateful for that, but I also must grieve the loss of memories made here for my younger children. That dream died with Da. This place needs children to fill it with laughter as it did during my childhood. And I worry that will never be the case."

I took a deep breath. "I think you and Ellie would agree on that, ma'am."

"And what are your thoughts?"

"Your daughter is broody," I said. "And this is her home. Of course, we will have children here. It will be different than the way I was raised where children were to be seen and not heard, but that's for the best."

Lady Danna raised an eyebrow. "So, you know?"

"Ma'am, I have seen the way she fusses over her niece. There is no 'fixing' that. I'm not going to tell her not to love our children or to keep the house quiet. And as I said, attempting to order Lanie to do anything is an exercise in futility."

Danna smiled slightly in the softest gesture I imagined I would get.

"Ma'am, this is Lanie's home now, too. And you? I welcome you here. It should be a place you visit often. This was your home, after all."

"I shall be back after you father is buried in the grave-yard," Danna said.

"Why?"

"Your wife promised me a dance on his grave, and I intend to take her up on that offer."

I chuckled. "Lady Danna, you may have the first dance, but not the last."

PART THREE

Mission Accomplished

CHAPTER 32
Independence

BAZ

"Baz, I don't have time. The car is in the alley," Lanie pled.

"Lady Osgoode, you're going to be gone for weeks. I won't see you until God knows when. I'm not letting you leave yet," I said.

"I want you. I need you, but I also—"

I'd pinned Lanie against my living room wall. Her luggage sat by the door. We survived the holidays—somehow playing husband and wife remarkably well at Eldergrove. It was the most fun I had in ages. But just as soon as I'd adjusted to the role of doting husband, Lanie was headed away to shoot in Wales. It was the role of a lifetime for her, and I wouldn't hold her back. Meanwhile, I was torn between Caleb's project, owning a football team, running an estate in Scotland, and a development in Copenhagen. I'd see very little of Lanie now that she couldn't travel with me.

"I need to go," Lanie gasped as I slipped my hand into her leggings.

"Fuck," Lanie moaned, pressing her hips into me.

I bit her earlobe and played with her clit.

"Fuck me, then. Quickly," Lanie begged.

I'd said nothing, but she was putty in my hands.

We undressed enough to make this work. I pinned her back to the wall once more. She craved me. I loved the way she looked—excited, flushed, desperate. But, I realized I'd not roughed her up in a while.

"Over the couch," I pointed. "Go."

Lanie followed my orders, leaning over the arm. She looked back at me as I slid inside her tight, wet little pussy. It elicited a long moan—relief. I intended to send her off desperate to have me again. I would leave her knowing I was the best she ever had.

"I should have sat on your face," Lanie panted.

I spanked her ass. "Who says you get to decide, Lanie? You're mine right now. You'll do what I say."

Holding on for dear life, she cried out in nonsense. Her breath quickened with each thrust. I awaited the beautiful sound of her orgasm. I'd miss that most of all. Pulling her auburn ponytail, I drove her over the edge. She screamed my name and pulsed around me. I felt her go limp, spent for now.

"Oh, God, Baz," Lanie said. "You are so good!"

"I know. Never doubt me, Lanie."

I debated how I wanted to finish. On one hand, I wanted to mark her as if she were my territory. There was a special satisfaction in that. So, knowing I wouldn't last much longer, I pulled out. Lanie turned, as if dissatisfied.

"I want you to know who owns you, Lanie. I want *everyone* to know. This is all you deserve," I pumped my shaft and pressed the head of my cock against her ass.

"You really think that will work?" Lanie asked.

"I think you know where your bread is buttered, yes."

I smacked her ass even harder. She moaned, satisfied. She loved a good spanking.

I enjoyed the handprint I left on her rough, pale asscheek. So, that became the target of my release. I focused on that as I came, my cum running down her ass onto her full thighs.

"Baz, you're an asshole!" Lanie groaned and scowled. "Clean me up. I must go."

Satisfied with her cross expression, I grabbed a kitchen towel and mopped the semen dripping down her leg. After a final rough spank, she turned to face me.

"I need to go."

I tossed the towel aside and pulled her chin to me. "Go, but you're always mine, Lanie. Don't forget who owns you."

She gave me a slight smile. "Bad boy, Baz! You can think that all you like."

"I know it, Lanie."

She said nothing, just left. I pulled myself back together, having little time to myself before I packed off to the stadium to meet Caleb at the club level.

"Where is the wife?" He joked.

"Finally headed to Wales at the mercy of Leah Roughy."

"Well, in that case, I have someone to introduce you to."

I wasn't sure what he meant until he led me to two tall women he brought as guests. The brunette was obviously more interested in Caleb. In early conversation, however, it became clear the blonde was little more than an offering at my altar—a prize for surviving a few months of newlywed life.

"You like her, right?"

"Jessica?" I asked. "She's fit."

"And single. I plan to head to the club after this," Caleb said. "Fancy joining us?"

I thought about it a moment. Any other time, I would have taken him up on it. This was a situation where a woman was dangled before me. She didn't care about the wedding band on my left hand. She was an easy lay. I could have a bit of fun. Caleb was good with that promise. Then, I thought about how it might get back to Lanie. I knew our agreement remained, but would she still feel the same?

"I don't know. I should probably turn in early today," I said.

"Mate, don't get boring on me. I thought Lanie would be cool with it. And she doesn't have to know. We're just friends."

I ignored my gut as I watched the Dyers go 4 to 1 against Newcastle. I told myself I enjoyed the ability to blow off steam with friends. Didn't I deserve a bit of fun? After all, Lanie left *me*. Baz Osgoode wasn't good at celibacy and Lanie wanted us to be independent, right? Instead of listening to the angel on my shoulder, I packed off to the club and gave into my deviant side. I ignored the ring on my finger as I let Jessica kiss me and drank more, knowing full well what I was about to do.

As I went to get us more drinks, I checked my mobile.

LANIE

I'm a sap. I miss you.

I heard her say it in her sweet little American accent. And suddenly, it wasn't worth it. All the hall passes in the world didn't feel right now. Who was I to chase tail when Lanie had hardly been gone and was missing me? Instead, I went home and turned in, wondering if Lanie had finally broken me. I always swore monogamy wasn't for me, but perhaps I was too old for this shit. I'd take Caleb's judgement over my sudden transition to good boy if it meant I wouldn't hurt the woman I realized I was falling for. Instead of bedding a woman I didn't know, I texted my wife.

ME

I miss you, too. I'll be there soon.

LANIE

Promise?

ME

I cannot be away from you for long, love.

LANIE

Good. I'll keep the bed warm.

I was in love with my wife.

———

LANIE

Crew introductions began two days after we arrived for a table read on the grounds of Leah's family castle in Wales. This was the actual home of the former Countess of Dwyfor. This is where Annie spent her entire adulthood. It's where she arrived—alone, a frightened American girl—and raised her children. She became a local celebrity and a favorite of Princess Maud when she travelled to London. But as I took the place in and the crew set up for our first day of shooting, I was overwhelmed at the sheer size.

The castle was big. It was lovely, but dizzyingly so. I still didn't feel like the lady of the house. However, this castle was usually open only to the public for weddings or for the enjoyment of Royals. Leah's father inherited the place and was on hand to watch shooting begin. It didn't feel accessible. In a way, I knew I'd be able to draw on that as I played Annie.

Then, I realized what I would have to contend with. It was much more than the scope of the set or how I had to film an uncomfortable love scene in two days. No, it was upon crew introductions.

"Hello, Lanie."

I was walking the hall between the library and the former Countess's bedchamber that I ran into my ex. Sam Clarendon stood in one of his typical vintage t-shirts. He was effortlessly sexy without trying. And here I was—a bit of a sloppy mess. It was as if I were once more the young actress who'd arrived on the set of a low-budget indie flick years before. He was the older, wiser, more important man. Or, at least that's what I'd felt. And when his career really took off, he dumped me.

"You're working here?" I asked. "I wasn't... aware."

"I am, yes," Sam said. "Leah's people reached out when their guy went to rehab. So, as of three hours ago, I'm on set for the foreseeable future as DP."

"Great," I lied, wanting to escape into the walls.

"I hope we can work together, Lanie," he said. "I hope we can… coexist?"

"We can, yeah," I said. "Of course. I'm cool if you're cool."

After he'd broken my heart, I wasn't keen on letting bygones be bygones, but Leah got what she wanted. She only worked with the best, and Sam was good at his job—perhaps the best in prestige dramas like this right now.

"Lady Morgan! Or, should I say Lady Osgoode?" Leah's voice cut through my worries.

She swept me up in a big, excited hug. "How the hell are you?"

"I am… good, thanks," I said. "This place is gorgeous. I met Prince George. Your dad is so sweet."

"He is… something," Leah snickered. "I promised he has *no* desire to be on set for the big, awkward scene. We'll lock it down. Have you met the intimacy coordinator yet?"

"First thing this morning. Brian worked through it," I tried not to think about how hard it would be to do a very awkward love scene—one written to be deliberately so— before my ex-boyfriend.

Thankfully, I wasn't nude in this scene. That wouldn't happen for a few more weeks. I wondered if I could ask to exclude Sam somehow, but I knew it would just make me look "difficult". I'd finally *made it*. I'd have to let it go and be a professional.

"Okay, well good. If you need anything, I'm around. Just ask for me."

"I will do so," I agreed.

She left.

"She is just… so very interesting," Sam said. "She's got energy for days."

"Stage actresses are another breed. You should know that by now, Sam. It takes a lot to perform that many times a week."

"You never did struggle to perform." He rubbed his temples nervously, realizing that sounded like an innuendo. "Shit, Lanie, I didn't mean it like that. Promise. I know you're married. Let's just get that elephant in the room out of the way, okay?"

"I am, yes."

"I was a little surprised, honestly."

It was the first vulnerability I'd seen in Sam. He was *hurt*. I was nearly drunk on his discomfort, turning from embarrassed to satisfied.

"Baz moved fast. He didn't want to lose out on the best thing he ever had," I twisted the knife. "What can I say?"

"Sometimes, I feel that in ways you'll never know, Lanie," Sam said.

That wounded me more than I'd wounded him. I still loved this man—not Baz. I wanted him. Had I made a major mistake? And if I Sam came onto me, would I be able to resist him? And if I did, would that be an overreach? I knew it was best to stay away—far, far away. Sam was bad for me. He hurt me once. I was married to Baz. Baz treated me with respect. He treated me like a queen. The impulse to respect Baz won out over my feelings for Sam.

I texted Baz when I got back to the hotel, needing some words of affirmation.

ME

How is Sweden?

Baz typed immediately. I wondered if he missed me as much as I missed him right now.

BAZ

It's Denmark now, darling. And it's bloody cold.

ME

I'm sorry.

BAZ

I miss you, Lanie. I will try to swing down to you next weekend.

ME

Really?

BAZ

I don't think I can make it another week
without you. I'm selfish

I smiled. I wanted him to be selfish. He adored me. We may not have had a love for one another quite yet, but we had this. And whatever it was, it grew over time. I pulled on his favorite shirt—the one I'd stole—and climbed into bed. I was allowed to miss him, wasn't I?

CHAPTER 33
A Short Visit

BAZ

I hadn't wanked quite so furiously for so long as I did in the week and a half apart from Lanie. I had no time to spend even one night in rural Wales, but I chose to spend three and work half the time I was there. I missed the way she tasted, smelled, and sounded. I'd been thinking about all the aforementioned since we parted.

"I will make calls to Bath," Jeremy said. "If you can take the—"

"Jeremy, I need to see Lanie first," I said. "She's my priority right now. We can talk business before dinner, but we both deserve some time off, I think. You can ring Bath again in the morning."

"What is wrong with you, Basil? Have you missed her?"

"Wipe the smirk off your face," I said. "What is this?"

"I never thought I would see the day that Basil Osgoode IV developed an *actual* attachment to another living human. You're in love!"

"And what if I were in love? It makes no difference. We've been on the move for almost ten days with no reprieve. I need a break—and a distraction—and if you could find one, I wouldn't judge you."

"I feel like the list of gay men in Cardigan is probably summed up on one hand and I doubt the prospects really shine. Besides, we're out in BFE. I pity the man doing that walk of shame tomorrow."

"He could hang out with film stars. Isn't Leah a gay icon?"

"Wrong type of gays for me. We are not all the same. I'm not into theatre people."

"Theatre people," I snickered. "I hardly think I am theatre people."

"Well, you married one. Unless you forgot?"

That silenced me. I still lacked most of the context of Lanie's past career achievements. Instead of thinking about all I missed, I thought about all I'd soon gain. We roved through the countryside through an endless array of green fields covered in dew. The morning was chilly, but not too cold. I was glad to be back on British soil again even if it meant I was the middle of nowhere.

Since Lanie texted they were still on set, I dropped Jeremy at the cottages near the castle where everyone stayed and proceeded to set where I hoped to catch a glimpse of Lanie doing whatever it was she did so well. I walked up to the first person who looked official—well, somewhat. Even in the cold of winter he was in basketball shorts. However, he had a lanyard and a headset.

"I'm here for Lanie Day. I'm her husband," I said. "She told me to come to set."

"You're the… royal dude?" The American kid asked.

I furrowed my brow. "Not in the least. I'm Baz."

"No. Sorry, bro. Uh, come with me. I think she's on a break while they shoot things with Harrison."

Harrison was Lanie's costar. He played the Earl of Dwyfor. I followed the kid through lines of lights, people milling, electrical equipment and down a dark hallway near a full spread of food. There, I recognized one face.

"If it isn't Baz Osgoode," Lourdes, Leah's wife, greeted. "How are you?"

I hadn't seen Lourdes in ages apart from the odd time she

and Leah came by Vesper. But, since I'd been in the good boy routine and home by ten, no one knew I existed these days.

"I'm good. Have you seen Lanie? Is she on set? She told me to come here—"

"They are filming down in the conservatory," Lourdes answered. "With the Earl and his mother. Lanie is…"

She looked around as if listening.

"They're in the library now."

I followed her, expecting to find her there with another costar. Instead, Lanie was on the floor in a long dress, rolling a toy plane over to Leah and Lourdes's twin ginger toddlers. They laughed gleefully, picking it up and running it back.

"Oh, look at you go," Lanie said. "Roll it to me, Victoria."

The little girl ran the toy back.

"I meant on the floor, but that works."

"They never are reliable," Lourdes said.

Lanie said, slowly turning, "Well, they're two, so I didn't expect much." She spotted me and smiled. "Baz, you made it!"

"I did. Although, this place is dizzying and I wasn't sure I did."

The other twin approached, holding the plane she just passed to his sister.

"Oh, thank you," Lanie said, brightly. "You are a doll, Bobby."

"They *adore* her," Lourdes said. "She's kept them busy off and on all day. I think they have a thing for ginger Americans."

I snickered. "But Leah isn't actually ginger, is she?"

"No. But at this point, does anyone but me remember her blonde?"

I did. She'd been a notable blonde everyone chased in my younger years.

"Lou! She's not a fucking babysitter!" Leah walked in. "And if you knew how expensive that costume was, you'd understand."

"Sorry. They were fussy and I was trying to help," Lanie looked upset.

Leah held out her hand to help Lanie up. A woman I'm assumed dealt with costumes swept in to fix the hem of Lanie's dress.

"Oh, I'm not mad. I just don't want you to assume that's your job."

"Oh, I love it," Lanie laughed. "It's not a problem. I cannot help myself."

"You're too much. Okay, I need to set up the scene in the dining room. Harrison said he was grabbing a bite."

"The argument will be amazing," Lanie assured.

"Don't talk to him. It's part of his… process." Leah rolled her eyes and picked up her son.

It was only then she spotted me.

"Oh, the husband *did* make it!" She laid it on thick. "Lanie told me, but I never thought you'd show?"

"I inspire little confidence," I said. "Well, that's nothing new."

"Catch up. It's going to take me probably twenty minutes to turn things over."

Leah and Lourdes left the twins. So, despite a swarming group of extras, I finally got to say a few words to Lanie.

"I'm glad you came," Lanie said.

I kissed her forehead as she wrapped her arms around me, burying her face in my chest.

"Me, too," I agreed. "Although, it seems you've been plenty busy."

"Sometimes the kids come on set. They like to watch their mom work. I don't blame them. But they're so sweet."

"I didn't realize you could get broodier," I joked.

"Don't panic."

"I'm not," I cupped her face. "I have missed you, Lanie. So much."

"Same," Lanie gave me a slow kiss.

"Miss Day, can I bother you?" A man with a thick Geordie accent, asked.

Lanie pulled away and turned. "Yes?"

"I need you to change. Can you come with me?"

Lanie turned back, giving one last kiss. "Sorry, it's a whole thing. Leah has changed her mind about the dress. I promise. This is our last scene of the day. I will be all yours in a jiff, baby."

LANIE

I loved to be wanted. It rushed over me like a flood whenever Baz stared from across a room. It wasn't a hard stretch to feel as though he did this very moment. His eyes met mine from across a crowded pub in a sleepy Welsh village with the crew. It was time to blow off steam. Baz chatted with Leah's friend Mac, while I caught up with Claire, another one of the Dollar Princesses. She was on set to shoot a few bits and pieces from a visit post-wedding to see me. I was supposed to act unhappy, but in this moment, I was almost overjoyed.

I hadn't had enough time alone with him, but somehow a look from Baz from across a crowded room made my heart flutter. I *missed* this man. I have wanted to crawl into his arms and tell him how much I wanted him since I saw him standing behind me. However, we were still doing this awkward too-cool-for-school dance about actually liking one another in public. We were newlyweds, but also independent people asserting neither of us was much into PDA. Secretly, I thought Baz *was* into PDA and longed to let people know I was his.

"Ah, Lanie, there you are," Sam walked up to Claire and me.

My happy eyefucking stopped as soon as he arrived. The way he looked at me made me both melt and want to vomit. I didn't want this man—not now—and I didn't want Baz thinking that I wanted Sam, either. Somehow, I knew my ex was off-limits even if we've not set that boundary. And, either way, he'd been staring at me like a lost puppy all day. This wouldn't start up anew. I had Baz—the man who looks at me like I am the end—right across the room.

"I wanted to talk to you about the love scene," he said.

"I'll leave you to it," Claire ditched me.

I called after, "Claire, you don't—"

She was long gone. I didn't want her to leave me.

"I know it will be awkward, but we will get through it, right?" Sam asked.

"I don't really want to talk about it. The intimacy coordinator will be there to go over everything with the crew."

Sam reached for my arm. "Lanie, it's just me. We don't need the intimacy coordinator to talk about this. I wanted to speak to you one-on-one."

He softened, then whispered, I've seen every bit of you without a shred of clothes."

It was strangely intimate—far too intimate for coworkers. I was *married*. I had a *husband* only fifty feet away. looked for Baz, hoping he'd meet my gaze and rescue me.

Same continued, "I know it's a little odd. I'll grant you, I could understand if I wasn't you *first* choice for a DP—"

"Sam," I pulled back. "All I'd asked is that you respect me. You must treat me like any other actor you work with. Be professional."

"We both know that's going to be hard given that I've *been* in this man's place."

"Are you like that with all the actors you work with?" I demanded.

"What do you mean?"

"Do you always put yourself in the male character's POV when shooting?" I asked, very annoyed.

"It's my job."

"To think of yourself with female leads in their most vulnerable state?"

"I don't think about having sex with actresses on shoots, no," Sam said. "Although, it'd be rich for you to accuse me—"

He stopped, gaze shifting to a newcomer. Baz muscled in, staring down at Sam. Baz had half a foot and a bit of bulk when compared with Sam. I'd not thought about it until this moment. I knew Sam was the brooding artist while Baz was the serious businessman. The contrast hit me for the first time.

"Is everything alright, my love?" Baz rubbed my back. "Do you need anything? Another drink, perhaps?"

I smiled, grateful for the reprieve, "I'm alright, thanks. In fact, I'm just a bit tired. It's probably time to call it a night."

"I think that's not a bad idea," Baz said. "Let's walk back. Can you excuse us… I'm sorry."

Baz cocked his head and held out his hand. "I didn't catch your name. I'm Baz. Lanie is my wife."

Lanie is my wife. He didn't say he was my *husband*, instead invoking a sense of ownership I should have found annoying as hell. Instead, it was hot. Baz wanted Sam to back off, knowing well-enough when a man made me uncomfortable.

Sam gingerly shook Baz's hand. "Sam."

I debated telling Baz who Sam *was*, but that didn't seem to appeal to Baz. He wanted to get me out of there.

"Nice meeting you," Baz said.

Then, without a beat, he took my hand in his and brought me through the mélange of people into the street outside the pub. We walked down the lane towards our idyllic little cottage.

"I appreciate you sparing me from that awkward conversation," I said.

"You looked confused and I struggled *not* to be polite, but took rescuing you as a sign it was time to leave."

"Polite?"

"Yes, well, I didn't want to appear *too* giddy to see what I could possibly get up to with my beautiful young wife who shot me impressive glances across the bar all night."

I blushed.

"You're thirstier than usual, Lanie."

"I feel the need to climb you like a tree. Maybe I'm

ovulating or maybe I just missed you. Either way, I wanted you."

Baz stopped, pulling me towards him. He wrapped me up in a delicious kiss that made my knees weak. I'd barely said two words to him since we'd arrived. I'd introduced him to everyone. At the time, I'd still had on makeup, so a big kiss wasn't in the cards. By the time we were free, we had social obligations and niceties. Now, standing on this street corner in Wales, I was all his again.

He put me back fully on my feet and said, "And if you *are* ovulating?"

"I doubt I am," I said.

"I saw you with the twins earlier," Baz said. "It seems cruel to deny you when it clearly appeals, love."

I shrugged, trying to appear care. "And what if we *did* get pregnant?"

"Well, we're married. You want children. I told you it was your timeline."

"And that... doesn't freak you out?"

"It could be fun," Baz shrugged. "To... try... I mean."

"Daddy vibes has a breeding kink?" I teased.

"Jesus, Lanie!" Baz looked like he might die of embarrassment.

I giggled. "Come on. Let's go home. I'll let you fuck me. Like the good little wife I am."

CHAPTER 34
To London, With Love

LANIE

WORD CAME that my love scene was flipped with others due
to concerns about seasons changing. So, we pushed off the
inevitably painful, awkward scenes for a few more weeks. We
filmed a less daring scene where only my right breast was
visible outside the family's greenhouse, all because it snowed.
In movies, *real* snow was gold. We thought we'd have to pay
to have it made. It allowed everyone to save time, money, and
setup considerations to use what we had.

In all honesty, as my costar and I kissed and ground
against the side of a tree by the greenhouse door, I didn't
think about the fact that my ex watched on. I didn't worry
about much at all. I was in character. I leaned into being The
Countess as she found herself sexually gratified in the wild
after what basically amounted to primal play. He pulled my
bodice down to suck on my nipple and all I could think about
was portraying Annie's sheer joy of being touched and
wanted. But I didn't want him. I wanted, instead, my *husband*.
I couldn't help but think about Baz and what we'd decided.
I'd not started a new pack of pills. And yet, Baz didn't flinch.
Instead, our sexting grew hungrier. I thought about the fact
that he said he wanted to mark my face with his cum that

morning rather than the current reality I was in. It worked to make it look authentic. I successfully ignored Sam.

After my first official nude scene, the crew began to pack. Tomorrow, we'd return to London for a short break to film scenes from Annie's wedding to The Earl. Leah would also be filming a bit of an epilogue with next season's story. So, it was a mixed bag. I told Baz we were coming "home" to London to his sheer surprise. He didn't understand shows weren't always filmed in story order—especially when locations were an issue.

Regardless of the reason *why*, I arrived home to Baz's house before he even came back from his most recent visit to Berlin. I relaxed for a few hours before it was call time. We were shooting a late-night party at a historic mansion owned by close friends of Leah's family.. Baz texted he would be home by midnight. I told him to meet me at the afterparty if he wanted. We'd reserved the VIP at a Soho club.

Tonight was different than usual. Leah was set to play my mother—a domineering, demanding Chicagoan a la Mrs. Vanderbilt herself. Annie's real-life mother was described as a "ball buster" and "hellraiser" in her own biography. I was there to play her excited, hopeful daughter. Leah snapped right into character, but didn't seem to get what she needed from me. I grew embarrassed.

"Lanie, let's chat," Leah pulled me aside after a take. "You're too joyful."

"Oh, really. I think of Annie as being hopeful here," I said. "She's excited to get married."

"She's confused. She wants to please her parents and wants to follow the rules, but she's also scared of what's to come. She's marrying a man she doesn't know. What could be scarier for an eighteen-year-old?"

I fought the urge to laugh. "I've done worst, honestly. Okay, I get what you are saying. Excitement, but trepidation."

"Exactly," Leah said.

As I played across from Leah, I began to draw on my own discomfort and worry as I waited for Baz at the registry office, terrified he'd never come. I felt lonely, a little used, and frightened. Even if I now knew being married to Baz wasn't a terrible loss, I didn't know that then.

My mother explained the expectations to me as my *own* mother had months before—knowing full well what I had agreed to.

"You're not just going to be a famous lady in a grand house," Leah said. "You will, Annie, be expected to contribute."

"How so?" I asked, innocently.

"He will expect some things of you."

"Like help?"

"No, dear," Leah turned from me and walked towards the mirror hanging above a grand fireplace. "He will expect you to give him children."

"And I can do that. I want to have babies of my own," I said.

"And how does that happen?"

Confused, I stammered, "I do not know, Mother, but—"

Leah spun around, looking pained. "He will need to reach… marital Congress… with you. It is the only way you can have children. Tomorrow night or in a few nights, when he comes to your bedchamber, you must let him in."

"Alright. I can… do that."

"What happens next…" Leah turned away again, this time speaking to me from the mirror. "It may shock you. It may also be painful. But, if you can endure it—and you should, for his benefit—then you will produce a child."

"Oh…"

"Eventually, you will fall pregnant—and for your sake, I hope it is soon. Once you are with child, he will leave you alone until he feels the desire to produce another. Pregnancy is a happy time where you can guarantee you have the bed to yourself."

"To myself?"

"He won't dare bother with you. It is better this way. Let

him do what he must, and the pain will end sooner than later."

"Mother, I don't… I don't understand."

"You will," Leah said.

She spun, nodded at me, then left.

I looked in the mirror, walking towards it to stare up at myself. There is a long pause then Leah yelled, "Fucking cut!"

I turned, trying to read her face.

"I think we're done. Great job, Lanie!"

I smiled, satisfied. The truth wasn't all that much stranger from fiction. That was the issue. Tonight, I'd let Baz use all of me—I'd luxuriate in the way he wanted me—knowing full well what might happen. And after that? I didn't know. The truth was, I didn't want Baz to stop coming to my bed. I wanted him to *always* be there. But would that happen? Or would he give up on me as soon as I'd granted him the last thing on our list—an heir?

It made me worry I signed my own death warrant.

Baz leaving was the last thing I wanted.

CHAPTER 35
Watching

BAZ

Lanie did her rounds while I kept to myself at the bar. The crew and stars were in their prime of social interactions—taking over a spot not far from their filming grounds. Lanie dazzled in some tiny mini dress. She never lacked flash clothes. I loved watching her in her element. She returned, reaching for me with her left hand—her ring finger noticeably bare.

"Come with me. Don't be a fun suck, Baz?"

I chuckled. "I'm not. I'm quite alright."

She pouted.

"Really. You do as you do. I like to watch you, Lady Osgoode."

Lanie bit her lip. "You're naughty."

"And you're mine," I said.

Lanie pulled back, tossing her auburn hair over her shoulder.

"You should wear your ring."

"He's suddenly possessive," she noted as if I were a character in a story she narrated.

"You're my wife, Lanie."

"It's stored properly," she promised. "I have to take it off for filming."

"Be mindful."

Lanie rolled her eyes, taunting me.

I pulled her close to me, gripping her by the hips. "Mind yourself. Be a good girl, Lanie. Go on, mingle."

With a firm slap on the ass, I sent her back out to the party. If people saw us, I didn't care. If she were any other woman, I assumed she'd have been mortified. Instead, she thrived on admonishment. I worried I might never find another woman who'd put up with this kink—or even drive it as she did.

Lanie passed by the Sam fellow—her idiotic ex. I assumed there was more to that story. She said he didn't want children, but it was never *just* that. It certainly wasn't that way with my friends. There was usually someone else. But, this time, as I watched his eyes follow her around the bar, I began to feel pangs of jealousy.

Unsatisfied with voyeurism, he approached. Sidling up to the bar, Sam's arm grazed her hip. He then pretended as if it were a mistake, chuckling. She merely nodded, talking to the bartender. As the bartender worked on his drink, he chatted with her. I wondered what his line was? Was it any good. She smiled and blushed about something. Was she *flirting* with him?

This prick got hours a day with Lanie. I decided to set him straight. He wasn't about to move in on her just because they were together on set.

"Lanie," I approached.

She turned, stopping mid-sentence. Sam looked at me, annoyed.

"Apologies, but could I butt in? Just need a refill."

I set an empty rocks glass down on the bar top. "Order me whatever you think is good, darling."

"Alright," Lanie peered over the bar and pointing at her glass. "Can I get second one of these?"

The bartender nodded affirmatively.

Looping my arm around Lanie's waist, I turned to Sam. "So, Sam what do you do? I never asked."

"I'm the DP or cinematographer," Sam answered. "Not something you *always* find on a TV set, but when you have Leah Roughy level bankroll, you can afford to be picky."

He sipped his drink, hoping I was impressed. Lanie shot me a questioning look.

The wanker turned back to Lanie and gestured with his drink, "Did you tell him how we met?"

"No," Lanie said. "We generally don't talk about things like that."

"Oh, it's good," Sam chuckled. "We were filming together in LA. It was this little indie movie. I had to set up this scene on a pool deck. The problem? We were under the gun to get it done in a pinch before weather. There was about time for approximately one take. I meet the actress playing a one-night-stand the main character is hooking up with. She's this young actress, the director says. I immediately doubt she can pull it off. Then, I met her."

He gave her a boyish grin. "I was wholly unprepared for the tornado that is Lanie Day. She comes in, does the scene with no direction. I have no notes. The director is happy. The camera *loves* her. And I'm like… that girl will be famous someday. Then, I gave her my number and she didn't call me."

"I didn't have time. I was back here for three months," Lanie insisted. "It wasn't some snub."

"She's definitely hard to ignore," I said.

"Well, especially then. She's good at projecting sexpot. It worked great in that scene. Of course, it took you… what? Seven years to strip naked. We've really upped the game on this shoot."

Lanie's face dropped. She stared at her toes.

"Excuse me?" I said.

"She didn't tell you? This whole show has a lot of nudity. Lanie is the lead. It's the first time you've done it, isn't it?" Sam looked at me, not Lanie.

I resisted reacting to his provocation, but my face gave away my disdain.

"Oh, you didn't know?" Sam laughed. "You didn't tell him, Lanie?"

"I… it was the part," Lanie said. "I never did it before Dad died. Baz, it wasn't—"

"So, you think it's cute… you seeing my wife naked and commenting on it?" I asked. "As if it's… what? Sexy? For you?"

I stepped forward, standing taller than ever. He was short in comparison and began to show his nerves at the prospect of fisticuffs.

Lanie said nothing. She stared in disbelief at the standoff.

Sam shook his head, raised his hands, and backed up. "It's just business."

"That's what I thought," I backed off slightly. "Because that would be unprofessional, wouldn't it?"

"Of… of course," Sam said.

"You'd not want me to say anything to Ms. Roughy about that, either. That would be *dreadful* for your career." I invoked his boss's name.

My drink arrived. Lanie handed it to me, still silent.

I sucked down the whiskey, neat as they both watched me, waiting for me to lose it in jealousy. I'd never give Sam that satisfaction. And while I could play it up with Lanie for fun later, I'd never lose my cool here. Doing so showed weakness.

"We should go," I told Lanie. "See you later, Sam!"

I nodded.

Lanie said goodbye to everyone, my hand on the small of her back as she navigated through the fray. Leah gave her a hug and waved us goodbye. We called our car and rushed into the rain together to get inside quickly. Then, once the doors were closed, we could chat.

"That was incredibly sexy," Lanie said. "I want you to take me home and fuck me like you mean it. I love playing this game."

I said, "You'll get it as soon as we get in the door, Lady Osgoode."

As much as I wanted to say it was a game, and I enjoyed the idea of sharing her for a minute only to take her home at the end of the evening, I couldn't let it go. Each time we did this, playtime gave way to something else. I only wanted to share a few glimpses of her. If it got beyond that, I couldn't handle it. Finding out her ex salivated over her naked body set me over the edge. She wasn't his to ogle. She was mine and mine alone.

———

LANIE

I freshened up after a long day of filming and changed into a piece of lingerie I bought at a boutique—in Wales of all places. I made sure to pop my rings back on, trying to show Baz I did genuinely want to behave. His aggro spat with Sam revved my engine, but I didn't want him to think I was *trying* to hurt him. There was something different about their interaction. This wasn't like when we went to a club and he watched me flirt. There was some genuine threat in Baz's voice when he leveled with Sam.

Once I returned to the bedroom, Baz sat in bed. I half expected I'd still find him in the living room or somewhere else—just leering. He'd gone traditional for this round.

"Come here," he demanded.

I followed suit, climbing into bed.

He patted his lap. "Here."

I hesitated, so he picked me up, pulling me like a rag doll until I lay over his lap—my ass in the air, basically on all fours.

"Are you going to misbehave again, Lanie?"

Oh, fuck.

He massaged my ass, lifting my chemise to reveal bare cheeks. I shivered.

"I... I won't," I lied, knowing full-well I loved to misbehave.

Baz smacked my ass, a loud clap filling the room. "You're incapable of promising that."

I bit my lip.

"You're supposed to be a lady and you're anything but."

Another slap.

"Yes," I moaned.

"Yes, what?"

"I will be a good girl, Baz."

"Lady Osgoode, you've never been a good girl a day in your life. You don't behave as a wife—my wife—should."

I ate it up like candy. Every spanking got a little harder. It delighted me. I lived for him being so rough.

"I haven't. I deserve punishment."

"Get up!" Baz's hand left my ass hot and a little sore—a prize for my misdeeds.

I moved aside.

"Suck my cock," Baz growled. "Think of it as penance."

"Yes, Baz," I promised, straddling his leg.

His cock had been pressed tight up against my midsection moments before—hard, ready, hungry for me. I rolled my hand up and down it, staring at the precum lacing the head. I licked from the shaft up to the head, sucking the precum up before spitting it back on to his cock.

"Fuck," Baz moaned.

I stopped, looking back.

"No, get to work," Baz pressed my head down.

Taking him completely tested my gag reflex, but I did it. While I played fragile and submissive, I was powerful and owned him right now. With every bob of my head, I brought Baz closer. He gripped my hair tighter.

Slow, he moaned, "Oh, fuck, Lanie. Oh, good girl."

I pulled back, wishing for more punishment and flirting with the idea of him cumming inside me. If I *was* ovulating, this would do me no good.

"You're not finishing in my mouth," I said.

"What?"

"I want you inside me. I *need* you inside me."

"Then work for it," Baz smacked my ass again.

"No. You should fuck me," I said.

"For that, I won't touch you at all," Baz threatened.

I scowled.

"Get yourself off first. Show me you can do it yourself. Don't be lazy, Lanie."

He *loved* watching me get myself off. I'd never had a man request it, nor did I know why it felt so unusually vulnerable. I'd just had his desperate cock inside my mouth for fuck's sake! So why did touching myself—something I did near daily when he wasn't around—feel so different? And why did he always love to watch?

I settled back on the pillows, maintaining strong eye contact with Baz. I dipped two fingers inside myself, picking up my own wetness. For effect, I sucked my fingers. Baz's face lit up, even if he tried to play it cool. He watched me eagerly as I began to stroke my clit slowly. I picked up speed, moaning. It felt wonderful. I focused on his cock. He slowly pumped his fist, staring at me as he did.

"Cum for me, Lanie," he moaned. "Cum for me and show me you've earned my cock."

I wanted to. As my breathing picked up, my fingers dove into my pussy—again and again. My thumb slapped my clit, bringing me closer.

The sound of my wetness rang out until I reached my climax, screaming, "Oh, fuck, yes!"

"Get on all fours!" Baz barked, flipping me before I had time to recover.

"Yes… Lord… Osgoode," I panted.

He pulled me onto his cock, smacking the cheek he mostly neglected so hard, I bounced forward. He pulled me back, his cock slipping back inside to fill me.

"Oh, fuck," I moaned. "Oh fuck, that is good!"

"So, are you going to behave? Are you going to be a good girl?"

He reached down to swirl his fingers around my clit.

"Uh… uh-huh," I shuddered.

Baz pumped harder. His fingers made good work. I lost myself again.

"Who owns you, Lanie?"

"You… you do."

Breath ragged and body pulsing, I wanted to cum so badly.

"What's my name?"

"Lord Osgoode," I moaned.

"So who owns you, baby?"

"Lord… Osgoode," I let out a sharp scream. "Oh, fuck. Yes, Baz!"

He pounded into me, both hands now on my hips. I tried to recover from my second orgasm, but there was little hope. I'd seen stars. I lived through something so wonderful I couldn't explain it. When he did this to me—played this game —I could escape reality and find the sweetest release. I'd never felt that with anyone else. The game topped all others.

Baz bounced into me hardest before stopping, holding my hips for dear life as he let out a low grunt. His cock pulsed inside me. I hung there until he pulled out, flopping to the side. I rolled onto my back, pressing my hips up slightly, legs pressed together.

"What's wrong?" Baz threw me a pair of boxers.

"Well, I think I'm probably near ovulation if I haven't already hit it. I didn't want to waste it."

He gave me a crooked grin. "You're dreadful."

"What? For wanting to conceive a child with my husband? Does Lord Osgoode not want an heir?"

"It's quite alright," Baz said. "But I doubt any of that will matter."

"Hard disagree," I said. "Sex that earth-shattering has to count for something."

CHAPTER 36

Surprises

LANIE

"The dailies all came back great," Leah said. "Honestly, it's coming along well."

"I am still able to sell myself as a brooding, straight earl?" Harrison joked.

"You read sexy as fuck," Leah joked. "And Lanie, you're good?"

"I am," I said. "I'm ready for this scene."

Today was another love scene. It was awkward. I never practiced my lines and blocking in my head as much as I did in the makeup trailer before one of these days. Love scenes took forever to shoot. The more accurate you were *before* in how you visualized it, the faster it went. By now, Harrison and I had good rapport. We trusted one another. Moreover, I had the added benefit of him never popping an accidental boner. He was gay as a post. Also in my corner this time was the fact that I would not need to be coated in body makeup to make it through.

After my time in London with Baz, I ended up with some very large handprints on my ass. The entire crew got to have a bit of a laugh at my expense. Sam, of course, did *not* laugh. I didn't know if that was Baz's plan, but my black and blue butt cheeks had to be carefully covered between the bedspread, lighting, and body makeup. If anyone thought our marriage of convenience was fake before, they weren't doubting it now. By now, they assumed Baz and I had the kinkiest marriage around. Which, to be fair, was mostly true.

"Okay, so, are we ready?" Leah looked at us as well as our intimacy coordinator.

She only saw nodding heads.

"Let's do it," I sighed.

"It will be great," Harrison said.

The scene began with Harrison arriving unexpectedly in my bedroom. I'd been sleeping, so I stirred. He dipped into bed, and we made out for an almost uncomfortable amount of time—far more than Baz and I ever would have. In all honesty, Baz and I didn't often kiss. We got down to business. Harrison was not a bad stage kisser. He was tender and kind, but we needed to really sell it. We set some strong boundaries here. Thankfully, Leah was happy with everything and moved on.

We cut for a minute, readjusted, and moved onto the second part. I started on bottom. Harrison gently rolled me onto my back, but I gained agency, flipping on top of him. Normally, I'd lose myself at this moment and pull through it, but I struggled. In front of me—with a handheld—was Sam. I was about to take my top off with him inches away from where we lay. It made my tummy flip in a nervous way.

"No," I shook my head. "No."

Harrison looked at me, nervously.

"Not you," I rolled off to the side. "I'm… I'm not comfortable. It's not anything you did."

Harrison immediately helped me into my robe, concerned. Leah rushed over.

"What's happened?" She whispered.

I climbed out of bed and rushed to the side. Our makeup person followed.

I paced, then said, "Why is there a handheld?"

"We've had the handheld before," Leah said. "You didn't—"

"I don't like it now," I said. "And it was from behind before. It's right in my face as I'm about to take my nightdress off. I don't want that. I'm not comfortable."

"What if…" Leah said, "I switch with Sam? So the DP would be back there, and I'd be up here. Is that comfortable for you?"

I nodded. "That would work."

"I am really sorry," Leah said. "I don't want to make you uncomfortable."

"I know. I should be a professional and just roll with it, but he's right in front of me and it feels odd."

We went back to where we began, our bodies diagonal on the bed. We did the roll, then the flip. I took my nightgown off slowly. Harrison pretended to be mesmerized by me. I did *not* have to pretend to be self-conscious, as I was very much feeling this way. I leaned into the shyness, pretending to gyrate against him.

Just as I thought we were selling it," I heard "Cut!"

The assistant direct called it.

"What?" Leah looked over. Her approach to sets was very horizontal. She wasn't offended by the call, just confused.

"You're in our shot," Sam laughed.

"Oh, shit," Leah said. "Well, fuck."

We reset, taking a minute so hair and makeup could deal with Harrison's t-zone. The smell of the powder felt stronger than ever. And, as I settled back into place atop him, the powder remained strong smelling—to the point I felt it all around me.

I couldn't handle it anymore. I felt as though I might puke. So, without thinking and without anything but a stringless G-string affixed to me, I rushed off to the side of the set and lost my breakfast on the floor about two feet away from a PA.

"Let's take thirty," Leah said.

I sensed frustration, but it was more worry.

Her tone went maternal, "Is anyone else feeling sick?"

Everyone stared at craft services. The set was closed—so we had a skeleton crew today. All I'd had was a croissant, jam, and an orange. I didn't like to eat much on stressful shooting days.

"What's wrong?" Harrison asked as someone cleaned up my puke. "Did I do something?"

I cringed, feeling terrible.

"The powder is really overpowering," I said. "The smell. I think it just hung in the air."

"Can we get a fan to air it out?" Leah called before turning back, worried. "Are you sure it's not food poisoning?"

The more I thought about it, the less likely that was. No. As I did the math, the timing was ripe for the one thing you couldn't catch or get from a bad thing of lox. I sensed soon, there would *be* no lox for me.

BAZ

Leaving Lanie became more difficult over time. Normally, traveling pleased me—new places, new people. Instead, I found myself wishing to be back in Wales with Lanie. I cursed her schedule—and mine. We were too busy to enjoy one another. I should have been grateful for the distraction. She was my wife on paper, right? I promised her little else, but couldn't bring myself to think about anything other than Lanie. And the more I thought about how her ex was seeing her naked on set, the more it angered me. I should let it go.

I needed to get my head out of the clouds and back to the wonderful game we started. We had fun. She'd been remarkably good at getting me off in the most deviant ways. Now, Lanie left me wanting more than just a release or images for the spank bank. I suddenly desired lazy mornings and late-night chats. I didn't *do* those things. This was a business arrangement.

It surprised me to receive an invite to the American state dinner at the last minute, but I figured that being newly married to an American heiress who was now in the "squad" of Her Majesty's favorite niece earned one such accolade. Usually, I'd ignore it. I'd instead do *anything* than engage in aristocratic bullshit but lacked that protection right now. We were selling it. I agreed to take Lanie on her one break in however long.

"Sir, you asked for updates." Jeremy stood at my door.

I nodded. "Yes?"

"Lady Osgoode has arrived back home, and the tiara is ready at Garrard. They have offered to send a courier to bring it by."

"Have it delivered to her," I said. "Let it be a surprise."

"Very well, sir."

"Thanks."

Jeremy disappeared. I drummed my fingers on the desk. I hoped Lanie would love this bit. The family tiara was available, so I asked to have it sent to me and have it cleaned for her. Lanie was as beautiful as any woman to wear it. If there was ever an occasion, it was now. It would buy me a bit of goodwill. I hated to admit I loved spoiling Lanie.

Jeremy poked back in. "Do you want me to make dinner reservations somewhere?"

I shrugged. "You don't *need* to."

"You have the wife home for the first time in weeks, and you don't want me to make a reservation?" Jeremy's face— rife with judgement—said it all.

"Fine," I said. "I will take her out."

"Is it so difficult to treat her to dinner?"

It wasn't, but it made everything feel genuine. The more I took her places to converse, the more I wanted to keep her to myself—for all the wrong, most complicated reasons.

"No. She's fine," I said. "Go ahead."

He rolled his eyes, leaving me to my own devices. I thought about plans all the way home—even after he landed a Hail Mary reservation at a Japanese place she'd find suitable. How could I have it both ways? How could I manage to keep this woman I adored at arm's length? I needed to bring us back to how it all began.

Off the Rails

LANIE

"I THINK we should go to The Vesper Room after this," Baz said as I devoured a chocolate souffle.

The suggestion surprised me. This afternoon, he'd sent me the family tiara—something my mother would be most excited to hear—and offered to take me to dinner. That was a complicated matter since he'd chosen a Japanese place where I couldn't eat most of the menu. The scent of the place bothered me most of all. Now, diving into chocolate, I felt a bit better. I felt like a *wife*. But now, he wanted to play again?

"Is that the best idea?" I asked.

"Well, I'd like to try if you would."

Baz's voice suggested a challenge. He expected me to be game. Instead, I was knackered. I wanted my bed. I wanted to tell the truth, but didn't want to here. I didn't feel like having a go in public, either. But it's what he wanted. This was our arrangement, and I wanted to please him. To deny him was to *not* hold up some part of a bargain I took far too seriously. I hadn't seen Baz in weeks. I longed to be his. So, if this is what it took, I'd do it.

"Sure," I said.

We arrived at The Vesper Room. I nursed a drink,

pretending to sip a rum and coke—an odd choice. The Thursday evening crowd was just beginning to file in. I assessed the situation. The thing that surprised me the most about the crowd on any evening was the average age of patrons. They were mostly in their mid-thirties and up. I was one of the younger people last time. I assumed it was a fluke but tonight solidified that was the usual crowd.

"What?" Baz read my expression.

"Just people watching and observing."

"Uh-huh. What do you think, Lanie Day?"

"I think everyone here is older than I expected," I said. "Not that I *mind*. I just didn't expect people over thirty-five to be so..."

I looked for the words.

"Interested?"

"I was gonna say *horny* but yeah," I giggled.

"People have time and money—professionals and couples with nannies, I suppose. And someone of us never grow up, Lanie."

I shrugged. "I think I'm pretty grown up. And right now, I have time."

"Says the important actress who has no time. You're an heiress. Not everyone here is born into wealth like we were. Some earned their ascension through actual work."

"I may be a nepo baby, Baz, but I worked my ass off as well. I know I'm a woman under thirty. You don't have to remind me."

"Oh..." he looked down. "That was more of a joke. I have seen your work. You're no slouch."

"You're a fan?"

"I try not to think about watching this series," Baz chuckled. "One, because of the *content*. Two, because you're supposed to be underage."

"Not your thing?" I asked, making eye contact with a man with a strong jaw across the bar.

"Not my thing. You're too young for me like this," Baz

said. "The idea of thirsting after eighteen-year-old you—in real life—perturbs me."

"That's refreshing," I admitted.

Baz turned to see the object of my gaze as a woman walked into view.

"Could be fun?" He asked.

"I thought so, but they're a couple."

"No interest in a couple?"

"I am not into girls," I said. "I've said this."

"The bloke last time was in a couple."

"She's making eye contact," I said. "They want to either swing or play together. I'd guess play together."

"Well, could be fun."

"I mean it. It's not for me. It feels fake. I'm not going to fake orgasms for all of you. I don't fake it—not anymore."

He chuckled.

"What? Did I just destroy a fantasy for you?"

"It would be a dream to watch you with another woman —I won't lie—but if you aren't into it, I'll keep those thoughts to myself."

"Why is that so entertaining? You didn't mind your best mate balls deep in me before," I said.

"So no swinging?" He raised an eyebrow.

"That never appealed to you before, Baz." I suspected it didn't now, either. "But it bothers me. So, no, unless you want to row—"

"I don't," Baz asserted.

My gaze transferred to another man alone at the bar wearing a sharp sportscoat. His eyes perused me. He'd do.

"I want to talk to him," I said. "What is your comfort level?"

"You want to fuck him, Lanie?"

"Uh-huh," I said. "If I stay interested. I want to torture you."

Baz shook his head, then brushed my cheek, cupping it. "You're greedy, Lanie."

"When you look like me right now, you get to be greedy."

Baz kissed me slowly, pulling away to whisper, "But don't you want me to cum inside you. Don't we still have a mission to accomplish?"

We didn't. *Mission accomplished.*

"There will be time," I lied. "I rather like the idea of making you squirm. Unless that won't work for you? Does the idea of us together bother you?"

He shrugged, "Then take what you want, Lady Osgoode. Just remember who owns you."

"I know," I assured. "You're going to get the last word, Baz. I save the best for you."

———

BAZ

The game no longer played the same. I should have lived to watch Lanie give herself over to someone else. I should have lived to listen to her get off. It should have added to the fun to watch him take her in a room full of people. Instead, it angered me to watch her with another man. What was hot at the beginning, now tortured me. I hoped she'd be satisfied going at it with another woman. That dream died. I wouldn't force the issue. I committed to this and I told myself this would snap me out of it—we'd return to the game, and I'd let this silliness subside.

Watching him kiss her and pin her to the wall felt fine. As he kissed her neck and ran his hand up her dress. She moaned, her eyes meeting mine. I hardened at her gaze and the sound of her excitement. I thought about how wet she must be with his fingers on her clit and inside her. This was fine. I handled this.

They moved to the bed in the center of the room where this paramour went down on her for a good long while. She looked back at me, breathing heavily. I marveled at the way her chest rose—her beautiful breasts nearly spilling out of her dress. I loved this image of her—the one I didn't get to see when my face was buried in her pussy.

Say my name. Say my name. I pleaded silently as she began to reach her climax.

Reading my mind, she cried out—eyes never leaving mine. "Oh, Baz! Fuck!"

My cock revolted against the binding presence of my trousers. I wanted her so badly. Then, everything shifted. I could lie to myself and say everything was the same until the point where I watched them exchange commentary about a condom. I stepped forward, handing one over. It was going to happen—against my will.

I don't want this. I fought what I knew I *should* feel. I wanted to be aroused, but as this hot stranger thrust inside my wife—the woman I wanted to be all mine—it faded. I fought the urge to turn away, suddenly horrified by what I agreed to. Unable to watch, I left. I let him finish. I'd not interrupt them, but needed another drink just to cope.

"You alright, mate?" The bartender asked.

I nodded, lying. No. I felt betrayed, jealous, and broken. "Just another whisky."

"Coming up," he agreed.

"Baz! Baz!"

I turned to see a frantic Lanie.

"Why are you here?" I asked, voice harsher than I intended.

"Because you left… why—"

"You were just fine on your own, Lanie. I didn't—"

"I did this for you, Baz."

"Don't lie to yourself, Lanie," I said as the drink appeared.

I took a long sip as she stood silently to my right.

"Baz, I… I didn't do this against your will."

"Your mind was made up, Lanie."

"You were the one—"

"I didn't want to bore you, okay? You were the one who was selfish. You wanted him to fuck you!"

Lanie's face turned from concern to anger. "We will not do this here."

"Fine," I said. "Let's row in the car, then."

"I will get my coat." Lanie stormed off.

I slammed my drink as the bartender closed our tab. The car was on the way to the entrance. By the time I reached the lobby, Lanie stood stock still, arms crossed. Expression livid, I didn't dare speak.

I tried to reach for her hand, to tell her I didn't mean to get cross, but she batted me away.

"Don't touch me!" Tears welled in her eyes.

I hated to hurt her. I wanted to wrap her in a kiss and apologize.

The car arrived. We climbed in, silent. I wanted—and needed—to apologize. Instead, she sobbed without a word from me. We arrived at my place and she raced off, unable to even look at me. I gave her space, pacing in the kitchen. I longed to tell her everything, but cowardice got the best of me. I'd lost the thread and the game. I needed to confess.

Do it now or you'll regret it, Baz.

I strode into the bedroom, finding Lanie asleep in the fetal position still in her dress. Tears soaked her pillow. She was exhausted. I didn't dare wake her. Instead, I tucked her in, then sat on the bed by her, rubbing her back. I couldn't leave her, but couldn't stay.

"I love you, Lanie. I'm sorry," I whispered.

Why couldn't I just say it out loud? I needed to be honest. She needed to hear it. Even if she didn't love me back, she deserved that clarity. She was my wife. All I promised her at the beginning of this was respect and honesty. I'd given her neither tonight. Instead, I'd publicly admonished her like she was a child—all because I couldn't tell her I was done playing this game. My cowardice cost me her affections, but there was time to make up for it.

CHAPTER 38

The Truth

LANIE

"Fucking asshole," I muttered, waking to a note and flowers rather than my husband.

Baz said he took the day off, but I woke to him gone. I knew he didn't have the balls to apologize for last night. He was a coward, but wasn't the only one. I'd still not told him my news. He deserved to know that much, but I didn't want to let go of the secret. I worried he'd never touch me again. I didn't want that. I wanted my husband in my bed. Why was it so hard to admit that?

> Lanie,
>
> I have business to attend to. I am sorry about last night. I don't know why I did that.
>
> Let Jeremy know if you need something today.
>
> I will be home with plenty of time to take you to the banquet. You'll be beautiful.
>
> -B

He thought flowers and offering his assistant fixed every-thing. I rolled my eyes. It was ridiculous!

I spent the day resting—grateful for a reprieve. Shooting all day while newly pregnant was not for the faint of heart. Leah told me she did at least one performance a day of *Victoria the Great* when she was in her first trimester with the twins. They fixed up her costumes accordingly, but she managed to keep going. I didn't know how. A musical was a lot more demanding than hours on set, right?

After a good long nap and bath, I waited for my hair and makeup team. I was grateful I hired someone once the tiara arrived. I had no idea how I would have managed on my own. And, as I looked at the result, I teared.

Somehow, the tiara my mother longed to wear again sat proudly atop my head. It was *mine*—for now, anyway. It was heavy and not the most comfortable I'd worn. Lately, I'd been wearing more of them. It also wasn't the worst. Here I was, as my mother had been on her wedding day in this beautiful diadem. I fought tears.

We accomplished our mission, so would this all go away? Would he cast me aside? Would the next time I wore this be a farce and only for show? Or would I ever wear it again? Questions swirled. Baz returned home, but didn't look partic-ularly ready to discuss his outburst. He mooned over me in a way I didn't expect.

"You look beautiful," he gushed. "Gorgeous."

My makeup artist stepped back, giving us a moment.

"Thanks," I said, confused.

"I am sorry to be in a rush, but I need to shower and shave, and we have all of forty-five minutes."

"I know," I said. "Go."

He stepped away.

The makeup artist said, "He's different than I expected from what you said."

I snickered. "Baz is nothing if not different."

Baz showered, shaved, and darted quickly into the closet in a dressing gown. By that point, I was in my evening gown

—a draped tulle off-the-shoulder dress in gold. I'd gone with a classic look from an American designer. Neither blue nor red felt particularly good. I assumed everyone would rock either color. I wanted to be different.

Still fastening cufflinks, Baz emerged, jaw dropping as he spotted me.

"Lady Osgoode, don't you know it's a dreadful idea to upstage Her Majesty and The First Lady?"

I blushed.

"There is no way they will compete with you."

"Good. Then, you can take a picture for proof-of-life. Mum would appreciate it, too."

"Do you want to take a photo with me, too?" Baz scoffed.

"It depends on how much you grovel tonight," I sighed.

"I can take one," the stylist said. "You look too good not to share."

"Give me just a moment," Baz pulled on his jacket.

"In front of the piano no one plays." I said. "Yes?"

"Sure," Baz said. "Whatever you think is best, darling."

We posed before the grand piano in the formal living room.

"I'll credit you all," I addressed the stylist and makeup artist. "Promise. You did a fabulous job. And hopefully this one is a good one. It should blow up."

"I mean… with you looking like that," Baz said.

"No," I said. "Just wait."

In the car on the way there, I typed out a post while we languished in evening traffic.

"Here," I said. "My publicist will want to strangle me."

I handed Baz my phone, almost as a peace offering. Even if he hadn't groveled yet, he seemed good-natured enough.

"State Dinner with the hubby," Baz chuckled. "That is almost… wholesome."

"I've never commented on our status. I've never confirmed anything," I said. "This is the first post, Baz."

His jaw dropped. "Really?"

"Yeah. I mean, the world knows, but I've never been out with you—not officially. So, it's a big deal. I held off releasing a statement because... I dunno. It was a business deal. It *is* I suppose, but I think we need to talk about this honestly—all of it."

He squeezed my hand. "I agree. Completely."

"I must tell you something. I hope you're not angry," I winced, turning off my social notifications and putting my phone away.

"Last night was the worst bit of me," Baz said. "I am so sorry. I set you up. It was... I didn't mean for that, but I also didn't expect to feel that way. In the future—"

I had to get this out before he groveled about things I cared far less about.

"Baz, I'm pregnant. That's what I meant."

Baz did a double-take.

"I have *been* pregnant. It's been difficult. And last night, I only did that for you, but... I'm exhausted. It's why I pretended to drink all night."

Baz stared out the window, silence overcoming him. I shook, unable to think about anything until he responded.

"You... you're pregnant?"

"Yes, Baz. I'm pregnant. Whatever magic shit we got up to last time I was in London worked."

"That fast..."

"I'm sorry, I warned—"

Baz squeezed my hand again. "It's okay, Lanie. I am not upset... just surprised. Why didn't you just say that?"

"There wasn't time. And you wanted to play the game. I worried I'd offend you."

"You couldn't. And the game..." he looked down, voice trailing. "I want to talk about the game."

"Yes?"

"I think we should suspend the game for now."

Relief washed over me.

"I don't think it is appropriate given your current status. Do you?"

Appropriate. I was still a sexual being! I had to fake bone my costar off and on for the past few weeks all while pregnant. No one could tell yet. Who cared about that? It confirmed what I thought—Baz was done touching me. He was kind, but wanted to ignore me. We'd done what he needed us to do. That was all it was.

I could remain his wife, but I wasn't his lover. I fought tears. The reaction was exactly what I expected but nothing like I wanted it to be. I longed for him to tell me he was elated. I needed him to love me. He couldn't give me that. It was unfair to expect it.

"You're off the hook," I laughed, trying to stay positive.

I felt anything but. Deep down, I was heartbroken.

BAZ

Lanie dug into the role of society wife. She and Leah chatted, leaving me to discuss my football team's chances the following day with some aristocrats I knew from school. However, my mind couldn't have been farther away from the chatter of our cocktail hour in the picture gallery. Lanie's news shook me to the core. I planned to say I loved her, but she seemed satisfied to be pregnant. She was right. Our job was done if this pregnancy stuck. Our business deal worked out.

My father would have been relieved to hear I finally did it. He managed to get what he wanted. Beautiful Lanie Day had come through. This enigmatic woman ticked all the boxes. The only thing I hoped for was that it was a girl. If it wasn't a *male* heir, I'd have an opportunity to ask her to try again, right?

Lanie played a perfect baroness all night. Lady Osgoode never failed. She never faltered. She glowed, obviously happy with her news. Lanie wanted to be a mother. I didn't particularly want to be a father but hoped that feeling changed. I didn't want to be the same man my father was. This child deserved love.

"What do you need from me, Lanie?" I asked.

"With what?" Lanie looked up from her mobile on the car ride home.

"With the baby."

"My allowance. A plan for a house. That's about it."

Back to business.

"You're right. We need a proper house," I agreed.

"I don't want you to think I am opposed to a big apartment, but Baz... that house isn't going to work with a baby. And I have a feeling you won't want to give it up, will you?"

"What do you mean?"

"When we divorce, you're going to want to have it. I know that place means a lot to you."

When we divorce. Pangs of sadness filled me. I stared out the window at sleepy London.

"You're right. That's practical. But I was asking more about what you need. You'll have appointments with the midwives and such, correct?"

"I can handle those."

"And when will we know if it's a boy or a girl?"

She raised her eyebrows. "You'd discussed changing that rule if your dad died. He didn't long enough to have an opinion."

"I've decided I want to keep the family name alive," I said. "So, I'd prefer a male heir. We can discuss it after we know more."

"Oh... okay. I will ask the midwife. I'm going to go to the private hospital that my sister used. Is that okay?"

"Sure," I said. "And let me guess... Leah knows?"

Lanie winced. "I had to make her and Harrison aware. It's caused some unexpected production issues. I trust them both, okay? They won't say anything. But it's my work—"

"Of course," I tried not to be offended that my wife's costar and director knew she was pregnant before me.

"I know this isn't your idea of a good time, Baz," Lanie

said. "And if you want to sleep with someone else, that stands. Just not while I'm in London. Be discreet."

"Lanie, that's not my motivation—"

"It's fine," Lanie said. "I don't… I will be away. I booked another gig. I'm going to shoot in Chicago for a bit. I'll be back home. It's an indie project—a small role for a friend—but I look forward to it. That will be right after we wrap."

"But, you're… pregnant—"

"It's a short thing. I was going to have to wear a pregnancy belly but now I don't—at least not a big one, "she said. "It's an accidental pregnancy thing. We will only shoot for two months. I told the director. I booked it last week and wanted them to know."

"So your agent knows, too?"

"It's the business, Baz. Would you rather have me text you the news?"

"When are you coming home?" I asked. "For good?"

"Probably around five or six months. So, like I said, you're free to browse."

"So I won't see you for months?"

"You could come to Chicago. I will be back sometimes—at least once a month for my appointments, right? By the time they become a big deal, I'll be back here. I don't have to be—"

"Lanie, this is your home, too. You are welcome here in London. I want you here."

"Okay. Well, then I will talk to you about what works best when I know more."

I should have thanked her, but couldn't. My bed would be cold. I'd not do it. I knew if I even *tried* to approach a woman, I'd immediately shut down. I loved Lanie. Why couldn't I get my shit together and tell her? She deserved to know even if she didn't want to go there, right?

I never expected the biggest complication I'd face in my forties would be falling for my wife.

CHAPTER 39
The Interim

LANIE

"WE'RE IN BUTTFUCK, BABES," Chloe looked around the yard where we set up.

I held an umbrella over both of us, waiting for a classic kiss-in-the-rain op.

"It's beautiful, though. I stay in town," I said. "You'll think the cottage is cute. Promise."

"So, let's go out and get a drink then! A real pub with real people."

I needed to tell the truth. Chloe was my best friend, but I felt isolated. I knew she'd think having a baby with Baz was mental. I spent days trying to hide my pregnancy from everyone, even if all I wanted was to feel supported. Now, she was here, and I needed to say something but couldn't.

"We're resetting!"

I turned to a PA. "The boss has spoken. Here."

I handed Chloe the umbrella and raced over to the one the PA held out between takes.

I snapped back into action, standing again in the rain with Harrison. We took our places—twenty feet apart. I was supposed to run to him, my dress clinging to me in a romantic, somewhat-sexy way. He was supposed to lift and kiss me before putting me back down. Unfortunately, he had yet to nail it, afraid to drop me.

"You… came?" My voice trembled.

"Of course, Annie," Harrison called. "I would never leave you. I made a promise to you."

"You didn't have to," I protested.

"I am yours, Annie. I came back for you."

I hesitated for a moment before racing towards him. This time, Harrison picked me up, spinning me around in a triumphant kiss before setting me back on my feet. He thumbed my cheeks and wiped my tears—mixed with the rain pouring down my face. I fought the urge to close my eyes since now the rain pelted us hard. I prayed this was our last take because I was freezing.

"Annd… cut!" Leah announced. "Fabulous! That's it for the day. Thanks, everyone!"

"Fucking yes," Harrison laughed. "Brilliant."

Chloe came up, a wide smile crossing her face. "Babes, that was *amazing*! You are so good at this."

I blushed. "It's… just… my job."

"Miss Day, let's get you dry!" A wardrobe assistant worried.

She fussed more than ever these days. We already had to let out costumes in the bust just to make them tolerable. My tits were constantly on fire. After a change of clothes and time with a hair dryer, I was good as new and headed back to my cottage with Chloe.

"What's going on?" Chloe asked, reading me well.

"I… I have an appointment," I said. "You don't have to come with me, but I was hoping you would."

She cocked her head. "What? Why? Oh my God! Are you *finally* freezing your eggs?"

"What? No! I don't need to worry about it now. Promise."

"Oh. Well, I heard you cancel the thing a couple times now, so I figured you were up to that. Did you finally do it? No judgment. I know you're with Baz, but it makes sense.

Because… things with him are complicated and your career is taking off. Why ruin it? Give yourself time."

My face dropped and she gathered what was going on without a word.

"Oh, Lanie, I'm… shit," Chloe stammered. "Did you really? And… are we happy about it?"

"I don't want to hear why it's stupid or whatever. Baz is… he's trustworthy even if you don't believe me. We threw caution to the wind. We didn't expect it this fast, but it's fine. I wanted this."

"And how does *he* feel?"

Voice prickly, I responded. "He's fine. He's supportive. He's buying me a house."

"He doesn't need to buy you things. He needs to be a father."

"We're not like that, okay?" I shrugged. "It's fine. He *is* excited. He cares, even if he's not there every day talking to my stomach. We aren't those people. I don't want that. I don't need him to be obsessed like Davey is with Eva."

Chloe snickered. "The man loves her when she's pregnant —most of all."

"It's fucking weird."

"No, it's not. I think it's cringe, but adorable. If I ever have babies, that is the way I want it to be. It's okay to not want that, but… babe, c'mon!"

"He's a good man, believe it or not," I said. "He will be a fine father. He will take care of us and let me raise this child the way I should. It's okay to do it differently. And… I was planning on doing this alone if it didn't happen with a man in a couple of years. At least this way, the kid will have two parents, right? You are the one who told me not to wait around for a man!"

She sighed. "I firmly believe you are meant to be a mother and I will support the hell out of you, Lanie. However, I worry that Baz is not grown enough to be a good dad."

"I think you will be surprised," I said, hoping it was true.

"So, do we get to see the baby?" Chloe changed the subject. "Is it this sort of appointment?"

"Yes. Baz isn't here because I didn't attempt to consider his wild schedule. I figured I'd have you, you know?"

She squeezed my hand excitedly. "Well, regardless of my reservations, you know I am here for you. You're going to be an amazing mom, Lanie. I just know it."

I beamed. "And you will be the best auntie!"

––––––––

BAZ

"There you are!" Caleb chuckled, giving me a hug and a pat on the back. "He's not dead!"

I rolled my eyes. "I have been out of the country."

"Likely story. Look, I hope you don't mind that I have someone joining me."

My stomach turned. It was predictably Caleb. As he explained his girl-du-jour—a model named June—was in town from a job in Paris and she brought her friend, my focus filtered elsewhere. My mobile buzzed. Lanie's face popped up with a dubious look. It was her avatar. I hated how much I loved it.

"Oh, c'mon. You're not locked down are you? If you didn't tell me—"

"What?" I turned back to Caleb.

"The Wife," he said. "Why?"

"Oh, she put it in my phone like that. She was just fucking around," I said. "It's just how she is. Funny."

"Please do not be boring."

"Caleb, I came out to dinner to catch up. That is all. She's not locking me down, but just because you offer me a new catch doesn't mean I will take it. I don't need you to bring me women. I could find them if I wanted to."

"And you don't?"

"I don't have time." I lied. The truth? I only wanted Lanie.

I didn't thirst after other women like I did her. While I hated this version of me existed, I longed to have her with me even now.

I snapped open my phone, revealing her text.

LANIE

Got back from dinner.

ME

And are you alright? How did today go?

LANIE

It's good. Morning sickness is okay and Chloe is here. We had a nice dinner.

ME

Good.

I worried that every time she saw Chloe I was about to be thrown under the bus. Yes, Chloe had reasons to doubt our unconventional relationship was even remotely healthy, but I was trying to make it better. I wanted to take care of Lanie. Then, as I wondered what to say, she sent an unmistakable photo.

LANIE

So, that's the baby. He or she is doing well.

It took me a moment to ground myself as I took in the sight of our child—the first pictures I'd seen. Meanwhile, Caleb only wanted to drag me.

"What, Baz? Is she sexting you? She would, wouldn't she?"

I turned back, trying to shake it off. "Not really. That isn't much my thing. You know I don't live on my phone."

"Untrue. You are always on your email."

True.

LANIE

Sorry. If you don't want to hear about it, I
won't bother you.

She was hurt. I needed to text back, but I knew no matter
what I said, it wouldn't be good enough.

ME

No, I did. I'm with Caleb and he's talking my
ear off. I'm happy for you, Lanie.

LANIE

For us?

She caught me off guard. Yes. Lanie was right. It was *our*
baby. We'd both made this thing.

LANIE

It's your heir.

ME

It's my child. It's our child.

I protested, but then, needed to soften my words.

ME

I'm happy for this. I am glad the baby is well.
Are you?

LANIE

I'm fine, but I miss you.

ME

I miss you, too.

For once, I let my fingers outpace my brain and didn't
care. I missed her every time I left or she returned to Wales. I
worried about her leaving for Chicago soon and this being
done the minute our baby was delivered. I wanted to hold
onto her and this feeling for as long as I could.

"Mate, what is going on?" Caleb laughed.

"Oh, she was sick," I lied. "I needed to check in."

As I said it, two beautiful women approached. I realized I'd have to take care of this other woman and act cool all evening. Meanwhile, my wife was in Wales celebrating the health of our baby. It felt altogether dirty and underhanded, but what could I do? I was certain in a few months, she'd insist we go back to the game. Would I just box myself out and lose Caleb's friendship and partnership for being lovesick over a woman who didn't love me?

I chose to persist, even if I now had reservations.

CHAPTER 40

Appearances

BAZ

LANIE BOARDED the plane like it was hers. I'd forgotten how much I adored her authoritative, independent side. In a perfectly matched dress and heels, she was abject perfection in feminine form. I longed to kiss her and tell her how I missed her every night for the past few weeks. I settled for a simple hello. She sat by me, crossing her legs delicately. A flight attendant offered her a drink.

"Just a lemonade, please," Lanie said.

The flight attendant obliged as Lanie kicked off her shoes. I wondered if her feet swelled due to the pregnancy? I figured if I asked, I'd be fobbed off. She took any question about the pregnancy as a business partner might about a building nearing completion. I wanted to feel some sort of connection about this, but she refused to grant it.

"Was your journey up pleasant?" I asked.

"Not at all," Lanie chuckled. "According to Leah, Duncan doesn't care about what the cabin thinks of turbulence in some sort of power play, you know?"

"Duncan?" I asked. "You're running around with the Prince of Wales now?"

"He and Leah brought us back up. It just made more sense than us chartering something when he was on his way out."

I resisted the urge to roll my eyes. Prince Duncan was a notorious womanizer and exactly the type I assumed Lanie went for. Now he was flying her around? It made me uneasy.

"Duncan is a friend," Lanie said. "It's nothing you need to worry about."

"I'm not worried about it. The rules state—"

Lanie squeezed my knee. "It would draw attention. And, anyway, Duncan is too much fuckboy for me. Not my type. I like my men capable of doing things without calling Mummy first."

I snickered, relaxing because I believed her.

"How is Caleb? And what's her name? June? And June's friend?"

Bristling, I thought of how to respond. Part of me hoped this was the moment instead of launching into the air, we'd skid and slowly come to a stop. Instead, our ears popped as the plane left London City in a flash. When I'd gone out with Caleb and the models, we'd been photographed. Nothing happened and I wanted to forget it all. I hoped Lanie wouldn't hear—as if *The Sun* didn't sell papers there.

"Nothing happened," I said. "Caleb again attempted, but… Lanie, that isn't my goal. I don't want that."

"What? An attractive girl of what? Twenty-two."

"What part don't you get, Lanie. You're younger than I usually go. She was a *child*. I felt she might call me 'Papa' at any time."

That elicited a giggle. "Could be hot."

If Lanie wanted to call me Daddy, I'd let her. Lanie could call me *anything*. She didn't know how much I longed to cup her face in my palm and kiss her pretty pink lips. I *loved* her. I wanted to ride out every storm with her, to wake up next to her every morning, and to always say I-love-yous as we drifted to sleep. I was a full-blown sap, but if I admitted that, I showed weakness before a woman who still thought this was a great game.

"And how is the crew?" I asked.

"Uh, they are good. The production slowed for weather a bit, but we picked it up. Owning a grand house is… complicated."

"Correct," I said.

"Roofs aren't cheap."

"They are not. So, what do these people want?"

"Just your average sort of story," Lanie said. "How are we as a couple. What is it like being Baroness Oban? I show them around, tell them about our love affair, gush about you, and that's all there is. Oh, and try on dozens of dresses."

Tatler rang Lanie's agent about doing a feature on us in Braemoor. Lanie asked, assuming I would say no. Instead—in desperation to have alone time with her—I said yes. She had to follow through. So, she flew up and came to play Baroness for a moment.

"You don't need to do anything. Be your charming self, Basil."

"I am charming? I didn't know I was capable, Lady Osgoode!" My eyes met hers. I wanted to kiss her so badly.

"You can be if you try," Lanie's expression turned to flirtation.

I didn't drop her gaze, but ran my hand above her knee, pressing on her hem. "How am I doing right now?"

"I…" Lanie looked for words.

I pressed on, my fingers inching up her dress. "And now?"

Lanie grabbed my face, kissing me in what felt like sweet relief. I cupped her face, soaking her up. Her lips felt so good. It'd been too long. I needed her desperately. We hadn't had sex in more than a month. I was desperate to have her.

"We… can't," Lanie protested.

"Why not?" I asked.

"It gets… messy," Lanie said.

"I like messy," I panted.

We kissed until we felt the plane level off. She tossed her tights aside and straddled me.

As I gripped her ass, Lanie's nostrils flared, "I think if I don't get off, I'm gonna lose it. So, don't tease me."

"I would never do such a thing, my darling." I kissed her again.

Zippers, buttons, and all else fell by the wayside as we renewed old habits. There was nothing more I wanted than to watch Lanie come unglued. She bobbed, chasing an orgasm greedily. As the heat crept up her neck and face, she threw her head back and let out a low growl.

"Oh, fuck me, Baz!" Lanie said. "Oh, shit!"

And then, she devolved into jelly as she tried to recover from the orgasm that rocked her world. I pumped her hips with my hands, before she leaned forward and kissed me, going back up to her usual cadence. If I wasn't sober and fully aware of my surroundings, I would have told her I loved her. It felt so raw and genuine.

"Oh, God, that felt... so good," Lanie panted. "Are you gonna cum?"

I fought it, but yes. A moment later, I couldn't stop myself. We sat, tied up, breaths short and desperate, hearts pounding. I kissed her forehead lovingly, wishing to soak up as much as I could of Lanie before she left me.

———

LANIE

"You're so peckish this morning," Eleanor said sweetly. "Are you alright, Lanie?"

It was our last day in Braemoor. From here, we'd head our separate ways—Baz to London, me to Wales. For a couple of days, we'd been the perfect aristocratic couple. We'd been unhinged, too. I had two days with little morning sickness, allowing me to fuck Baz with abandon. Unfortunately, this morning I woke to the reality of pregnancy in all ways—bloated, breasts protesting, and stomach at sea.

"I'm... I'm fine."

I didn't wish to draw attention to it. Our baby thrived—draining my batteries, putting me through hell some mornings, and humbling me with worries. Despite it coloring my world, I never shared the woes of pregnancy with Baz. He didn't care, as far as I could tell.

"There's no secret you need to tell me?" Eleanor asked, eyebrows raised.

Her gaze flitted from Baz's face to mine.

His face suggested I should just say it.

"I'm… pregnant," I said. "About nine weeks now We're not really telling anyone. It's… very new."

"Oh, but I'm not just anyone," Eleanor's face lit up. "Congratulations!"

She teared, overcome. The reaction surprised me, warming my heart. For weeks, I wanted to tell someone I knew would care. I dreaded telling my own family. Beyond Leah, Chloe, and Harrison, no one had been all that happy about this status change.

Eleanor raced to hug me, then her brother. For a moment, as I watched them embrace, I thought I saw genuine happiness cross Baz's face.

"Papa would have been so glad to hear that," Ellie wiped tears. "Oh my God, Baz, you're going to be a father."

"I suppose that is the natural progression," Baz said.

Ellie joked, "No wonder you all weren't up here. You were busy on your own."

"Well, it's mostly been that Lanie is busy."

"And you, too, Baz," I said. "We're both people with lives."

"But you have a life *together*. When will you return?" Ellie asked. "I'd like to spend time with you both again. It's been so nice. I love my big brother, but I miss his lovely wife."

I smiled, wishing that it made sense. I wanted to be close to Ellie. I adored her sweet soul and now there was more to be learned. I wanted my child to know her. Getting more involved made me feel set up for pain and misery when it all fell apart.

"Someday," I said. "I have another shoot in America after this one, but I'll be back around twenty weeks. So, not too far off now."

"We'll welcome her back with open arms," Baz smiled. "Promise."

CHAPTER 41

Holding Off

LANIE

"Can I help you, miss?" An older man offered to grab my carry-on from the overhead bin as we landed at the gate in Chicago.

"You don't have to."

"Oh, I don't mind. You should rest," he lifted my suitcase gently down.

"Thanks."

Does he know?

The man smiled. "Take care of yourself."

As I left the jet bridge, I beamed. He was the first person to guess—even if he wasn't brave or stupid enough to say. I was fourteen weeks pregnant—just barely showing if you knew me, but *flagging*. I saw our baby live and kicking the week before. I had the photos to prove it. He or she was fine. At the gate, Chloe met me.

"My love, you've returned home," she hammed it up.

We hugged for a while. I missed my best friend all this time. She was busy with her own work, and we'd been all over the world—far apart.

"What is different about you?" Chloe asked.

I winced.

"I hate to offend you, but… you're *glowing*."

"I am *not* glowing."

"You are. How is the baby?"

"I'll show you in the car," I said.

I flipped through a list of beautiful pictures of our baby—still a bit of a potato in my belly.

"So sweet," Chloe said. "Oh, Lanie, this baby is going to be so pretty. Poor Baz. You *did* tell him you were one of six, right? And that your parents were always busy."

I smacked her. "Stop!"

She put her Porsche into gear, and we pulled out. At my mother's house, a welcome back dinner awaited. My niece and nephews ran wild in the family room. I couldn't help but feel I missed out on so much. Davey and Eva's daughter, born months before, lay on the floor kicking her legs. I unpacked a gift—a wooden carved sheep I bought in the village where we shot some exteriors. As she gnawed on the toy, my twin nephews bopped around, cruising the furniture for an open lap. Robbie, the oldest of my brother's twins careened into me.

"Hey bud, don't go too crazy," I laughed, pulling him into my lap.

For NICU babies, Robbie and his brother Max, were stout. They dwarfed Daphne's daughter, Cordelia, despite being several months younger. Cordelia was built slight and delicate like her mother. The boys were tanks, in comparison.

Robbie handed me a toy.

"Oh, thank you," I said brightly.

"So, where is the husband?" Mother asked.

"Mum, he's busy with work right now."

She tutted.

No one knew what to say to me. Everyone found my surprise marriage totally bizarre, but I was an actress. People expected me to be weird. That was just how it was. Mum was surprised we made it this far. I hadn't seen my husband in weeks. When I came back to London for a scan, it was only for a day, and I didn't tell him my plans. He'd been off in

Stockholm. No news from Baz was good news. He hadn't been in the press. That was the most I hoped for.

"And you're happy to be here without him?"

"Mum, they have busy jobs," Davey said. "People do work apart."

"Especially in Hollywood," Chloe chimed.

Mum shot her a look that said, "Don't try me."

Chloe wasn't one of us, but she might as well have been. Mum calmed, backing off. I focused on my niblings, enjoying the moments I finally got with them once more. It had been so long. It wasn't until everyone left for the evening that I found myself alone with the bear.

I sat on the couch with Mum.

"So, being so far apart. How does that work for the other part of your bargain?" She couldn't help herself.

I fell silent.

"Is he even interested in women? What is the game here?"

"Baz isn't gay," I scoffed.

"But he lets his wife run around all over god's green earth doing god only knows what?"

I took a deep breath. "I am working. And he has nothing to worry about—"

"No, he's just been spotted out with other women."

I firmly believed Baz wasn't cheating. He could, but didn't. He may have lacked in many ways conventional husbands did, but Baz felt some sort of obligation to me and whatever our agreement was. Whatever the gossip rags said, I dismissed them. I didn't know why I trusted my gut. I just felt—for better or worse—that I knew Baz better than anyone.

"He hasn't. He's…he's a good man, Mum."

She rolled her eyes.

I realized it was now or never. She was still convinced it was terrible, so how much worse could it go? I let the news rip.

"I'm… I'm pregnant," I said. "So, we're having a baby, and he will be in the family for good. So… just… let it go. I won't tolerate you being rude to Baz."

"You're… pregnant?"

"Yes, mother," I said. "I'm fourteen weeks pregnant."

Her mouth dropped. For a moment, I thought she might hug me. Instead, she stood.

"He will leave you. He will hurt you, Lanie. But you're too stupid to think about it. And now you've permanently tied yourself to a man who will never love you or prioritize you. I hope the money keeps you warm at night, Delanie. Your father didn't kill himself in business trying to support all of you so you could go over the ocean to attach yourself—"

"Mother, I did this for the family. I did this because you wanted—"

"Don't blame me for your bad choices, Lanie! I refuse to be blamed for my daughter's foolish behavior!"

She left. Tears fell. I again felt so alone. No matter what I did—no matter *why* I did it—she didn't see it as good enough. I sobbed and dialed Chloe.

"Can I stay with you? Mum went ballistic when I told her."

"Always," Chloe said. "Get a cab. I love you."

I needed someone in my corner. But the voice I really wanted to hear was my husband's.

———

BAZ

"Thanks for meeting me," I said to Caleb and our friend, an estate agent.

Within the gate of a beautiful palace in St. John's Wood, I contemplated where my life was headed. I resolved to buy a damn family house the minute I found out my wife went rogue and refused to warn me of her twelve-week scan. In truth, I'd been heartbroken. It hit me with all I missed out on. She didn't believe anything I said about my desire to be there for her—for our baby, too. Sometimes, Lanie's independence infuriated me. I hoped to buy a proper family house that wowed her.

"All the way over here?" Caleb asked.

Caleb was my gut check. Somehow, he would know if Lanie hated it. He appreciated a grand house standing on its own in a way I didn't. He understood this side of Lanie in a way I did not. She was more his type, after all. While it was unconventional, nothing about our triangle-of-fuckery made sense.

"Lanie wants something calm and family-focused," I said.

Caleb cocked his head.

"Yes," I sighed. "She is."

He did a double take before patting my back. "No wonder Baz has been a dull boy of late."

I rolled my eyes. "The German project is the perennial reason, but thanks for your concern."

Freddy, our friend, looked on confused.

"My wife is pregnant," I clarified. "She's due in about five months. So, we need a family house. It's all she's wanted."

"And is she joining us?"

"She has delegated this as she shooting in the States right now," I said.

I gathered Lanie wanted to be surprised.

"She's a very unconventional sort," Caleb added. "And after closing that Stockholm deal, Baz has money burning a hole in his pocket."

It wasn't a lie.

"This is certainly more of a family-friendly home than I ever expected you to inquire about," Freddy agreed. "Come on inside."

The white stone home looked impressive from the big iron fence and gorgeous white stone facade. Inside, stone floors and a grand entrance with a beautiful Georgian staircase greeted us. It would be grand enough for Lanie.

The kitchen was modern and flowed into a grand dining room overlooking the garden. A small snug sat next to a library and office.

"The downstairs is the impressive part," Freddy said. "You won't lose your pool, Baz."

"Good. Lanie enjoys that bit," I said.

Downstairs, the basement gave way to a beautiful pool flanked by two entertaining spaces. It was enough to sell me. On the first floor, the primary suite had more garden views. The typical Georgian stone exterior would delight my American wife, I suspected.

"This carpet needs to be replaced. It will need work," I said.

"It's new," Freddy said.

"Doesn't matter. I loathe it. Lanie doesn't like carpet, either. We could put down some hardwoods or stone, but I don't like it."

Freddy shook his head. I knew I was a nightmare client, but anything I bought would need some renovation to make it ours. I fancied delegating the interior design to Lanie. She'd be a proper lady of the house. I'd tell her it was a blank canvas, and it was hers alone to paint. The house wasn't for me. She was right. I had a place that fulfilled that goal. However, it was my intent to live here with her until she set me free. I wanted a happy place to raise a family. This would be proof of that intent.

"There is a second bedroom with a bath across the way perfect for a baby," Freddy said. "A nice, cheerful room. Upstairs, you have two more bedrooms. You could either put the nanny down here in the other room or move her upstairs."

I loved that Freddy assumed we'd have a nanny. Maybe we would? It would make sense, but Lanie never discussed it. I wondered if Americans had nannies? It seemed they loved to exhaust themselves raising their children with their abilities alone. I never understood it, but Lanie was a working woman. I didn't see her giving up her career—even for a baby.

After the tour, I turned to Caleb for honesty.

"I don't know. I think you should run it by her," Caleb

said. "Truthfully, she'll love it, but maybe she will want to give feedback?"

"I think it would please her," I admitted. "It's perfect for a family and it's private."

"These listings rarely come on the market, as you know well, Baz."

"I know," I sighed. "Give me a couple hours to try and ring her. It would be a cash offer."

"Of course," Freddy said, unfazed that I'd drop forty million in cash.

Caleb was correct that I made a killing in Sweden, but it could have been double that and I would have been happy to spend it on Lanie. She was worth it—all of it.

As if on cue, she rang me while Freddy locked the place up.

"Yes, Lanie?" I asked.

"Baz… I am sorry to call," she said.

Her voice was emotional.

"Don't apologize. What do you need, darling?"

"Things fell apart."

"What do you mean?" My heart stopped.

I panicked, thinking something was wrong with the baby.

"Mum reacted in anger, so I fled to Chloe's house," Lanie answered. "But I cannot stay here. She's off soon and I cannot impose any longer. Plus, I just… I'm an emotional wreck."

She rang me because she needed to hear my voice. I worried about her, but couldn't resist gloating internally because she needed me. She trusted me.

"I told Mum," she continued. "I cannot go home and… I feel like a teenager who fucked around and found out."

"You're not, love." I spotted Caleb's confused face as he listened in.

"I don't even know why I called. It's not like you could do anything."

"I have business in Chicago to attend to," I lied. "I'll come to you. I have a suite booked. I'll send you the details."

By now, Jeremy—waiting outside my car—stared at me, confused.

"Oh… okay. Why didn't you tell me?" Lanie asked.

"I wanted it to be a surprise, darling," I said. "Also, I'm buying us a property in St. John's Wood. I will send you the details."

"Really?" That got a hopeful response.

"Yeah. I miss you. I will be there as soon as I can get a flight," I said. "I'll just bump up my trip a bit."

I hung up, narrowly missing an incriminating *I love you*.

"Let's put in a bid at 37. Cash. We'll go from there," I told Freddy. "She didn't bat an eye or complain."

"I will write it up," Freddy said.

"And Chicago?" Caleb asked.

"I have something to do," I lied. "Jeremy, I need a hotel room and flight ASAP."

Jeremy sighed, already exhausted.

CHAPTER 42
Vindicated

BAZ

Lanie's childhood home in a posh neighborhood in Chicago further supported Caleb's assessment of her status as an American Princess. I'd never seen this place, but Chicago didn't disappoint in views. It was a big American city. And jet lagged, I had to finish this mission before I even found Lanie. I hoped the address she'd given Jeremy was the correct one as I stood on the doorstep.

I knocked. A woman in a pair of slacks and a crisp white shirt answered.

"I am looking for Lady Danna Delphine," I said.

She looked me over. "I will see if she is accepting visitors. Who should I say is calling?"

"Basil," I answered. "She will know who that is."

I waited a moment on the doorstep, awkwardly, until the woman returned. "She will see you in the conservatory."

I followed the woman through the impeccably appointed townhome. Lady Danna new how to decorate a grand house. It further affirmed my purchase the day before. The owners accepted our bid after I granted them a 60-day requirement for them to vacate. I expected Lanie would be happy to hear.

Lady Danna barely gave me a casual gaze. If I'd surprised her, the poker face remained intimidating.

"What are you doing here, Lord Osgoode?" She sighed in annoyance.

In an attempt to humble me, I was neither invited to sit or to take tea.

"I must speak to you about your daughter."

"Yes? The one you impregnated?"

"Yes, my wife."

She chuckled. "On paper."

I ignored her tone. "Lady Danna, you risk your daughter and I writing you off completely over this. I would be less casual about it."

"For what? For being right? I will be here to pick her up when you discard her for something less complicated."

"That is not my intent. It is your brutish treatment—"

"She is better to hear the reality of her situation from me than from polite society. No one believes you are capable of being a proper husband."

"Regardless of what people say, Lady Danna, I haven't strayed or betrayed her. It is my true intent to do well by Lanie. I adore her. I miss her. That is why I am here."

"Did she ring you with a sob story?"

"No. She is hurt—wounded. All that woman wants is for you to love and affirm her, Lady Danna."

Lady Danna rolled her eyes. "She knows that."

"She doesn't. Ever since you told her that her father would be appalled by her behavior, she took all your words to heart more than anyone knows. She is brave. She won't tell you that this hurts her. And as her husband—as a man who loves her—I am telling you to please stop with this. I don't need you to think I am good. I just need you to respect her for being the wonderful woman she is. She's perfection. She deserves to know that, Lady Danna."

"You *love* her?" Lady Danna scoffed.

Why could I say it to everyone but the woman who needed it most?

"I do. Our love is unconventional. This… is odd for you. However, I will do right by Lanie. I want a good life with her. I want to take care of her. I'd like to think your late husband would find that admirable. I'd also think he'd be over-the-moon about Lanie's career. I know *I* am proud of her. I hope you are, too."

"He'd be mortified to hear Lanie decided to degrade herself with nude scenes. That doesn't bother you, Baz? You aren't angered by your wife parading around naked for all to see?"

"It's part of her job. Do I love it? No. But she comes home to me. She does good work—she tells stories. And she's brilliant to watch. She deserves your love and support as much as anyone's. I say this as someone who lost the only parent who loved him at a young age, it is *wrong* for you to take out her choice of husband on her like this."

Lady Danna fell silent. "You're just like your father."

"I refuse to let that be the case," I said. "I understand why you think that and I don't blame you for being cross with me. But even if it takes another thirty years to prove to you that I'm even slightly worthy of your daughter, I will do it. You can have a dim view of me, but not your daughter—not in my house, not ever. And I will protect my child as much as I must. I'd hate to think I have to protect them from their only living grandparent, but I will."

Lady Danna looked at her tea. "I am offended by your assertion that I do not love my child."

"I know you do," I said. "But that is how she feels. Apologize. Do better."

———

LANIE

Baz arrived in our hotel room, finding me in bed. His gaze intent, rather than sympathetic, he switched off the television, and gave me the longest kiss. Shivers ran down my spine. I didn't want to speak. I couldn't chat. I wanted him to give me everything. I wanted to feel something—to feel chosen. And for a moment, I got to be his.

There was no talking. Without a word, I signaled all I wanted was for him to take me. I didn't have the emotional bandwidth for words. As we both shed clothes and Baz drifted south, I lost myself to the way he chose me. It was almost like a dream. As he got me off, I felt everything come back to life. Doubts faded for a moment. Once more, this felt like an actual marriage. My husband adored me. As I climaxed, I remarked on how safe I felt.

As Baz kissed back up my body and parted my legs around his hips, I gaped in awe at him. My hands on his face, I pulled him in for another deep kiss. In that moment, I loved him. This wasn't fucking. For the first time, I admitted we were making love. It was raw in a different way. It was earnest and beautiful.

Baz kissed my neck as I wound up to another climax. Then, he pulled back, feasting on my expression as I came— exhausted and so wrapped up in how he looked at me. His gaze loving, I gave myself to him—not because he wanted to own me but because he'd flown across an ocean when I needed him.

As we lay in bed, our limbs in a tangle, I said nothing. I wanted to tell him I loved him, but felt it might ruin this perfect moment.

"I'm sorry I wasn't here faster," Baz apologized.

"There was a geographical challenge," I giggled. "It's okay."

"Have you had food? I'm famished," Baz said.

"I could eat. It seems I always can."

"Good. Let's order room service."

"Get me a cheeseburger, fries, and a massive slice of cake."

Baz rolled over to grab the room service menu, then dialed. He got himself a steak—predictably—then left bed.

"I should at least grab some clothes," Baz said.

I groaned, not wanting to move.

"No. Stay there. Just like that. Don't move on my account, darling."

His gaze remained uncharacteristically sweet. Realizing he could see the changes in my body clear as day, I self-consciously climbed under the covers.

"You're beautiful, Lanie."

"I… I don't know what to say."

Baz climbed into bed by me, running his hand to my stomach under the covers. He tenderly kissed my temple.

"You don't need to say anything. Just let me take care of you. It's infuriating watching you traipse all over and knowing I'm not even allowed to dote, Lanie."

I rolled towards him. "I am sorry. I didn't think you cared. I'm trying to be uncomplicated."

"I've just parted with an obscene amount of money to prove to you that I care, Lanie," Baz chuckled. "Please give me the benefit of the doubt."

I nuzzled his nose with mine. "How much now?"

"About forty mil," Baz chuckled. "And I regret nothing after this. I really should be smarter about my investments, but you drive me mad, darling."

He kissed me deep and sweet. I melted.

"Now, this child… how is it? Given that you're not telling me anything…"

"The baby is well."

"And you know the sex?"

"I declined," I said. "I decided to wait, hoping you might come to the next scan with me and be there."

He pulled back, surprised. "If you thought that, why didn't you tell me? I would have taken the time—"

"You were busy. I didn't want to bother you."

"It's no bother. It's my son or daughter. You're my *wife*, Lanie."

I smiled. "I will be back that week. We can go to the scan together. And with any luck, we'll have a new house."

"Unfortunately, given what I agreed to, we've got a house, but it's not going to be ready until shortly after that. Also, when you see it, I have a feeling you'll want to make some changes."

I brushed his cheek. "That's fine, Baz. A girl can't complain about a surprise house."

CHAPTER 43

Delay Tacticts

LANIE

"So, do we want to find the sex out?" The tech asked.

Baz deferred to me. My heart raced. I thought I knew definitively already. I'd done a lot of research on the Internet in between takes to know what I was looking at. I'd seen a ton of ultrasounds of my nephews to know. This was a boy.

I didn't want to know. Or, more, I didn't want Baz to know.

Ever since Chicago, Baz and I had been so happy. He'd been sweet as pie, trying to make time to visit. We mostly went at it like rabbits. To my surprise, he didn't mind my body at all. While most of these visits were hotel room trysts, he did come to dinner at Mum's. She apologized weeks before and took an interest in my prenatal appointments. My transatlantic pregnancy was odd, but nothing with me was normal.

My biggest fear now was for the tech to tell us this was a boy and for Baz to go cold. He wasn't exactly obsessed with fatherhood, but the look on his face had been one of awe upon seeing our baby on the monitor. I worried he'd assume his work was done and would leave.

I felt the reins slipping through my hands, "No. I want it to be a surprise."

Baz furrowed his brow. "Lanie, you said—"

"I changed my mind. Wouldn't it be wonderful to have a surprise?" I asked.

Baz didn't protest, instead nodding at the tech in agreement. "If that is what my wife wants, it's her choice."

Baz squeezed my hand. It wasn't the reaction I expected.

"Well, then, we shall wrap this up with a bow and a few more photos."

I looked at Baz, watching him take in the fact that this baby wasn't just an idea anymore. It was real. And while I still feared him leaving, I had a bit more heart. I wanted to believe that we'd still have a great love story to tell.

CHAPTER 44
Final Countdown

BAZ

THE BABY'S sex didn't matter, but her wavering confused me. I expected her to want to know—for her own sanity. She'd feel relief, wouldn't she? If she had options, she'd be happy. Instead, she balked. Her punt delighted me. I'd come into this praying for a girl and fearing her going cold, but now she leaned on me.

I lapped up whatever oxytocin we built anytime we were together. If absence made the heart grow fonder for most, it made us hornier. It brought about important conversations. She let me in. I listened to her hopes and dreams, foolishly thinking I might be included in those plans.

And as her stomach grew, we tore apart the house— replacing the floors as I suspected she'd demand. By the time we moved in, she had decorated the nursery. She was due in three weeks, but we still made it in. Now, she was nesting.

I prepared for my entire life to change, but the closer we got, I didn't fight. Instead, I appreciated lazy days in bed with her feeling our baby kick. It didn't seem possible I could be attached to something that didn't exist, but here it was. While Lanie and I appeared the perfect couple, nothing with us was ever straightforward.

"We should pack your luggage for the hospital," I suggested one morning as Lanie folded baby clothes on the nursery floor.

"Chloe is coming by in the morning to help me," Lanie said.

It was an odd statement. I knew Chloe just landed. She wanted to be here for Lanie.

"We can pack it now before I go to Manchester tomorrow evening. Chloe doesn't need to be involved."

"Chloe will be at the hospital with me."

"With *us*," I corrected.

"Are you planning to be there?"

Dumbfounded, I answered, "Yes, Lanie. I'm your husband. I'm this baby's father."

"And you get squeamish. I figured you'd be glad to get the call and come see the baby after it is born."

"Lanie, I want to be there."

"Well, I want Chloe there."

I couldn't understand her. Why wouldn't *I* be there? I had been here for her all this time. Had I not proven myself in my steadfast support?

"Lanie, I will be there. Chloe doesn't—"

"I want Chloe there."

"Why do you not let me be involved? Why must you *always* exclude me?" I demanded, voice stern.

She bristled. "Baz, I am allowed to want Chloe there. You can join us—"

"*We* are us, Lanie! What more could I do? Do I need to hire a bloody skywriter to tell you how I feel?"

"Baz, this is—"

"No!" I cut her off. "How much more do you demand of a man in this circumstance? I have dropped everything to support you when you needed."

"I appreciate that, but—"

"I went to your mother—before you even knew I was in Chicago—to tell her she was making a great mistake treating you this way, Lanie."

"You didn't need to do that," Lanie said.

"No, I did. For fuck's sake, I bought you this beautiful house! Is that not enough?"

Lanie scoffed, "There it is. I spent all this money on you. Don't you believe I love you now?"

"It's not that, Lanie. It's not that at all. It's—"

"You don't get to throw money in my face. I don't need your money. Our agreement was our agreement—for the sake of our child and the estate. This was never supposed to be about the house or—"

"It's because I fucking *love* you, Lanie! That's what it is. And because of that, I want to be there. It's why I do everything."

"Don't say what you don't mean, Baz!"

"I do mean it, Lanie. God, you're so fucking obnoxious. It's infuriating loving you! I wish I didn't sometimes!"

Tears rolled down her cheeks. I immediately regretted my words.

She cried, "You don't. You're free! I'm sure we're having a boy, so you'll soon be off the hook."

"I don't want off the hook, Lanie. I want you. I want us. I want this family! I *need* this."

"Well, I don't need to be reminded all the time about how much you spend on me. Or have it thrown in my face. I'm sorry loving me is shitty. Don't think you're alone in feeling this way. Take a number. The queue is a long one."

I wounded her unintentionally. I kicked myself. *Couldn't I just love her properly and at a better time?*

"I love you, Lanie. You're the only woman I've ever loved. It's *still* not enough? What assurance do you need—"

"I cannot do this. Not right now," Lanie said.

"Delanie, I—"

"No, Baz. You should go I'm perfectly fine on my own, thanks."

"Lanie, do not do this," I said, voice strong. "You are not thinking straight—"

"It's better if we just end this friends and—"

"I don't want to end this."

"No, you'd rather break my heart while I'm nursing an infant and you find a shinier object—one whose vagina wasn't laid waste to by a massively oversized head, right?"

"Lanie, I won't… I cannot move on. I will wait. If I must wait—"

"Out. Go!" She sobbed. "You're giving me contractions. I don't want to argue. I don't have the energy."

I packed off to my old house, a broken man. I wasn't giving up, but I was tired of giving Lanie everything and receiving nothing. Loving her hurt. Not hearing it back broke me unexpectedly. I wanted a life with this woman in a way I never felt with anyone. How could she still play the game while I'd fallen so hopelessly?

CHAPTER 45

Birth Plan

LANIE

Chloe arrived in the morning to pack my hospital bag, but found me in early labor and a puddle of tears. I didn't want to call it, but the pain continued. I didn't want to admit I wanted Baz here and regretted sending him away. That felt foolish. I didn't want to have my heart broken while I welcomed this thing I already loved into the world.

"You aren't okay," Chloe said. "You're infuriating."

"I'm fine."

"This baby is coming. Where the hell is Baz? Why did he leave you like this?"

"We got into an argument while I was in terrible pain," I said. "I could have handled it better, but he pissed me off. I sent him away."

"Lanie, you're about to give birth to *his* baby. Why would you send him off?"

"Because I didn't think he honestly wanted to go with me. Then he went off on this heart wrenching rant about spending all this money on the house and rushing to Chicago and that he loved me. It was ridiculous. He *thinks* he loves me."

"He very well could," Chloe said. "Lanie, he has done nothing but show up—when you allowed him to, which is rarely. Let him love you. What harm does it do? Don't you love him?"

I shrugged.

She tossed a onesie at me. "Damn it, Lanie! I know you do!"

I groaned through a contraction that brought tears to my eyes. "Maybe. Maybe I do, but it does no good, Chlo. The baby is a boy."

"So?"

"It's all he needs—an heir. And he will be free and move on."

"How do you know that?"

"We signed the agreement."

"Lanie, he loves you. Why the hell would having a boy matter?"

"It's his heir—"

"That doesn't matter. I am telling you that even if Daddy Vibes got my ire earlier, it's not how I feel. I love you, but sometimes you annoy me. You have this man waiting on you hand a foot—buying you a motherfucking palace, Delanie! Let Daddy Vibes love you!"

"It hurts. He could end it all when I need him most if he's there. It's easier for me to see this as an agreement so I don't get hurt."

"Lanie, you already will get hurt if something happens. But that is the case no matter what. I want to believe it will work."

"I am not in a position to just let it go, okay?"

She zipped the bag. "Ta dah. Done."

I grimaced.

"Okay, that's it. We're calling the hospital. We're going!" Chloe said.

———

BAZ

Lanie texted the next morning.

LANIE

I'm in labor. Headed to the hospital.

In a panic, I replied.

ME

Do you want me there?

LANIE

I need you. Please come.

She slept it off. We weren't done. My heart leapt as I raced back across the city to the posh maternity ward. The issue? When I arrived, a surly nurse held me at the front desk, doubting Lanie's request.

"I swear she told me to come. Her friend is here," I insisted. "She's my wife and this is our first child. I need to be there with her."

"That may be the case, sir, but we need to confirm with your wife."

The nurse left. My heart stayed in my throat the entire time. Did Lanie change her mind? Was this all a sick, terrible game? The nurse returned.

"She said you can come back," she said.

Relieved, I raced to Lanie's room, finding her hooked to a million monitors. Nurses raced around. Chloe gave an inviting smile. Lanie said nothing, looking annoyed.

"I didn't tell you to come," Lanie said.

"You literally did," I held up my phone. "I have it in writing, love."

Lanie glared at Chloe. "Did you fucking text him?"

"I'm going to step out," Chloe patted my shoulder. "Come get me when the baby arrives. I will be waiting. Shouldn't be too long."

"Chloe, I'm going to kill you!"

"Curse me now but thank me later, bitch," Chloe said.

I didn't understand these women, but thought Chloe handed me a mulligan. I would not fuck this chance up.

"I love you, Lanie," I said. "What do you need?"

"She's in transition and she needs support and quiet," a nurse admonished.

"Do you want us to remove him?" Another nurse asked.

I was appalled at that assumption.

"No, no. He's my husband. We had an…" Lanie's words faded into a scream. "Oh fuck!'

She never finished her sentence, and the nurses didn't ask more. I assumed they'd seen worse.

"It feels like my asshole is erupting!" Lanie sobbed.

"Breathe through these contractions," a nurse said. "Can we get a check here?"

The other nurse nodded.

Lanie sobbed in pain before saying, "I'm gonna puke."

"Here," a nurse said, "be useful."

She handed me a dish, and I was unaware of what the purpose was until Lanie grabbed it, puked, and handed it back.

"Is this normal?" I worried.

"She's in a great deal of pain in unmedicated labor, so yes," another woman said. "Cervical check! Lady Osgoode, can we take a peek?"

"Oh, fuck, it hurts!"

"Just breathe," the woman parted Lanie's legs.

"Why didn't you give her anything?" I demanded.

"Your wife spent early labor at home. She presented six centimeters dilated. She elected to avoid the epidural given she was already so far along."

"Baz, I'm gonna die."

A nurse took the vomit receptacle, and I brushed Lanie's hair from her face. "I know you won't. You're brave and strong. It will be fine."

I had no idea if that was true.

"Love, it's time to push," a nurse said.

"Oh, fuck. No, no, I'm not ready," Lanie sobbed. "I cannot."

"There are no hand-delivered invites from the queen for this," the newest arriving nurse said. "How do you want to push?"

"I just want it out. Get it out!"

Lanie's cool demeanor the day before devolved into panic.

"Lanie, you are going to be fine," I promised.

"All fours," Lanie said.

"We can try that," a nurse agreed.

What followed was the most terrifying, nerve-wracking experience of my life—worse than even the most torturous loss at home. The stakes couldn't have been higher, and it couldn't have lasted longer.

CHAPTER 46
The Heir

LANIE

"I'm DYING! I am actually dying!"

"You're not, Lanie," Baz assured.

"Stop looking! Stop fucking looking!" I screamed.

"Dad, let's stay up here." A nurse beckoned.

I knew Baz was squeamish. Ellie said he passed out at the sight of blood regularly. And, as I labored on all fours, my body felt like it might split, I screamed. I was sure there was blood and all manner of things happening. I didn't need that being the vision he saw of my pussy anytime he thought about me.

"Fuck! Fuck, Baz! It hurts!"

"Deep breaths, darling," Baz said. "You are doing beautifully."

He was solid. I never expected this. Who was this man?

"Push, push, push!" The midwife called. "We're going to catch the baby!"

I pushed with all I had, then felt relief as a body left *my* body. A scream erupted. And for the first time in ages, it wasn't my own. I looked down to see a baby in the midwife's hands, screaming angrily. For a moment, I was transfixed on its little face. That was *my* baby. Then, I realized it was a boy, confirming my worst fears.

The nurses helped me onto my back. Baz elected to let the midwife cut the cord, wisely focusing on staying upright.

The nurse put the baby on my belly as I sobbed tears of joy and sadness. The baby's perfect face turned to me. A beautiful blend of us, I couldn't imagine a better being. He was beyond my wildest dreams. This was our baby boy, but I couldn't help but fight my worst fears.

"He's beautiful," Baz murmured.

"He is," the nurse swooped him up. "We're not taking him far, Mum. We just need to do final checks and he's all yours."

Baz kissed my forehead. "Well done, Lanie. That was terrifying."

"For all of us, I'm sure," I said. "You have your boy."

"I do," Baz said. "And he's brilliant. You did such a good job."

"You don't have to—"

"I am not leaving you for a billion dollars," Baz cut me off. "No. Not now. Not ever if I get it my way. Lanie, he's my son. You're my wife. I'm not leaving you in a million years."

His words were strong. He meant it.

Tears continued to run as I held the baby close, trusting somehow that Baz wasn't about to run. This baby would never leave me, but the feeling that his father was here to stay made everything feel safer. For the first time, I trusted Baz unequivocally. It wasn't just his words, either. The way Baz stroked our baby's mostly bald head and ate up the feeling of this new life assured me he meant it.

"I'm sorry I lost it on you," I said, guilt hitting.

"You had your reasons," Baz kissed my forehead. "And I could have been less stubborn and told you how I felt long before then. I mean it, Lanie. I'm not going anywhere. I love you."

"I know." I murmured and took in the sweet scent of a new baby—*our* baby.

———

BAZ

Our baby was perfect. His mother had won a battle I couldn't have imagined in a million years. In awe, I cradled our son against my chest as Lanie looked on lovingly. It couldn't have been more precious. I was a full-blown sentimental sap, and nothing would change it.

"I love you, Lanie. And him. What shall we call this little soul?"

"Not Basil," Lanie said.

"Please god no," I chuckled. "What about George after your grandfather?"

"George, really?"

"George, yes," I agreed.

"George Ewan," Lanie said. "I always liked that pairing."

"George Ewan Carlisle Osgoode," I murmured.

"Really?"

"Yes, my love." I kissed the baby's head, soaking up the sweet new baby smell. "He's both yours and mine."

"He's the best."

I nodded, feeling firmly that was the case.

"Baz, I love you," Lanie said. "So much. I'm so scared, but… I love the fuck out of you."

Startled, I stared at her.

"Don't rush to say anything, Baz."

My face broke into a smile, "Lanie, I have waited so long to hear you say that. I get it. I was terrified to tell you I loved you, too. God, I adore you. You're the best thing that has ever happened—and you gave me the other best thing."

"You cannot have two best things," Lanie giggled.

"And you cannot make me choose, Lady Osgoode."

The baby fussed in my arms.

"He's hungry," Lanie said. "I would bet it's hunger."

I handed the baby over, giving his hand another kiss.

Lanie cradled George in her arms, lining him up to nurse.

Somehow, she knew what she was doing. Despite all my fears, we made it. Against all reason, I'd fallen for this woman and now this baby. I was capable of attachment after all.

Lanie turned her gaze from the baby to me.

"Baz, are you crying?"

"I am," I admitted. "I'm just so glad to have this little soul in our lives. I'm relieved for so many reasons."

"It's going to be okay."

"You don't understand," I said. "I feared I'd be a shit Dad like my father—that I'd never be able to love something like this. Now, I cannot imagine loving anything more in my life, Lanie. I'm also livid. Because… he should have loved me like this."

Lanie smiled. "Channel all that anger into breaking generational trauma, okay? You're enough. Somehow, we'll do this. We'll probably scar him a little, but he's got two loving parents."

I leaned to kiss her. For the first time in my life, I felt like doing nothing—nothing but being in the moment right here. I didn't want more excitement. I didn't need to chase a deal. I wasn't keen to move. Everything I loved was here. Everything I needed right now was right here.

LANIE

"He's asleep," I announced, entering the place we turned into a family room. I just put George down for a nap.

Ellie looked up from her crossword and smiled. "He fights them like mad."

"He does. But there is so much to do, and his aunt is in town."

Dora Elizabeth sat in the window overlooking the sea, arms wrapped around her knees. Her tan arms indicated just how far she'd been from Braemoor. She was here for a short visit, taking a break from her time in the DRC feeding people and being otherwise saintly.

My sister sensed I was staring and turned. "What?"

"Nothing, you're just sun kissed and I'm a little bit jealous," I admitted.

"I'd tell you to visit. Even if you stayed in Gisenyi, it would be nice," Dora Elizabeth offered. "Not that I suspect Baz would let you bring Georgie."

I snickered. "I'd guess not, but what fun would such an adventure be with a baby?"

"Probably not much," Dora Elizabeth said. "Of course, if

he came by the convent, he'd have dozens of friends to play with. There are always children. I'm usually holding a baby—not that I mind."

I didn't mind, either. Motherhood suited me. I always knew I wanted to be a mother, but I didn't realize just how much I craved this time until we had a baby. Watching Baz dote on our boy only affirmed how perfect it was—perfectly imperfect, perhaps. The show had gone bananas but apart from a short appearance in season three, I elected to take a break from work to stay home with Georgie.

"I'm going to go find Mum," Ellie declared. "I should take a walk. Even if I freeze to death."

"You're from Chicago. You can manage."

She stuck her tongue out.

"Go on," I giggled. "Go find her in her wandering. Even if she tells you she won't like the company, you know she does."

"It will do you good," Ellie said.

We watched her leave before Ellie asked, "She's still a baby, isn't she?"

"She is completely innocent, yes," I giggled. "But she's an absolute sweetheart. You two have much in common. You love to serve everyone around you. I only worry that some man will take advantage of it. Thankfully, I don't think she's much interested in dating. I don't understand it."

Ellie shrugged. "I'd rather be happy on my own with all my hobbies. I'll settle for the right man if he ever presents himself. Until then, I have my work and Georgie and maybe more?"

She raised an eyebrow as if she knew. *How did she know?*

"I haven't told anyone yet," I whispered. "And Mum will kill me if I say anything before I tell her."

Ellie brimmed. "And Baz?"

It was his idea.

I didn't want to admit just how much Baz begged for another baby or how little I'd resisted. George was only seven months old but thriving. We wasted no time with baby number two. I was barely pregnant, but so excited at the possibility of having a little girl this time.

"He's excited, yes," I said. "He'll have a hard time keeping it under wraps when he gets here."

Baz had been abroad off and on for the last month. I'd taken the test with Chloe on the line last week before calling Baz to let him know that our shag in the butler's pantry in London had borne fruit.

"Is he not back yet?" I looked up to find Mum standing in the doorway. Based on her face, she'd not heard any of my news, just the mention of Baz getting in.

Ellie checked her watch, a gift from Baz at Christmas. "He's due really anytime now."

"Did you not see Dora?" I asked.

"Briefly. She came to see me, then promptly left me to see if the man with the ponies down the lane is about." She pulled a face.

"Oh, Tim?" Ellie asked. "Those ponies are adorable."

"Every chance she gets, it's always a horse," Mum sighed.

"I don't know. Tim is charming," Ellie said. "And rather handsome. Might be more than the ponies?"

Mum shook her head. "It should not be. She must go back to Africa in two days' time. What good does that do her?"

"How much longer?" Ellie asked.

"She's only a couple months out from the end of that contract," Mum answered. "I keep asking her what is next and pray she will just stay a bit and maybe meet a nice man from a good family."

"A nice man from a good family? What good is that?" Baz's voice rang out as he entered, looking handsome with a fair bit of stubble.

I rushed to greet him. He bent down to give me a sweet kiss, leaving me longing for what we might do later.

"You know, Lord Osgoode, she's a good girl. She lives in a convent," Mum protested. "And she's still very much a practicing Catholic unlike some of us."

Mum glared our way.

"I went to mass with you two weeks ago!" I protested.

"For the baby's christening. It does not count. This weekend—"

"She wasn't feeling well," Ellie said. "It wasn't her fault."

Ellie's protective streak always warmed my heart.

"She was unwell?" Baz asked, concerned.

I turned to him. "It's fine. I am fine. Stop."

"This weekend, you are *all* coming to mass and I won't have any protests."

"If the place catches fire, it's on your head, Lady Danna," Baz said. "Go, Lanie, sit. Can I get you anything?"

"Are the rest of us merely chopped liver?" Ellie joked.

"Can I get *anyone* anything?" Baz asked. "Or ring the staff we pay to help?"

Ellie knew he only fussed over me for obvious reasons. She loved to rib him, and I loved to be fussed over.

"I'm fine. Sit. You're the one who has been traveling."

"Don't worry about me. Worry about you." He kissed my forehead and sat.

Mum stared suspiciously in our direction. "Now, I hate to say it, but your father always got like this when I was pregnant. I found it rather annoying."

"I remember you when you were pregnant with Dora," I protested. "And you seemed to be quite happy to let him do everything for you. He worshipped the ground you walked on, and you were quite fine with it."

It wasn't a denial, nor was it an acceptance. She knew, though. Somehow.

Baz looked for confirmation and I shrugged.

"Well, I am a bit nervous, yes. As you say, Danna, I'm being annoying because I worry about her when it's early days like this."

"I knew it!" Mum said. "How far along?"

"Super early," I said. "Like six weeks. But I promise you, I'm fine. And I didn't lose my mind, and you don't have to worry."

The baby fussed on the monitor and I groaned.

"I'll get him."

"No, Baz, he just went down. Let him settle," I insisted.

"Sorry, but I missed him."

Baz departed and Mum turned to me. "This is exactly how your father and I ended up with Daphne, you realize?

"What, the two of you had sex? I am *so* surprised. I had no idea how it worked!"

Ellie stifled a laugh.

"Well, I… I am happy if you both are. It seems Baz is pleased."

"He is," I said. "It was his idea, so…"

She did a double-take.

"Oh, Danna, he loves that boy so much."

"It doesn't surprise me at all," I admitted. "He's been wrapped up in Georgie since day one."

"When he's around." Mum would never admit that despite our odd beginnings, her concerns about Baz were unfounded.

"Yes," I said. "But I don't mind it. When he's here, he's like this. He always is the first to go grab George."

The baby continued to fuss on the monitor, but by now Baz swooped him up, something I could see in real time from my phone if I wanted. Instead, we got to hear him baby talk to George in a way that melted me every time.

Voice excited and sweet, he cooed, "There you are. Mummy told me *not* to get you, but I ignored her. C'mon."

Mum said nothing, but Ellie laughed. I couldn't help but love him for it. Yes, he was a sap. No one would believe that Baz Osgoode was capable of being the baby-talking family man he was, but I knew the truth. In a way, that made it even better.

Baz returned minutes later with a happy baby.

"He's not fussing. He just had FOMO," I joked. "Didn't you?"

George, bright-eyed and excited, blew me a raspberry. I leaned over and kissed the baby on the cheek, so happy he was all smiles. George gripped my hair but thankfully let it go.

"Be nice to your mother," Baz said. "Don't bite her, either."

"Yes, that is wise or else no more boobs," I said. "What a nasty surprise the other night."

"Has he done it again since?" Baz asked.

"No. But I worry I traumatized him by getting up and leaving him with Mum."

"Am I traumatizing?" Mum scoffed.

"No. He just… he didn't want to take that bottle and crying hurts me something fierce."

"I told you it was the right thing to do, darling. It was. You're a wonderful mother. You'd never hurt him," Mum said.

I was nearly dumbfounded by her words.

"What? You two have done well by Georgie. He is a happy boy," Mum cooed, walking up and taking Georgie from Baz's lap.

Baz looked at me, astounded by her statement, not that she stole the baby.

He rubbed my back and whispered, "Well, that is a first."

"Write down the date," I snickered. "I doubt we will hear it again."

He chuckled. "I'll take what I can get. That and a week with you. Fuck, how I've missed you."

I rested my head on his shoulder, lapping up how deeply I felt his words. "Even if you're stuck going to Mass?"

"For you and to skirt her ire, I will," Baz whispered. "But in an act of protest, I plan to do all manner of things to you afterwards which will make up for any expression of piety, Lanie."

I wanted to run him off to the bedroom right then.

I whispered back, "Tonight, I plan to torture you for leaving by forcing you to watch me get myself off first."

"You think that will work?" He asked. "That that is torture?"

"It has worked before," I said.

"You'll get as good as you give then. And I will not hold back, Lady Osgoode."

I kissed him, not even minding we weren't alone. "I expect nothing less."

Also by Maude Winters

Want a free book?

Read how Baz's father stole Braemoor from the Carlisles? Grab *Love Match* here or by scanning the code below:

For more billionaire fun, read the Lakeshore Empire Series (a prequel to Wickedly His)

Executive Decision - The beginning on the Delphine Family's arc in Chicago where Daphne chooses to move on and give her father's best friend a second chance.

Power Move - When Eva met Davey at her friend's bachelorette party, she never expected him to get her pregnant. She also didn't expect to show up for the first day of her new job to find out he's David Delphine, the CEO and her new boss.

For more high-spice fun and an indecent bargain, check out *Royally Redeemed*.

Duncan is a late-thirties bad boy prince in a media firestorm. Eloise is the twenty-something babysitter sent to keep him honest. The problem? He wants to drive an indecent bargain with the young handler unafraid to make him beg on his knees.

This femme domme romance will leave you begging for mercy. Out Spring 2026.

www.ingramcontent.com/pod-product-compliance
Lightning Source LLC
Chambersburg PA
CBHW030138310726
48970CB00005B/1478